WILL & TOM

Also by Matthew Plampin

The Street Philosopher
The Devil's Acre
Illumination

WILL & TOM

Matthew Plampin

THE BOROUGH PRESS

The Borough Press
An imprint of HarperCollins*Publishers*
1 London Bridge Street
London SE1 9GF
www.harpercollins.co.uk

Published by HarperCollins*Publishers* 2015

1

A catalogue record for this book
is available from the British Library

ISBN: 978-0-00-756086-8

This novel is entirely a work of fiction.
The names, characters and incidents portrayed in it, while at times
based on historical figures, are the work of the author's imagination.

Set in Perpetua

Printed and bound in Great Britain by
Clays Ltd, St Ives plc

For KP,
who made me think of golden aeroplanes

Historical Note

In this period, watercolour paintings were commonly referred to as 'drawings', and watercolour brushes as 'pencils'; this was partly to distinguish them from paintings in oil, which was considered the far superior medium. Artists who aspired to join the Royal Academy (the professional body that dominated British art until well into the nineteenth century) would often begin their careers exhibiting works in watercolour, proceeding to oil as their skills and reputations developed. When depicting landscape, the conventional approach was to make detailed open-air sketches in lead or graphite, before painting the actual watercolour in the studio. Simple colour studies were sometimes taken on the spot, but they tended to be crude, partial views, created for reference only. To depart from this method was highly unusual.

'The enquiry in England is not whether a man has talents and genius, but whether he is passive and polite and a virtuous ass, and obedient to noblemen's opinions in art and science. If he is, he is a good man: if not, he must be starved.'

WILLIAM BLAKE

Harewood, West Yorkshire

August 1797

Tuesday

First sight of the house prompts a hard exhalation. Will's fingers play a scale on the stick balanced over his shoulder. Sunlight swells between the scattered clouds, growing immensely bright, charging the pristine parkland around him with colour. His new blue coat feels hot and heavy; he notices the dampness gathering in his armpits and the droplets of perspiration wobbling on his freshly shaved lip.

'Come now,' he says. 'Onwards.'

The driveway curves past a bank of elms and more of the vast mansion inches into view. Will smells bark and the resin oozing beneath; the leathery lushness of leaves; the faint, sour tang of livestock. He tries to calm himself by inwardly mapping out a composition and blending pigments to match the golden hue of the stone. The result of this exercise, unexpectedly, is disappointment. For all its size and grandeur, Harewood House is a simple structure, little more than an even line of boxes. There would be no challenge here.

Three large carts stand before the service entrance at the building's eastern end. Servants are streaming in and out, unloading boxes, bags and packages. Mr Lascelles' letter instructed Will to delay his arrival until a week into August, and here is the reason: that eminently fashionable gentleman has only just returned from London, despite the season having concluded some weeks previously. Will doesn't try to imagine why this might be. Already, from his limited experience of their patronage, he's learned not to second-guess the whims of the rich. A few glances are thrown his way – at his new clothes, his stick and bundle, the two leather-bound books clamped under his right arm – but no one asks his business. Their chief isn't difficult to identify. A looming, fleshy fellow, clad in impeccable butler's black, he watches from the sidelines, issuing orders and rebukes while doing none of the real work. Will steels himself and approaches. The man eyes him impatiently as he begins the introduction he rehearsed in the stage.

'I have here a letter from Mr Lascelles, dated fifth of July, requesting that I attend him at—'

The butler, or whatever he is, breaks away to harass a pair of footmen bearing flat crates stamped with the mark of a London auction house – telling them to be extremely careful, that their positions are at stake and so on. Will follows, talking still, a strong, sudden indignation banishing any vestige of nervousness; and he crosses the threshold of the mighty house without even noticing.

They weave down a corridor littered with luggage. Will

is determined to have this man hear him out, but cannot prise his attention from those accursed crates. In an effort to push himself forwards, he stumbles against a trunk and knocks the umbrella from the end of his stick. This umbrella is a quality item, not cheap, purchased on Oxford Street especially for the northern tour, and has proved its worth many times. Will wheels about, searching for it – and the butler is gone, around a corner, through a door.

The umbrella is trapped between a stack of shoe boxes and a wickerwork hamper. Will stands over it protectively. A retrieval would involve putting down his books or his bundle, and he's unwilling to do either; it seems all too likely that something could be mixed up in the clutter and accidentally carried off. After the still, luminous heat of the driveway, this basement has an unsettling effect. The air reeks of tallow and boot polish, and it is quite dark; the only light is admitted through the service entrance and a narrow court somewhere up ahead, broken blue-white reflections gleaming across the floor tiles. Every variety of servant hurries by, focused on specific, pressing duties, disappearing down passages and into rooms. It is like a bustling underground village, or the lower deck of a huge merchant ship.

Will is attempting to lift the umbrella free with his shoe – to work the toe into the curved cane handle – when a hand comes to rest in the crook of his elbow. He starts, turning again; the person beside him ducks to avoid being clobbered by his bundle. It is a woman, two or three inches taller than he is. She is wearing a maid's mob-cap over a mass of black hair and carries a shallow basket piled with plants. The eastern doorway is at her back, the daylight beyond making it hard to see much of her face. Will apologises, indicating his conundrum. In one movement, she crouches, plucks up the umbrella and hangs it where her hand was two seconds before.

'Much obliged,' he mutters.

The maid is studying his person, the bundle, the leatherbound books. 'You're the draughtsman,' she says, 'up from London. I've heard them talking about you.'

Her voice has a ripe, rough edge to it, the Yorkshire inflections mingled with something Will can't place. She's older than he'd first thought, though how old precisely he wouldn't like to say. Her hips are broad and arranged at a slight angle; her bosom (he can't help noticing) is remarkably ample; her forearms, exposed by rolled-up sleeves, are sun-tanned and etched with muscle. There is no deference in her manner, such as a personal guest of Lord Harewood's son might expect as his due – just a powerful, amiable curiosity.

'In't you a mite early, sir? Weren't you supposed to be joining us at the end of the week?'

Will shakes his head. He won't have this. 'A letter was waiting for me in York. At the Black Horse. The dates were clear.'

The maid moves by him, further into the house, and now Will can discern the roundness of chin; her ink-black eyes with their long lashes; her wide lips and the lines at their sides. A heath gypsy, he thinks. Will has been travelling in the north for six weeks now. He's caught the occasional glimpse of these people, camped out on the moors or at the fringes of the smaller towns. They're commonly held to be inveterate criminals, or mystics with unnatural pagan allegiances. That one has managed to find herself a position beneath Harewood's exalted roof seems unusual, to say the least.

'Well then, I must be mistaken. Heavens, sir, that'd be no great novelty! Come, this way – we'll pay a visit to Mr Noakes, our steward. He'll straighten this out.' She smiles, her teeth white in the murk. 'Would you have me carry them books of yours?'

Will firms his grip, his fingertips sinking very slightly into the leather. 'I am well.'

The gypsy maid leads him through the basement, cruising three steps ahead. Others, younger girls, hop smartly from her path; this is no drudge from the scullery. A sweet, hedgerow fragrance trails from the basket on her arm. Will looks at it more closely. Amidst the leaves and stems are clusters of tiny pale flowers and a twisted seam of purple berries.

They cross a bare, vaulted area; beyond it, along another passage, a latticed interior window provides a view of a large, formidably neat office. Two men are within, standing on either side of a desk. One, bearded and dressed for the outdoors, is plainly a gardener; the other, Will senses, is the fellow in overall charge down here, senior even to the butler figure he chased inside. Barely half the bulk of the gardener before him, he is entirely bald, the unified expanse of his scalp and forehead seeming to compress the face beneath, to squash it under the line of his brow. He is listening to his subordinate report some difficulty or other; his thin arms are crossed and his expression ill-tempered.

Will's guide enters the office without knocking. 'The draughtsman's here, Mr Noakes,' she announces, 'the one from London. Found him out in the east corridor, I did, quite adrift.'

The gnome-like Mr Noakes glances over at Will. He is unimpressed. 'You're early,' he says. 'What's your name?'

'William Turner.' Will's limbs are tense; his blood is humming. It's always like this with servants. They'll do whatever they can to pin an error on an innocent outsider. Keeping steady, he sets down his bundle, unclasps the smaller sketchbook and slides the letter from inside the front cover. The Harewood crest is at the top, and Beau Lascelles' swooping signature at the base. He walks forward to hand it over. 'Mr Lascelles asked me to come here in the second week of August.' He pauses. 'The mistake ain't mine.'

This alters the situation somewhat. A footman is summoned and dispatched upstairs to obtain clarification from the family. Mr Noakes returns the letter, rather more politely than he received it. Will calms; things will now be put on their proper course. He'll be taken to his patron and they'll set out their business together. The house itself may not inspire, but inspiration, in truth, is a luxury for a young artist. Harewood remains a great chance.

The office begins to feel close. A stripe of sunlight falls in through a high window, tinted with the first fiery note of dusk; running diagonally between Mr Noakes and the gardener, it ends at Will's stockings, blazing on the white wool, making it prickle against his skin. He looks about him. A snowy tie-wig rests on a stand; a bookcase groans with ledgers; a framed engraving of the King, taken indifferently from Zoffany's portrait, hangs upon the wall.

The gypsy maid, Mrs Lamb, is lingering close by, the scent of those pale flowers seeping through the room. 'You must excuse us, Mr Turner,' she says. 'The family came back only yesterday, along with Mr Noakes here – and as you saw, most of their luggage arrived just an hour or so ago. We're all a-shambles at present! Why, it is—'

'Mrs Lamb, do you not have duties to see to?' interrupts Mr Noakes. 'If you're lacking for work, I'm sure Monsieur Blossier would welcome your assistance in the kitchens.'

She meets his irritability with a smile, which she then directs towards the gardener. 'As it happens, Mr Noakes, I do require a word with our Stephen.'

Several detailed questions follow, concerning Harewood's crop of peaches. The gardener, obviously uncomfortable, keeps his replies brief. It's plain enough that Mrs Lamb already knows the answers – her aim is to rile her superior. Will stares down fixedly at his bundle; he considers lifting it to his shoulder again, so that he's ready to go upstairs the moment the footman reappears.

Before he can act, someone strides along the corridor

9

outside and enters the office. Mrs Lamb looks across at the newcomer and promptly falls quiet. It is not the man who was sent up. At first, Will assumes he must be a member of the family, or a guest perhaps, so fine are his clothes. The coat, though, is a sober black, the stock a modest grey, and no jewels or gold adorn his person; the impression, taken with his short sandy hair, is more that of a professional gentleman, an engineer or architect. He is imposingly tall, dipping his head slightly as he comes through the door. His tapering face, with its straight nose and sharp chin, makes Will think of greyhounds.

Mr Noakes had been preparing to launch another rebuke at Mrs Lamb, but seeing this man he pulls himself up and makes a small, stiff bow. 'Mr Cope,' he says, 'good day to you, sir. I trust all is well with Mr Lascelles. Did his first night at Harewood pass pleasantly?'

Mr Cope does not respond. He looks at each of the three servants in turn. Mr Noakes smiles thinly; the gardener quite literally backs away; Mrs Lamb meets his gaze but remains disinclined to speak.

Then Mr Cope turns to Will. His eyes are a flat hazel and rather narrow-set; their scrutiny feels inescapable. Several seconds pass. Will is clutching his sketchbooks more tightly than ever, with not a single idea what to expect; and this Mr Cope is bowing, bowing lower than anyone has bowed to him before.

'Welcome to Harewood, Mr Turner.' The man's voice is even, expressionless, without accent. 'Mr Lascelles extends his fondest greetings and most sincere regards, and hopes that your journey from York was not too onerous.'

Will nods; he mumbles something.

'I am Mr Cope, his valet. He offers his apologies for the unfortunate circumstances of your arrival, and asks that you accompany me.' Mr Cope's attention returns to the servants. 'Understand that Mr Turner is the guest of our master. We must grant him every courtesy from now on.'

Will is consumed by a violent blush. For an instant he is intensely grateful towards Mr Cope, but then he corrects himself. This is how it's supposed to be. This is how a visiting artist should be received. He looks down at his bundle – and Mr Cope is scooping it up, umbrella and all, and making for the door. They leave the office, valet then artist, watched by the others. Mrs Lamb sighs, chuckles almost, as if tickled by a private joke.

Another sequence of corridors follows. The pace, this time, is swifter; Will feels like a child, a Covent Garden guttersnipe, scurrying behind some upright officer of the parish. He is confused, momentarily, when they pass a staircase – but decides that they must be going outside rather than upstairs. It makes sense. Mr Lascelles must be in the park, intending that they discuss potential prospects of the house in the last of the day's light. Beau Lascelles is known to be a man of advanced tastes; perhaps it is the effects of dusk that he'll desire in these drawings. Will's enthusiasm for the commission begins to return.

They halt before a door on one of the longer passages.

Mr Cope reaches into the pocket of his mustard-coloured waistcoat for a key. The door is unlocked and opened; beyond is a dingy bedchamber, barely more than a closet. Only when a key is held out to Will does he realise that this room is to be his.

'Ain't we—' Will stops. His dismay, the abrupt dashing of his expectations, is disorientating. 'Are we not going to Mr Lascelles? Weren't that your purpose in fetching me?'

Mr Cope remains impassive. 'No, Mr Turner. My instructions were to escort you to your quarters, and to inform you that dinner will be called at half-past six. Someone will come to show you upstairs.' He leans into the room and sets down the bundle. 'I take it, sir, that you have evening clothes?'

'I have,' Will answers. He's angry now. Course I have, he nearly snaps. I know very well where I am! He scours the valet's face for a sign of judgement or disdain. There is nothing. Years of going with Father on his rounds has acquainted Will with more or less every variety of servant. This one is from the top flight, the dearest there is, available only to men of the highest rank or the most capacious coffers. These uncanny creatures are capable of screening their characters entirely; of becoming vessels, embodiments of their master's will. There is no more chance of a normal human response from Mr Cope than from a guardsman on parade.

Will steps through the doorway, thinking that perhaps the chamber will seem larger once he's inside. It's like a casket. The bed seems to have been made for a child. Will is short enough, God knows, but he wonders if he'll even be able to lie down on it at his full extent. The single window, furthermore, is high and dull – north-facing, he reckons, and devoid of direct sunlight, lacking even the slanting beam enjoyed by Mr Noakes. Will glares at the wall, at the chalky, unpainted plaster, and is gripped by the urge to object. Surely, as a practising painter he is at least entitled to some decent light?

But something about Mr Cope prohibits complaint. Will stands, glowering silently, while the valet issues a stream of perfectly enunciated information: a plain prelude to his withdrawal.

'Water can be obtained from the pump in the sluice room, and candles from the still room. Laundry will be collected each morning and returned the following day. Any queries should be directed towards Mr Noakes. He will be more helpful when next you speak.'

There is a second bow, less fulsome than the first, and Will is left alone in his casket chamber. Besides the bed, which nearly fills the floor, it contains just a washstand and a small wooden chair. For a minute he doesn't move, trying hard to weigh every element and not be hasty or extreme. He's defeated, though; he can't understand it. Having over-looked his arrival, his host sends down a valet, a personal servant, to soothe him with flattery – only then to consign him to what must be the most wretched accommodation in the entire house. It isn't proper lordly behaviour. It isn't even polite.

Leave, says a voice, *right away. No other painter would stand for such treatment.*

The notion comes as a relief, and seems wholly excellent and right. What, honestly, is to stop him? He doesn't need this man. There's material enough in these two sketchbooks to fuel a decade's worth of painting. Of this he is certain. His northern tour, with its crags and blue hills and endless, rain-swept valleys, has been no less than a revelation – the opening up of a new and brilliant territory. He's on the cusp of something. He's convinced of it. Beau Lascelles can go hang.

But no. He can't do this. He *mustn't*. Father's warning, given just as he was setting out from Maiden Lane to catch that first coach, sounds unbidden in his ears. Standing at the parlour hearth, the old man recited every expulsion and exclusion Will Turner had earned over the course of his life – the opportunities missed, the would-be allies lost, through shows of temper.

You fight off your friends, boy, he said. *You defy the very men who seek to help you.*

Will sits down on the bed. It is hard as a bench. He sets the sketchbooks on the meagre pillow and forces himself to consider his broader circumstances. He must operate, as all of his profession must, in the art world of London: a not over-large stage upon which Beau Lascelles, with his many friends and mountains of ready gold, is assigned a significant part. The man is simply too influential to risk offending. Will scratches at his calf through his stocking. He has to be reasonable. This room isn't so very bad. And it is a bolt-hole only. Above are the saloons of Harewood – as splendorous as man's wealth could summon, it is claimed – and outside is Nature, basking in the full-blown glory of summer. He'll hardly have need of it at all.

Will unwinds the white stock from around his neck. The muslin is damp, the starched collar beneath soaked with perspiration. He lays it on the bed beside him and reaches for the bundle.

He has to see this through.

*

The dark mahogany door, gigantic and glossy, swings back on silent hinges. Will slips through, crossing from carpet to stone, and discovers that he is at the rear of the entrance hall. It is laid out like a mock temple, dedicated to the transcendent wealth of the Lascelles; around him are classical reliefs and statues, a table of dove marble upon a Grecian frame and a dozen fluted columns, all steeped in an atmosphere of cool, gloomy magnificence. And overhead, dear God, overhead is a moulded ceiling of such Attic intricacy – such divisions and subdivisions, such a profusion of loops and laurels and minute, interlocking patterns – that it makes the eyeballs ache to study it. The effect is oppressive. Will looks elsewhere.

The door closes; the surly chambermaid who led him upstairs hasn't followed him through it. He's to find his own way from here. Six quick steps take him to a shallow niche, occupied by a bronze Minerva. The moment is approaching, advancing on him, impossible to avoid. Trembling slightly, he makes an adjustment to his plum waistcoat and catches a whiff of fresh sweat beneath his jacket. This is vexing – it's been barely a half-hour since he performed his ablutions. He's consoled, however, by his fine Vandyck-brown suit, the best York's tailors could provide, which remained largely uncreased during its time in the bundle; his hair, plaited and powdered as well as Father could have done it; and his new evening shoes, little more than black leather slippers, which glisten wetly against the hall's hexagonal flagging like the eyes of oxen.

There is laughter close by, a blast of male laughter, free and full of casual authority. Will's head snaps up. A liveried footman is standing beside an urn on the far side of the hall. As if activated by his notice, this servant goes to a door, and holds it open. The sounds of merriment increase. Will scowls; this footman has been observing him, has recognised his reticence and is giving him a shove. He tugs again at the waistcoat and gathers his breath. What can he do now but go in?

Do not take fright, he tells himself, striding towards the very faintly smirking footman. *Do not*. You were invited here. This man wishes to see you – to give you patronage. You have to grow used to this, to the toadying, to the bowing and chattering and incessant smiling. It is part of painting. You have to master it.

Will enters a library. Tall white pilasters flank shelves loaded with gilded volumes; above is another of those staggering ceilings. At the other end of the room — and it is at least thirty feet in length — four gentlemen are roaming around a billiard table, engaged in a boisterous argument over some point of play. Cues are waved in the air and brandished like rapiers; insults are exchanged with jocular relish.

'I call a two-ball carom — a *two-ball carom* — and no soul on God's earth but *this bounder here* could possibly deny it were so!'

'It ran wide, I tell you! That shot, you damnable villain, that shot struck my *cue ball only!*'

Three ladies are half-watching this overblown dispute from a suite of delicate furniture, away in the early evening shadows at the back of the library. Another is off on an armchair, closer to Will, apart from the company — on purpose, it seems. All are dressed at the height of aristocratic fashion: pastels and greys, silks and satins, festooned with frills and a glittering variety of ornaments. The ladies also hold their fans, and both sexes have been dusted liberally with hair powder.

Will Turner, born and raised on Maiden Lane, has landed among the *bon ton*. He experiences a new spasm of self-consciousness, a crumpling, contorting sensation in his stomach that quite paralyses him. Brown and plum! he thinks. You look like a parson, for God's sake, next to these people — a plain little dumpling, simple and poor, brought in for general ridicule. He is relieved, though, that he opted to leave his sketchbooks downstairs. That was the correct decision.

It would have cast him as a tradesman, coming to call with his samples – of no more significance than a fellow touting wallpaper or curtains.

Edward Lascelles the younger, known to his intimates as Beau, is one of the four gentlemen at the billiard table. Clad in a coat of mulberry velvet, his fleshy face is warmed by exertion and hilarity. He is trying to speak, to make a riposte; but then a new joke is broached and the laughter resumes. Will wonders what exactly he is to do. No one seems to have noticed his arrival. He glances back through the doorway, at the motionless footman out in the hall. Weren't the servants supposed to announce you? Wasn't that the usual form?

A figure slides from beside one of the windows and approaches the billiard table. It is Mr Cope, the valet from earlier; he touches Beau's shoulder, just once, and has his master's immediate attention. A few words are murmured. Beau looks over with evident satisfaction, then passes Cope his cue and starts towards this latest guest.

Will orders his thoughts. He is to talk with his patron at last. Terms can be laid down, a contract agreed. This visit can be given its proper purpose. He makes the bow he has practised: tidy and brief, one foot drawn back, an arm held momentarily across his waist.

Close sight does not inspire confidence. The heir to Harewood has a decent frame – Will's eyes are level only with his Adam's apple – but he's rather plumper than Will remembers, a globular belly nestled comfortably within his well-tailored breeches. His hair, powdered to the uniform smoky tone, has been crafted into a dense cap of curls, each one carefully teased out and arranged to create an impression of graceful, manly nonchalance. Beneath are full cheeks, coloured with just a fleck of carmine, Will reckons – he knows from Father's shop that plenty of gentlemen still use it – a protuberant chin and small, hooded eyes. His expression, his bearing, every single aspect of his person, is shot through with a sense of easy dominion, over Will and the rest of humankind: a dominion brought about and upheld by the all-conquering power of cash.

Will feels a pang of disgust. He wishes himself in his painting room, amidst its smells of damp, coal-smoke and mice, cork pellets pressed in his ears and a drawing taken from one of his Buttermere sketches clamped to the stand before him. He stares, unblinking, fighting the sensation down. It passes.

'My dear Mr Turner,' Beau begins, 'how you must loathe me!'

Will's eyebrow twitches; he opens his mouth to speak. 'I—'

'Such short notice, such a steep imposition, such an interruption to your plans! Yes, you must positively *loathe* me – but I remain, for my part, unapologetic, so very glad does it make me that you were able to join us.'

Will inclines his head. 'A—'

'Determining your itinerary was straightforward enough, out among the landscapists of London, along with the address of your tavern in York. I confess, though, that I was not hopeful. I had convinced myself that you would cast my letter on the fire and forget it at once.' Beau takes Will's left shoulder, enclosing the joint with his hand. 'But here you are. *Here you are*, by Jove!'

The hand squeezes; Will wants very much to shrug it off. Beau's last remark strikes him as profoundly disingenuous. The Lascelles fortune is such that any young artist would give a finger to win their benefaction. He stays quiet.

Beau looks to Mr Cope, who is back by his window. 'I trust that your accommodation is adequate? I'm afraid that we are rather full at present. This house, Heaven protect her, is not so spacious as might sometimes be desired.'

Will considers this. Harewood can surely hold more than are gathered in the library. Others must be upstairs. He shifts, his new shoes squeaking, and clears his throat. 'Perfectly,' he replies. 'My needs are few, sir, in truth.'

There is an unfriendly cackle from the billiard table; off in the shadows, fans flutter open to hide smiles. The cause is obvious. Will sees that he should have given more time to smoothing out his accent and rather less to buffing his buttons.

'So, Lascelles,' says one of the gentlemen – another well-fed specimen in a coat cut just like Beau's but the colour of lemon curd, 'this must be your cockney project.'

An odd word to select. Will senses an objection building inside him; again, he quells it, keeping his face as blank as he can manage. *Project* may imply a refashioning, as if he is somehow inadequate in his current form – but it also clearly indicates an intention to invest. Be patient, he instructs himself. Wait for the terms.

Beau is grinning, doubling the number of chins that quiver upon his collar. 'If you were any less of a philistine, Purkiss,' he declares, 'you'd be aware that Mr Turner here, despite being scarcely out of boyhood, had two fine oils shown at the Academy Exhibition, and as many drawings in watercolour. He is a veritable phenomenon.'

'Four,' Will corrects – taking care to say *forr* rather than *fowah*, as he might in other circumstances. 'Beg pardon, sir, but it was four drawings.'

Beau pauses for a moment, deciding how much license he will allow. 'Of course,' he concedes. He releases Will's shoulder. 'Views of Ely Cathedral, if I recall correctly, and quite divine.'

'Salisbury,' murmurs Will, but he is not heard; Beau has turned about and is strolling to the billiard table.

'I found Mr Turner, would you believe, in the house of a *mad-doctor* – one Thomas Monro, an illustrious fellow indeed within his field. He was prominent among the party of physicians assembled to minister to our King, God save him, during His Majesty's most recent deterioration.'

Beau's manner had grown confidential while revealing this sensitive yet impressive detail; once it is out, though, and Monro's cachet established beyond question, he moves briskly onwards. Discussing the royal travails is not thought patriotic.

'The good doctor is a collector, and a devoted friend to the arts. He has a villa on Adelphi Terrace, from where he conducts a copying society – an academy, you might call it. On certain evenings, I have seen upwards of a half-dozen young draughtsmen at work in his rooms, setting down their own versions of drawings and prints from Monro's albums. It is a fascinating undertaking for anyone interested in the visual arts in England, and several noble connoisseurs number among the doctor's regular visitors. Viscount Malden introduced me there, in fact.' Beau's voice becomes mocking. 'You know Malden, don't you, Purkiss?'

The gentleman in the lemon-curd coat levels his cue, returning pointedly to the billiards game. His complexion, beneath whatever cosmetics have been applied to it, is pock-marked; the bulb at the end of his nose is cleaved like the cheeks of a tiny bottom. 'No need to revive that old tale, Lascelles,' he says, 'in front of the ladies and all.'

This embarrassment is false. Mr Purkiss is perversely proud of whatever Beau is about to reveal. A lively back-and-forth ensues, drawing guffaws from the other two gentlemen and disapproving sighs from the ladies. Will learns that on one infamous occasion, while staying at Viscount Malden's country seat at Cassiobury Park, Mr Purkiss embarked on a brandy-fuelled rampage across the formal gardens, under the impression that the peacocks purchased to strut thereabouts were intended to serve as game. The conclusion was predictable: iridescent feathers strewn over the lawn, the Viscount's young children wailing at windows and a dead bird crushed in a flowerbed, buried beneath their father's insensible guest.

Will, still standing, is forgotten completely. Mr Cope snags his eye and gestures discreetly to a chair. It is a fancy thing, all scrolls and flourishes, painted a soapy green with cushions of pink satin. Will sits as naturally as he can, flapping up the tails of his jacket. He is close to the lone lady, the one who appears to have deliberately isolated herself from the party. A sidelong glance reveals that she is younger than the rest of them – who range, by Will's estimate, between thirty and forty years of age – being no more than twenty-five. She slouches in her chair with none of the poise affected by the other women. Her legs are crossed inside her loose fawn gown, a silken slipper dangling from her toe. There is a clear familial resemblance to Beau, the eyes heavy-lidded, the nose straight, with the same generosity of figure; it fits her better, though, Will decides – lending her a sleek, almost classical quality, akin to the larger women of Tiziano, or Peter-Paul Rubens – and she is hugely, aggressively bored. No notice whatever is granted to the artist seated beside her. Will summons his knowledge of the Lascelles family, gleaned from the portrait commissions they have made. This is surely Mary Ann, Lord Harewood's younger daughter.

It won't do to sit there mutely. Will knows that he has to talk; to ingratiate and flatter. He draws breath, makes an introduction and asks Miss Lascelles if her father is at home. She says that he is not, and nothing more – neatly snipping this first, somewhat feeble line of discourse and dropping them back into silence.

Will girds himself to try again. The library is growing quite dark now, but he opts nonetheless to undertake an assessment of the paintings displayed above the bookshelves and in other suitable places. These are Grecian in character, simple decorative pieces done without use of local colour or atmospheric effect; hack work, basically, and too late he realises that he must admire them, yet cannot hope to sound remotely sincere whilst doing so. He is growing tongue-tied when Miss Lascelles interrupts him.

'You are well used to praise, aren't you, Mr Turner? You rather expect it, I think.'

Her voice, in contrast with her careless pose, has a tart refinement, suggestive of governesses and tutors, private balls and carriages, the best of everything. Will begs her pardon.

'Just then, when you were talking to my brother – he called you a *phenomenon*, for goodness sake, and you gave next to no reaction. You are accustomed to people falling at your feet. Lauding you to the heavens.' She looks away. 'I would worry, if I were you, that it had made me proud.'

A bristling heat blooms across Will's face and closes around his throat; he turns a little in his chair. There are no thoughts or words within him, only a sense of having reached a boundary beyond which he cannot proceed. He feels the usual impulse to retreat, to plan and prepare, to seek the advice of more experienced men. This can't be done, of course. He needs to meet this bizarre slur with modest good humour, a deferential quip; but the precise remark required, the sentiment he has to frame, eludes him utterly.

Someone enters the library and begins to speak over the billiard-table prattle in the assertive yet respectful tone of a senior servant. It is Mr Noakes, resplendent in livery of emerald green and gold, the tie-wig from his basement office perched atop his head, come to announce that dinner is served. The ladies rise, the gentlemen lay down their cues and an informal procession saunters off into the palatial hallway. Will lifts himself from the soap-green chair, his shirt peeling clammily from his back. He glances out at the blue shadows of the park with vague longing; then he mops his brow on his sleeve and falls in behind.

*

The dining table is oblong, with a chair at one end and four down each side. Beau claims the head with a swagger and beckons for Mr Purkiss to sit at his right hand. The others slot in around them, in seconds it seems, leaving but one place vacant. It is as far from Beau as the arrangement will allow.

Mary Ann is opposite. Her appeal, Will finds, has quite vanished; *slovenly* is the word that comes to mind now. The blankness that beset him in the library has also gone. He itches to tell her that he has *never*, never once in his life, received undeserved praise, and name some of the notable connoisseurs and newspaper critics who have singled out William Turner for special attention. But, thinking of Father, he holds his peace. It would become an eruption, for certain; and an eruption at Harewood, directed at a member of the baron's family, would do him no favours at all.

The candles have been lit, perhaps three dozen of them – grouped along the table, set before massive, gilt-framed mirrors, positioned upon every available surface. This creates an extraordinary level of illumination, and makes the dining room disagreeably warm and airless despite its cavernous size. Beau orders the windows opened, admitting a barely perceptible breeze; and, soon afterwards, a horde of biting insects. During the entrée a papery moth hurtles in, butts against a candle and bursts into flames, prompting shrieks and exclamations as its smoking, flapping body spirals to the tablecloth. At once, a servant is on hand to dispose of it.

Will eats mechanically, scarcely registering the series of fussy, Frenchified dishes that are placed before him. Burying his puzzlement, he thinks only of the conversation he might make. Nothing comes, though: no topics, no opportunities. The company moves seamlessly from one society scandal to the next, an animated parade of disclosures, dropped names and allusions, interspersed with peals of nasty laughter. He forces a grin at a couple of Beau's jokes, and even at one of Mr Purkiss's – feeling a pinch of self-loathing as he does so.

Across the table, Mary Ann sets about her dinner with gusto, but otherwise manages to sustain her air of disconnection and ennui. This is not permitted for long. Her brother and his comrade begin to goad her, prodding and jibing, trying to draw her out by recounting details of nocturnal antics back in London.

'*Four o'clock in morning*, was it, before the fair Miss Lascelles deigned to return to Hanover Square? And was she really *quite alone?*'

'Indeed she was, dear Purkiss – and what's more, her gown appeared to have lost a number of, ah, *crucial components* over the course of the evening's revelry. Why, it was hardly sufficient to cover her person. Some slight recompense for the coachman, I suppose!'

Mary Ann merely rolls her shoulders like a sulky cat, much to her tormentors' amusement. Then a lady's voice bids Beau to leave her be – and reminds Mr Purkiss, none too fondly, that he is a guest at Harewood. The speaker, who has contributed little up to this point, is sitting further down the table on Will's side. He tilts back in his chair for a surreptitious survey. Although leaner and a shade more severe, she too is plainly a Lascelles. Will gathers from the gentlemen's apologies that this is Frances, the baron's eldest child. Mary Ann is annoyed by her sister's intervention; she lays a fork down noisily on her empty plate.

Will watches a spindly insect drift over the central candelabrum, lifting an inch or two in the flames' heat, and fits together a theory. The younger daughter is in disgrace. There has been a liaison during the spring, a grave blunder on her part, and it has ended badly both for her and her family. She is at Harewood as a punishment, under Frances and Beau's wardship, exiled so that memories of her misadventure can fade. This would account for her demeanour – and for her harsh treatment of wholly innocent house guests. Why her brother would refer to this matter before him, however, and these others to boot, and so *lightly*, is past Will's comprehension; unless, like so many of his type, Beau Lascelles has simply never learned to think better of a bit of drollery.

Firmly, Frances moves them on – asking another of the gentlemen, a slim, bland-looking fellow who Will perceives is her husband, to tell the table of an encounter he'd had the previous week with the Prince of Wales. The gentleman, addressed by all as Douglas, is glad to co-operate. It was at Almack's, he reveals – where, during a conversational hand of piquet, he informed the prince of his connection with Harewood and its family.

'His Majesty gave a laugh, looked to his friends and declared, in that winning way of his, that the last time he'd heard the name Lascelles it was being mistakenly applied to *him*.'

The similarity said to exist between Beau and the prince is quite famous. Will has observed George on two occasions, waddling around the Academy Exhibition; their likeness, in his view, is one only of overfed complacency. Beau, though, grown loud with wine, cannot conceal his pleasure. The prince remembers his name, who he is! To enjoy such an association with royalty, to edge past obeisance towards proper familiarity, is the fervid dream of every aristocrat

– especially those lodged on the lower rungs of the noble ladder, as the Lascelles undoubtedly are.

The company – Mary Ann excepted – attempts to be impressed by Douglas's tale. An awkwardness persists, however; and before ten more minutes have passed, Frances gathers in her silken shawl and rises from her chair, giving the ladies their cue to depart. Her sister is away immediately, rushing around the table in a wide circle and off through a door at the back of the room. The two other women follow at a more leisurely pace, arms linked, sharing a whispered joke that Will suspects is at Mary Ann's expense. Frances is equally unhurried, but she sweeps rather than strolls – stopping by a sideboard to murmur an order to the ever-present Mr Cope. He bends down to offer his ear, then nods once in obedient understanding.

The door closes behind her, to a collective release of breath. Costly jackets are removed, wrapped into balls and hurled aside; waistcoats are unbuttoned; sweat-sodden shirt-tails are wrenched free from breeches. Servants bring in crystal brandy decanters, large tumblers and trays of sweetmeats, folding back the tablecloth to set them upon the polished wood beneath. Intrigued, Will leans forward to scrutinise the jewel-bright confections – selecting one that is a rich raspberry red and moulded in the shape of a conical sea shell. He gives the point a cautious nibble; the soft, jellied flesh dissolves instantly, flooding his mouth with a taste of summer fruit so succulent and intense that he nearly blurts out an oath.

Beau wishes to clear the air. 'Gentlemen,' he says, 'please tell me that you are far too wise to pay any mind to that saucy talk concerning my younger sister.' He props a foot on the empty chair to his left. 'None of what we said was of any consequence. God knows, Mary Ann has had a miserable time of it lately. I'm sure you'll have heard the rumours – the scurrilous stories that swirl about London. It was not gallant of us to wave it before her up here as well.'

The others indicate that they understand Beau and Mr Purkiss spoke only in jest – Douglas adding that his wife was damnably prone to over-reaction where her sister was concerned. Will, for all his theorising, has heard none of these rumours about Mary Ann. Keen to learn more, he wonders how best to assure his host of his discretion.

Mr Purkiss is watching him, his pocked face heavy with contempt. 'An appropriate moment for you to withdraw, Mr Turnbull, wouldn't you say?'

Will looks to Beau. He is swilling brandy around in a tumbler; he makes no objection, not even to the error regarding Will's name. A silence settles upon the dining room. These fine gentlemen will say nothing else while the painter is present. He is being dismissed.

There is a second or two's numbness while Will fully apprehends what is happening – and then a jolt of furious, dizzying energy. Lips pursed hard, he clambers from his chair like a man dismounting a difficult horse. The plum waistcoat has gone awry and one of his stockings is coming loose from his breeches. He doesn't attempt to adjust them.

Drawing himself up, he announces that he will retire for the evening – adding, a little more pointedly than is politic, that he has *much work to do*. A cursory bow and he is off across the carpet, accelerating shoe-squeaks marking his progress to the door.

The music room beyond is far darker, lit by only a triple-stemmed candelabrum placed atop a pianoforte. Will slows, feeling a gummy sensation in his right palm: the remainder of the shell-shaped sweetmeat, carried with him from the table, is starting to liquefy against his skin. All appetite gone, he looks about distractedly for somewhere to dispose of it.

His mind teems with unpleasant questions. Was he asked here specifically to be mistreated? It's beginning to feel deliberate. Has he perhaps offended Beau in some way, or connected himself inadvertently to an enemy of the Lascelles? Is this all, in short, a *trick*? Have they dragged him out to Harewood in order to avenge a slight received during the season, in a London drawing room or pleasure garden? Will has grown up listening to the *ton* talk in Father's shop, gossiping unguardedly while they were shaved. He knows very well how they delight in their cruel games and obscure vendettas – in wreaking precisely this kind of humiliation. The only rational course for him is to leave, at first light if not that same evening. He makes for the hall door.

'Mr Turner.' It is Mr Cope, back at the entrance to the dining room. 'One moment, if you please.'

Beau saunters through. He glances at his valet with mild

resentment, like a man forcibly parted from his brandy and the company of his friends; but, nearing Will, he plasters on a rueful smile.

'My apologies for Purkiss, Mr Turner. The fellow is brusque as a baboon, really he is. And I am sorry, also, if I have appeared inattentive – not the case, I assure you. It has been a trying day for everyone at Harewood. Relocation, on the scale that we must perform it, is so very taxing. The clothes alone, great Jupiter . . .' He sighs, weaving drunkenly into a window alcove. 'I have been busy these past months, furthermore, in the auction rooms – specimens of finest porcelain, you understand, cast in the workshops of poor King Louis and several of his departed courtiers. Nothing that would be of interest to *you*, I daresay, but it must all be unpacked under close supervision. The servants simply cannot be relied upon to—'

Will has had enough. 'I want my terms, Mr Lascelles. Your letter let me believe that it was drawings you were after, drawings of your house. So I want my terms, sir. What views you'd have me do, and the money involved.'

Beau is blinking, amazed, as if he is entirely unused to being addressed in such a direct fashion. It is an act, deliberately unconvincing. 'Well, of course, Mr Turner. I suppose we have not . . . I mean to say, I am aware that we—'

Mr Cope intervenes. 'Mr Lascelles desires four views of the house, two close and two distant – you may select the orientation – and two other subjects of your choice, taken from the estate. For these six drawings, delivered in a complete condition to Lord Harewood's residence on Hanover Square, he will pay you sixty guineas.'

Will pauses, then nods; it's a solid contract, half the winter's work right there, not to mention the valuable additions he might make to his sketchbooks in the valley and woods around the house. But things still don't seem right. He's being dispensed with. This is not the manner in which commissions should be made – laid out by a businesslike valet whilst his lord sways in the background.

Now, though, Beau is walking towards him with disconcerting purpose. 'There are your *terms*, my solemn young sir,' he proclaims. 'I trust that they are to your satisfaction.'

He seizes Will's hand, as if to seal their agreement with a shake – but instead turns it in both of his, examining it closely. Will stiffens, acutely aware of the sweetmeat still stuck to his palm. Beau makes no comment, brushing the ruby-red stub onto the carpet; then he isolates the thumb and holds it up for his valet's inspection. Will is dragged to Beau's side – pressed against the damp, voluminous shirt and the slippery flab beneath.

'See here, Jim, look at that *nail!* A proper talon it is! Why, the damn thing must be half an inch long. The *scraper*, I believe they call it. Distinguishes the true watercolour man, the true artist, from the mere dabbler.'

Released abruptly, Will stumbles and almost falls to the floor. He regains his balance to find the two men contemplating him. Mr Cope is inscrutable, a towering silhouette in the bright dining room doorway; while Beau stands beside him in a boozy contrapposto, one hand on his hip, that over-sized, florid face split by a sardonic grin.

'Did I not say that our Mr Turner was the genuine article?'

*

Two days at most, thinks Will, hopping from the bottom step back onto the service floor. Two days to sketch this pile, and some bridge or lake in the vicinity, and I'll be gone. The fat villain can rot out here with his fine French china and troublesome sister and idiot idler friends – and that unaccountable valet, that *Jim*, stuck barnacle-like to his master's bloated hull. Their crude efforts to intimidate him, to humble him, won't be successful. He vows it.

A *cockney project* indeed! The *genuine article*! Will suddenly wants to break something, to kick in that door panel, to rip the buttons from his new brown jacket and send them skittering down the corridor. But instead he stops; swallows hard; loosens his stock. He has been undervalued before. He has known every sort of maddening condescension. *It is nothing to him.* All that matters is work, and finally he has his terms. So, two days of diligent sketching – and then away again into the hills and woods of England, never to return. It's not late. The studies could be started that same evening. Will is confident that he can recall enough of the house to lay in the beginnings of a close north-eastern view. He needs candles, though; he searched his bedchamber earlier and found none. The still room, Mr Cope said. Will corrects his waistcoat and stocking and sets off.

Few servants are about. Will reaches the middle of the floor, the bare vaults beneath the main hall, before he encounters anyone – a boy in an apron propped against a pillar, polishing his way through a sprawling herd of boots. This boy's directions take him past a dining room, where footmen and maids sit at separate tables, eating quietly in close rows. Mr Noakes stands beside the plain fireplace, still in his tie-wig and livery, detailing the day's lapses with stern, priestly disappointment. Will hurries by.

The still room is on the building's western side, off to the right at the end of a passage, the door wedged open at the bottom with a split log. Beyond is something between a well-stocked laboratory and a back-alley curiosity shop. Sturdy shelves hold a great archive of jars, bottles and drums; bushels of dried herbs, earthenware dishes and copper jelly-moulds hang across every remaining inch of wall. It is stiflingly hot, the single high window firmly shuttered. The smells are many, mingled and layered; vinegar, cloves, baked fruit, lavender, some kind of roasted meat. A low stove supplies the only light, washing the room's brown shadows with red and ochre, and adding a lambent edge to glass and tin. Will thinks of the Dutch paintings he has seen, at the houses of his London patrons – the cluttered huts and stables of Rembrandt or David Teniers. He walks in.

Mrs Lamb stands past the window, at a workbench invisible from the doorway. She has her back to Will, angling herself to catch the firelight, but has noticed his entrance. This, he sees, is her domain. It seems obvious now; the basket of purple berries, the interest in the gardener, the knowledge of the house's fruit stocks. She is Harewood's still-room maid. Her mob-cap is off and her hair unfastened, the tangled curls a vital, absolute black.

'You're down early, Mr Turner,' she says, turning slightly, showing a cheekbone and a curving eyelash. 'Supper was cleared but fifteen minutes ago. Did you not care to converse with Mr Lascelles and his friends?'

'I've work to do, madam. I need rest.'

'Such dedication.' Will can feel the spread of her smile; she's guessed the truth. 'Few men would walk so willingly from Mr Lascelles' table. He's on familiar terms with royalty, you know. Frequently mistaken for the Prince of Wales.'

'It was mentioned.'

Mrs Lamb faces Will now and he is struck anew by the *fullness* of her, her height and bearing, the span of her hips – a sheer womanly presence that dwarfs and bewilders him. She's grinding peppercorns in a pestle and mortar, twisting her wrist with slow strength.

'They're ambitious,' she says, 'this new branch of the family. Baron in't sufficient. Less than two years since they inherited and they already see themselves at the big palace, dining with King George. Half a dozen more mansions like this one affixed to their name.'

Will looks at the stove, at the pans bubbling gently atop it, and is unable to stop the thought of patronage entering his mind. *Do good work*, whispers Father's voice, *and this family will surely use you again*. 'Well,' he says; then nothing.

'Candles, is it?' Mrs Lamb asks, putting down the pestle and mortar. She opens a drawer and reaches inside. 'These was dipped only last week. Should burn decent enough.'

The candles are tallow, tapered and dirty grey. Shaped from animal fat, they smoke copiously and are prone to sputtering – and their light is poor, barely adequate for reading, let alone making a sketch. Will thinks of the candles that shone so brightly in the dining room upstairs: finest beeswax, white as milk and a clear foot long, superior even to those that he has Father buy back in Covent Garden.

'Ain't there nothing else?' He hears the curtness in his voice, the flat twang of London streets; immediately abashed, he wants to apologise, to revise his query, but can't locate the words.

Mrs Lamb, wrapping a dozen of the candles in a thin sheet of paper, appears unperturbed. 'There's no beeswax below stairs, sir,' she informs him, 'if that's your meaning. The cost, see. Our good steward has them locked away in his office.'

Will's incredulity overtakes his embarrassment. 'But Lord Harewood is one of the richest men in England.'

'Oh, Mr Turner.' Mrs Lamb walks over and presses the packet into his hands, holding them just an inch before her bosom. 'Don't you know the nobility at all?'

'But—'

'These are a special recipe of my own. They may surprise you.' She is near, disconcertingly so; she smells of orange peel and fresh pepper. Her expression is dryly sympathetic. *You are strange*, it seems to say, *but I like you nonetheless.*

37

Will tucks the packet under his arm and bids her good-night. His smile is faint; remarkable enough, though, after the day's myriad confusions and annoyances. It lasts almost the whole way back to the building's eastern side – when he lights one of the candles at a wall-bracket and knows at once that Mrs Lamb's creations are no better than any he's encountered before. The nimbus hardly seems to cover the length of his arm as he bears it to his chamber. He sets the candle in a saucer upon his chair, sooty smoke streaming from the flame like steam from a kettle. If three or four of the wretched things were grouped together, he thinks, there might just be enough light to work by. He starts to unwrap the rest of Mrs Lamb's packet – and sees that something is printed on the inside of the paper, a diagram of some sort. He shakes out the candles and unfolds it.

A cargo ship is shown from several different angles – profile, elevation, cross-section – each one packed with tiny forms, serried rows of supine human beings. The printing is rudimentary, yet care has been taken to render every individual body; there are so many, however, and laid so close together, that Will's eye struggles to separate them in the low light. He recognises it, of course. These sheets were ten a penny a few years ago, nailed up by the Abolitionists in certain coffee shops or taverns. For a time they were much discussed; then, gradually, they weren't, the attention of London shifting elsewhere. He didn't even register their eventual disappearance from view.

Will sits slowly on his bed, staring at the image. This is trouble. The wellspring of the Lascelles' fortune is no secret: their West Indian holdings pay for it all, from the seats in Parliament to the gold buckles on the footmen's boots. Any material pertaining to Abolition will be contraband under their roof. If he's discovered with such a thing in his possession, it will surely be taken as a grave affront. He'll be dismissed. Word will get about – a reputation swiftly acquired. This crude print could well harm his standing with an entire stratum of London society. He has to rid himself of it at once.

Yet he does not move. His mind, quite involuntarily, has started to generate a picture. Chained Negro captives, children and adults alike, wallowing in gloom and filth. The dead left among the living – mothers with daughters, husbands with wives, sisters with brothers – their naked limbs entwined in lamentation. White lines of sunlight slanting in hard through cracks in the deck, tormenting the multitudes entombed below. Parched mouths gaping open in hoarse, hopeless cries.

He recoils sharply; the paper crumples in his hands. It can't be done. The misery is too great. Too vivid. As he looks away, he notices the diagram's heading – concise, descriptive only, yet loaded with outrage.

Stowage of the British Slave Ship 'Brookes' Under the Regulated Slave Trade.

Wednesday

Climbing from the valley at twilight, Will arrives in a large flower garden. Up ahead, past tiered beds dark with blooms, is the house. The state floor is a raft of light, its brilliance deepening the surrounding dusk. Throughout the day, he has watched the fine carriages snake through the park, their panels flashing in the sun; the teams of gardeners rolling lawns and scrubbing stonework; the gathering of provisions from the farms and hothouses of the estate. A dinner is being thrown, and on a grander figure than that of the previous evening. The sounds of revelry grow clearer as he ascends – cheers and laughter, the chime of glass. Will carries on his way, pushing aside the fronds of a weeping ash. He wants none of it. Nothing useful could come of his attendance, not now. He is calm, steadied by labour and the practise of his art. Why disturb this by squeezing back into that Vandyck-brown suit?

To his undeniable satisfaction, Will is on schedule. Under his arm are the leather-bound sketchbooks, and inside the

larger, on loose leafs, are the close views: the north-east
in the morning, the south-west in the afternoon. These are
the more difficult, calling for passages of detailed draughts-
manship. He's confident that the remaining four, the distant views and the two other subjects, can all be completed
tomorrow. The sixty guineas are within reach.

Will turns to take in the shallow valley. The sun has all
but retreated, the sloping pasture and scattered woodlands
fading through a range of misty pinks and greys. It feels very
easy, this place, after the rugged sites of his northern tour.
The landscape of Harewood has been barbered, smoothed
out and rearranged, each element positioned merely to
please the eye; a tune composed to soothe rather than to stir.
The evening sky, at least, provides a constant – Sublimely
pure, immeasurably vast, forever beyond the designs of
man. Will gazes upwards and the darkening world around
him seems to contract, to sink beneath his feet. A pulse of
exhilaration beats through his chest and stomach, tingling
along his limbs. He sets himself the usual test of colouring
it – deciding on a deep indigo, luminously clear, blended
through a mix of gamboge and Indian red; with perhaps a
touch of the Venetian, stronger, along the western horizon.

A toast is proposed at the house. The party has assembled within the first-floor portico that adorns the mansion's
southern front, and throughout the long saloon behind it.
Every male arm is thrust aloft; the name of King George
repeated in an enthusiastic shout. Scowling now, Will leaves
the flower garden and cuts across a corner of lawn, making

for the western service door. Something to eat, he thinks, a brief survey of the day's work, and then to bed.

'Hoi, Will! I say, Will Turner!'

Will freezes, instinctively, as if this might somehow undo his detection. He knows this voice – yet he cannot know it. This is not Covent Garden. This is about as far from Covent Garden as you can get. His chin twitches an inch to the right. A lean, long-legged man, simply dressed, is clambering over the balustrade of the portico, between its columns. It appears, momentarily, like a vignette from a revolution: a looter or arsonist dangling from a grand house. He's escaping, though, abandoning ship – and those on board are encouraging him, applauding and whistling, even extending their hands to assist his descent.

Ignoring them, the man drops to a crouch on the grass below. His coat is plain, cheap, of a colour Will can't determine; his hair is close-cropped and unpowdered. He springs up and starts across the lawn. He wears a smile – not a smirk or an aristocratic simper but a broad, open smile of friendship. As he draws close, Will transfers the sketchbooks to his left side, flinching in anticipation. The handshake is firm, heartfelt; after only a couple of seconds it becomes a brotherly embrace. Will, the shorter by four or five inches, doesn't bother to resist.

'Tom,' he mumbles, his lips pressed against a lapel.

Released, clapped on the arm, Will staggers back. He sees the party watching them, a sneering gallery up on the state floor, and his first thought is one of relief. Tom Girtin is at Harewood. Here is an ally – a fellow Londoner, and a painter, and a commoner besides – someone to stand with him against these people. Tom is looking him over in the candlelight that falls from the house, quite oblivious to the scrutiny that accompanies it. His chuckle catches in his throat, bringing on a quick, hard cough.

'This is wonderful,' he croaks. '*Wonderful*. I hadn't the least idea. I've been here since two o'clock – but Beau mentioned it just now, for the first time, casual as you please. "And there", he says, "is dear Mr Turner, tramping up the hill." I swear I almost spat out my wine. You didn't know, did you? That I was coming here?'

'I did not,' Will replies – noting the *Beau*.

'Well, it was a rather last-minute arrangement. I was asked to Hanover Square a week or so ago, to discuss some drawing lessons – and then, from nowhere, Beau proposed I hop into his carriage and ride up the north road with him and his sisters.'

Will bites his cheek. It's one thing to use a patron's nickname when he is out of earshot; common enough among artists, a harmless bit of impertinence. Private drawing lessons, though, and an invitation to share a carriage all the way from London, with ladies on board – this is preference. 'Why didn't you?'

'Business with Moore,' says Tom, his head lowering. 'A regrettable matter. I was running late with a couple of the old dog's Lindisfarne drawings. You know the ones. I'd already had the money, there was talk of bailiffs . . . it had to be attended to. Four days' delay, then I took the stage.' His eyes, now, are on the sketchbooks. 'How about yourself? Did Beau send someone into the hills of Cumbria to hunt you down?'

'York,' Will answers. 'A letter at the Black Horse.'

Tom's ready smile returns. The inn was his recommendation; he lodged there during his own tour of the north the year before. He repeats the name fondly and launches into a string of reminiscences – the crust on the mutton pie, pots sunk around the fire, the pretty wrists of a certain kitchen maid – as if the place is an outpost of Paradise brought down to northern England. This does not match Will's experience. He kept to himself, found the food and drink to be adequate only and considered his bill a good deal too large.

'It was you, wasn't it?' he interrupts. 'You told Lascelles where I'd be.'

Tom stares in surprise. 'I ain't – I mean, I'd never—' He stops. 'I suppose it might've been mentioned. But he never let on that he was thinking of inviting you here as well.'

'You sure about that, Tom? Was there really no clue?'

Tom's reply is cut short by the appearance of their host, emerging majestically through the western service door.

'Hail, my artists! My youthful genii – votaries of Zeuxis, disciples of Saint Luke!'

Beau Lascelles seems large, larger even than he did the previous day. His stock and waistcoat are an immaculate white and a champagne flute glints in his hand. Tom adopts a mystified pose, his arms open. Beau laughs as he strolls over.

44

'I owe you an apology, Tom,' he says, 'and you as well, Mr Turner. You are the unwitting victims of a scheme of mine – a most cherished scheme, conceived in a flash at Somerset House. A *spontaneous encounter*, I thought. The two radiant stars of Dr Monro's academy, brought together at Harewood in high summer. Left to roam freely across these glorious parklands, sharing their observations.' He arrives before them, drains his glass and holds it out for a footman. 'How can such partnership fail to inspire you both to ever greater feats?'

Tom is nodding, smiling still. It's a splendid idea, he declares, and an excellent opportunity, most generously bestowed. Will manages something similar, but his mind bubbles with disquiet. Like him, Tom is a regular presence at Monro's – dependent, to a reasonable degree, on the doctor's modest stipends and the oyster suppers served at the end of the evening's labour; and he recalls now that it was at Tom's desk that Beau tended to linger during his rather self-important, disruptive visits to Adelphi Terrace. This other artist is not a companion or a brother-in-arms, as he imagined a minute earlier. He is a rival. There can be no *partnership* here, nor is there intended to be. Quite deliberately, Beau Lascelles has arranged a contest.

Will is not so vain or naive as to doubt Tom Girtin's ability. He has been studying the fellow's productions – with which Tom had always been careless, showing them to any who ask – since their boyhood. Will, however, has advanced further along the painter's path. This is indisputable. He has been exhibiting at the Royal Academy for longer, and in greater numbers. The press have begun to notice his paintings in admiring terms. A number of the senior Academicians know his name. He has worked hard to bring all of this about.

But Will does not delude himself. He knows how he appears, and he knows how the rich think. Any comparison between them, between their persons and bearing, must be unfavourable for him. There's the height, of course, and breadth of shoulder. He's the conspicuous loser on both counts. They share a certain largeness of nose, but Tom's is set in a face better favoured in every other regard. The jaw is nicely rounded, not pulled out to a point; the eyes are clear and direct, lacking Will's beady squint, so often taken for guile; the mouth suggests manly perseverance but is also quick to grin, in contrast to Will's habitual sour pout. Tom Girtin, in a word, is handsome. No one, not even Father, would make that claim for Will.

Beau and Tom are talking on, some breezy conjecture about how the house might be improved by a door and steps in the southern front, to offer access to the lawns from the state floor. Tom's accent, although never as strong as Will's, has grown yet milder, attuning to his circumstances. This is done unconsciously, without calculation; he'd surely be taken aback he was made aware of it. An intimacy exists here, Will sees, well beyond that normally found between a patron and an artist. It is obvious, too, that Tom has been to Harewood before, despite Beau's father having owned the estate for little more than a year. Will has never heard him mention this. He looks off into the shadowy valley and decides that he will head inside.

'A fruitful day, Mr Turner?' Beau enquires suddenly, with the artificial cheer of one attempting to remedy neglect. He glances at Tom; they have guessed Will's intention. 'The weather has certainly been fine.'

'Very, sir,' Will replies. 'Very fruitful. I believe that I'll be gone from here by this time tomorrow. I'll have all that I require.'

Their reaction is gratifying. Tom is wide-eyed with dismay; Beau takes a half step backwards, letting out a sigh of lordly disappointment.

'My dear Mr Turner,' he murmurs, 'there is no call what-ever for *that*. Perhaps you misunderstand this experiment of mine. *Collaboration*, my young friend, of the intellect at least.' Beau warms to his theme. 'Two kindred art-spirits drawing strength and vision from one another, like Raffaelo Sanzio and Michelangelo, Nicolas Poussin and Claude, Murillo and . . . and that other Spaniard, what was his name?'

'Velazquez?' Tom ventures; Beau snaps his fingers in approval.

You mean to pit us against each other for your entertain-ment, Will thinks, and by God, you've already picked your favourite. 'I have my terms, Mr Lascelles,' he says, 'which you were so kind as to give me. When the six sketches are done I shan't burden your household any longer.'

Beau waves this away, but he recognises the determination on Will's face. There is a pause; his smile becomes strained.

47

'Well,' he says, 'I can hardly *force* you to stay, Mr Turner. I am no gaoler. This house of mine is no damned gaol.'

'Come now, Will,' says Tom amiably, 'can't you be convinced to remain with us a while longer? How many hundred times, back in London, did we wish for a chance like this?'

Will addresses Beau. 'I am fatigued, sir, after my labours, and hungry too. I must ask your permission to retire.'

Beau gives it offhandedly, amusedly, with a faint nostril-flare of disdain; and as he speaks, his attention shifts to his dinner guests, who are still watching and chattering in the bright windows behind the portico. Will bows, then turns towards the service door. Tom Girtin stands in his way. He has hardened a little, affronted by Will's intransigence, and seems to consider holding the smaller man in place to hear another appeal. Past experience, however, has taught him to know better, and he steps aside.

'Be sure to wait for me in the morning,' he says. 'We'll have one good day out here together, Will Turner.'

*

The service floor is on high alert. Maids and footmen hurry along the corridors; orders and queries are shouted through the haze of tallow smoke. There is a crisis, Will soon learns – too many guests for the dining room. Nobody can agree whether this is due to faulty information from the family as to how many were invited, or late, unsanctioned additions, hidden in the larger carriages, but the talk is of relocating the dinner to the gallery. This would involve retrieving the banqueting table from a store-room, assembling it upstairs and then setting it for twenty-eight, all in a matter of minutes — an undertaking viewed with a mixture of panic and black resolve. Mr Noakes stands at a corner, up on a stool; clad in livery, the tie-wig in his hand, he dabs his shining pate with a handkerchief as he yells for the groom of chamber.

Will edges by unremarked. His goal is the kitchen, and the supper he hopes will be available within. He succeeds in reaching the doorway. Servants stream constantly in and out. Past them, he glimpses billowing steam clouds, a surface covered with gold-leafed plates, a spout of orange flame. There is a searing hiss, like fat sliding across a hot pan; someone, the chef presumably, curses loudly in French. Will moves on, further into the house. If he enters that kitchen now and asks to be fed he'll be lucky not to have a spoon thrown at him. Better to sit in the servants' hall until the weight of their duties has eased.

Suddenly the servants come to a stop, stepping against the walls, bowing their heads and dropping cramped curtseys. Beau walks through, unmindful of all, on his way to rejoin the festivities on the state floor; Tom Girtin is beside him, finishing a story. Will slips down a corridor, out of sight. He recognises this tale immediately. It's one of Tom's favourites.

When they were but fourteen years of age, the two of them had been due to join a sketching party to Hampton Court, under the stewardship of Tom's erstwhile master, Edward Dayes. A boat was hired, and the company of young artists and apprentices gathered on the wharf at Blackfriars. Will voiced a desire to sit at the prow; Dayes had this privilege marked for himself. The resulting clash, between a renowned watercolour artist and a barber's son from Maiden Lane, was terrible to behold, and resulted in Will remaining ashore, stalking back to Covent Garden as the boat and its mirthful cargo eased out onto the river.

'The pattern of Will's life was set that morning,' Tom concludes. 'Everything since has been mere reiteration.'

Beau laughs. 'It is fair to say, then, that Mr Turner tends towards obstinacy?'

'He's a brother to me, honestly; but the most ill-tempered old donkey, denied his feed-bag and left out in the rain, is a picture of good humour by comparison.'

They mount the stairs and are gone. The servants return to work as if freed from a spell. Will takes a breath; he rubs the frown lines from his brow. His capacity for astonishment or umbrage at this situation is exhausted. Tom's words, in truth, do not anger him particularly. Donkey, mule, ox – such epithets lost their sting long ago, and are now heard with something close to pride. Let them, he thinks. Let the Lascelles make Tom Girtin their pet. It's hardly a secret that the fellow has no diligence, no discipline and a host of other defects. Let them wait month upon month for his drawings, long after Will's are adorning their walls, winning widespread admiration. Let them——

'A hand, Mr Turner, if you please?'

Mrs Lamb is at Will's shoulder, standing close and smiling

wide. She has a small sack clasped to her chest and another resting between her boots.

'London brawn, sir, is what I need. Seems I've over-reached myself – this here load is more than I can manage.' She leans in yet closer, her mouth inches from Will's ear, and lowers her voice conspiratorially. 'I can promise you a fine reward.'

Will reaches for the sack on the ground. It holds only three slim silver trays – Mrs Lamb could surely have carried it without difficulty. This request for assistance is a ruse, but Will is content to play along. He has a question of his own for the still-room maid.

'Lead on,' he says.

She doesn't move. 'You're friendly with him, in't you – with this other artist, Mr Girtin. I saw you from my window, just now. Out on the lawn.'

'We've known each other a good while.'

Mrs Lamb catches the distinction; her mouth narrows very slightly. 'The gentleman's arrival this afternoon was the talk of the house. He was at Harewood last summer as well, you understand. Among the very first guests the new family admitted. Couple of the housemaids grew quite besotted with him. Our dashing young painter.'

Will has no response to this. He adjusts his hold on the leather-bound sketchbooks.

Mrs Lamb is studying him with her black, unblinking eyes. 'You weren't told that your friend was coming here, were you, sir?'

'Neither was he,' says Will quickly. 'Neither was Tom.'

The still-room maid brushes past, the stained cuff of her dress pressing against Will's sleeve, then tearing away with a syrupy tackiness. 'Goodness, Mr Turner, neither was anyone! You saw the confusion yesterday, when you showed up at our door. The family expect us to manage their little surprises, whatever they might be. Just look at the unholy bother down here this evening – twelve extra guests there are, and with no notice at all. A wonder we don't rise up against 'em.'

Swinging about, Mrs Lamb advances imperturbably into the crowded junction of corridors before the kitchens. Will follows, trying to keep in her wake and out of everyone's way. This is impossible: when a footman strides from the western stairwell, he has to skip sideways to avoid a collision. The servant is bearing a silver wine cooler, an ornate piece with lion's feet at its base, filled almost to the brim with fresh vomit. Mr Purkiss is named as the culprit; wearily, as if this is but the latest in a line of similar misdemeanours.

'Life in service, eh, lad?' says Mrs Lamb to the footman. 'Does it match your boyhood dreams?'

'Enough now,' calls Mr Noakes from his stool, over the laughter. 'Sluice room with that, Mr Jenkins.'

The passage to the still room is quieter, a rich, jammy smell thickening the air. They go inside; moulds and pans, recently used, are piled upon the dormant stove, and perhaps two dozen tallow candles burn in a range of improvised holders. A stout table has been brought in and stood in the centre of the room. Across its middle, in their hundreds, are jellied sweetmeats. This is their source. Dusted lightly with sugar, they are arranged in rainbow bands – ruby red sea shells, like the one Will sampled; stars of jade with trailing tails; azure fishes beside coral-pink piglets.

'My contribution,' says Mrs Lamb, 'to this most magical of nights. A new batch, Mr Turner, made especially. Pass over the trays, would you?'

They are alone, the door standing ajar behind them. Will sets down the sack. 'Them candles you gave me,' he says.

'Oh aye. How d'ye find them? Any better?'

Will unclasps the larger sketchbook and takes the *Brookes* print from under the front cover. The moment is not nearly as dramatic as he envisaged. Mrs Lamb looks at the page for a second only. It leaves her totally unconcerned. She starts to stack dirty bowls and utensils at the table's edge, clearing a space by the sweetmeats.

'Mr Turner,' she says, 'you must pay no mind to that. It's speakers in the markets, sir, over at Leeds and elsewhere. The scoundrels will stuff their pamphlets into a basket without so much as a by-your-leave. I use them for scrap.' She heaves a chopping board to the floor. 'I'm sorry, truly, if that one upset you.'

'It didn't *upset* me, madam,' Will lies hotly. 'It simply ... it ...' He stops, wrong-footed. 'It was chance, then? An accident?'

The still-room maid tosses a long knife into a dish, the bone handle clattering around the rim. 'Heavens, Mr Turner,

so mistrustful! Tell me, what else could it be? Why might I
have done such a thing on purpose?'

Will's gaze strays to the bowed hull of the *Brookes*. 'That
I don't know.'

'There's the blessed family for a start, and the minions
they have hereabouts. If Noakes or Cope found a body with
summat like that they'd see them whipped like they was
caught poaching rabbits. Why didn't you rid yourself of it?'

Staring now, Will is thinking of the slave ship upon the
open sea, and how it would move; the dreadful compres-
sion of humanity below deck as it rolled upon a wave; the
hundreds of gallons of freezing saltwater that would pour in
through the hatches. 'I don't know that either.'

Mrs Lamb comes around the table to retrieve her sack.
She slides out the silver trays and lays them in a row, upon
the knotted wood. 'There's more,' she says, almost casually,
'if you want them, that is. In that drawer.'

Will is snapped back to the still room. 'What d'you
mean?'

She shrugs. 'Just seems that you're holding on to that one
very tightly, Mr Turner. Perhaps it speaks to you. To your
Christian conscience.'

Will returns the *Brookes* to his sketchbook, refastens the
clasps and looks towards the door. Is this why she wanted
him in there? Why she snagged him in the corridor? He has
an instinctive wariness of causes. Painters of any ambition
take care to remain independent. He knows a couple of
politically minded artists back in London and it's proving a

pronounced obstacle to their rise. 'I don't, madam. I assure you.'

The still-room maid shrugs again and begins to transfer the sweetmeats from table to tray, plucking up three or four of the miniature piglets at a time; and then she changes the subject so deftly and completely that it's as if their discussion of the *Brookes* hadn't occurred.

'In't it *strange*, though,' she says, 'that the family should be choosing to put on such a large entertainment as this one upstairs. Word down here is that Mr Lascelles and his sisters – one of his sisters, anyhow – should rightfully be hiding themselves away.'

Will, still a little flustered and contemplating his exit, wasn't listening. 'Beg pardon?'

'And there's the death.' Mrs Lamb adjusts a couple of the piglets. 'Some might say that it's difficult to mourn an infant only a day old, already buried down in Huntingdonshire, and with a twin still living. But their brother Henry would be unimpressed, I reckon, and injured perhaps, to see all this jollity at Harewood barely two months later.'

This Will hears. Henry Lascelles is the second son, the politician. Will was unaware that he'd suffered such a loss. Small children die easily, though, and babies especially; it is not, in his experience, regarded as grounds for any prolonged seclusion. 'What was the first thing? The sisters?'

Mrs Lamb, starting on the fishes, is happy to tell him. 'They say that our Miss Lascelles found herself in a spot of trouble down in London. Quite compromised, she was.

The poor dear had to be whisked off post-haste, back to Harewood.'

Just as Will deduced. He sees Mary Ann flouncing from the dining room upstairs, her footfalls rattling the glassware; Beau's show of contrition once she was gone. 'What happened?'

'D'ye really not know, Mr Turner? D'ye not read the London papers? *The Intelligencer* and suchlike?'

Gutter rags were always heaped around Father's shop, pored over by the clientele, every veiled reference and pseudonym debated at length. Will, concerned only with art reviews, never looks at them. 'I confess that I don't.'

The first silver tray is covered, loaded with confectionary. Mrs Lamb switches to the stars, continuing her revelations with steely levity. 'You'll be unaware, then, that Miss Lascelles' mishaps are followed closely in their pages. All the available details. They find their way up here eventually. And those on the staff who wintered at Hanover Square saw plenty of it for themselves.' She taps a clot of sugar from a star's tail. 'There was an affair, Mr Turner, and a wild one at that, and then there was a jilting. Our young miss was knocked off some gentleman's boots like a lump of dung.'

'Who was he?'

'No one can discover. A mysterious nobleman so very rich that the prospect of the Lascelles' millions leaves him unmoved, and with enough sway on Grub Street to keep his name the subject of guesswork only.' Mrs Lamb straightens up for a few seconds, wiping a palm on her apron.

'It's a grand humiliation for her, to be sure. For the lot of them. Yet here they are inviting dozens to dine and drink in their home, and artists, *two* artists no less, to sketch in its grounds.' She begins to fill the final tray. 'It don't fit.'

'Perhaps they think it best to act as if unaffected.'

Again, her expression is doubtful; and then, noticing something behind him, it grows distinctly frosty. Will turns to find Mr Cope standing in the doorway. An uncomfortable pressure creeps up behind Will's ears. It is impossible to say how much the valet might have heard. He curses himself for indulging in such careless gossip.

'Mr Turner is a painter, Mrs Lamb,' says Mr Cope, calm and unforgiving. 'He is the guest of your master. He is not at Harewood for you to collar whenever you need an errand boy.'

The still-room maid's smile is terrifying, a parody of graciousness. 'Why, and a very good evening to you too, Mr Cope! The young gentleman has only been helping me for a minute. Besides which, might I point out that it is *dark?* What painting could he be doing now?'

Will's eyes go back to the valet.

'Mr Turner is here at the invitation of Lord Harewood's son.' Mr Cope speaks more slowly, as if for an idiot. 'He has specific tasks assigned to him and little time in which to perform them. You are not to distract him with duties that belong properly to domestic servants. Do you follow?'

The false smile drops away. Mrs Lamb shifts back from the table and plants a fist against her hip. 'It were common courtesy, that's all. I had a heavy burden and Mr Turner was good enough to offer me assistance. Few of your precious *domestic servants* would do the same.'

Mr Cope will not argue. He extends a long arm into the corridor. 'Mr Turner.'

The valet's manner, taking compliance utterly for granted, reminds Will of the music room, and the slighting way in which his terms were conveyed. He isn't about to refuse, though, or chance a bold remark – not with the *Brookes* inside his larger sketchbook. In fact, he finds it easy to imagine that Mr Cope might be drawn to the print somehow; that he might sniff it out and run barking to his master. The best course is to go with him, peel away as soon as he can, pleading tiredness, and then burn the thing back in the casket chamber. He bids Mrs Lamb good evening, but gets no response. She is bent over her table, making a great fuss of laying out the red sea shells on their tray, and ignoring everything else.

'Be careful, Mrs Lamb,' says the valet, once Will is through the door. 'Their tolerance is nearly at an end.'

The service floor has emptied. Many of the servants are upstairs, Will supposes, setting the banqueting table in the gallery. Valet and painter walk side by side. After a dozen yards or so Mr Cope says that he understands Will is not joining the company in the saloon; would he care for some supper in the servants' hall instead? Will's belly emits a joyful growl. He replies that he would, and despite his apprehension he is thankful, once again, for the valet's effectiveness.

They separate, Mr Cope heading for the kitchens. Only when seated on a bench in the servants' hall, the sketchbooks safely beside him, does Will properly consider what has happened. It is easy enough to work out how the fellow knew where he was – Mr Noakes must have told him when he went upstairs to marshal the dinner party. Why, though, had Mr Cope come at all? Why had he been so set on removing Will from the still room? What kind of a damn valet is this?

Mr Cope appears with a plate of food and a tin tankard. The few servants loitering in the hall disperse immediately. Will's meal is set upon the table, roast pork and potatoes and a pint of treacle-coloured ale, along with a plain knife and fork. He bolts it, more or less. This has become a ritual of his tour: the sating of his hunger after a productive day outdoors, shutting out the world to go face down in the trough. The food itself is almost unimportant – fortunately, given some of the tavern fare he has endured – but this is good, really good, the meat tender and the ale smooth. He's halfway through before he realises that Mr Cope is still there, at his shoulder, peering at him coolly like a stone saint up on a cathedral. Seeing that he has Will's attention, the valet beings to speak; his voice is different, quieter, with the trace of a London accent.

'Mrs Lamb isn't your friend.'

Will lays down his fork. 'Never thought she was, Mr Cope.'

'It's a game she plays. You must see this. She's trying to get you on her side.'

Will thinks of the *Brookes* print, hidden not six inches from his thigh; Mrs Lamb's rather flimsy explanation of how it came to be in his possession; her offer of more. 'Beg pardon?'

The ghost of a smile crosses Mr Cope's face. 'Some advice, Mr Turner. Resist it.'

And with that he's gone, departing the servants' hall for the nearest staircase. Will looks blankly at the strands of pork still upon his plate. Ale gurgles inside him; he smothers a belch against his sleeve. Then he rocks forward on the bench, shovels in the remainder of the meal and scrambles to his feet. He's at the casket chamber in less than two minutes, hunched over a tallow candle, feeding the *Brookes* print into the flame. The paper is dry and membrane-thin; it flares yellow, curling to a blackened wisp that floats up from his fingers, vanishing into the shadows overhead. Will slumps back on the bed. He is filled, more than anything, with a sense of monumental unfairness. Making drawings of an aristocratic estate is a simple enough proposition. It has been going on for centuries, and mostly without incident. Yet when he attempts it, bringing with him all of his assiduousness and ability, he is plunged into a dark farce – a mess of unwelcome complications. It truly defies belief.

Will rests a hand on his sketchbooks; a steadying breath becomes a yawn. He has to sleep. He has to keep to his schedule.

He has to get away from this place.

Thursday

It is well past noon when Tom appears. Will is sat against a fin of mossy rock; he lifts his porte-crayone from the paper and watches the other painter approach. Tom wears a faded travelling coat the colour of builder's clay, long riding trousers rather than breeches and a pair of scuffed boots. He is bare-headed and carries nothing: no umbrella, sketchbook or drawing board. That easy stride of his, that expression somehow light-hearted yet unyielding, causes Will to remember the last time he'd seen him in London, several weeks before the opening of the Academy Exhibition. There had been a pack of them, installed in a tavern after a day painting scenery at the Sans Souci. Full of punch and lively defiance, Tom had climbed atop a chair, set on defying the gagging acts by reciting a passage from one of his radicals. 'My own mind is my church!' he'd cried, swatting at Georgie Samuel as he tried to pull him back down. An unthinking grin curls the corner of Will's mouth.

Tom flops beside the rock. He gives Will's thigh a good-natured pat before stretching himself out, crossing his legs at the ankle and covering his eyes with his arm. Will says nothing. He's back in his sketch, the first of the long views, tracing a knotted thicket and the small farm building half hidden within. After a few minutes he realises that Tom has fallen asleep.

An hour or so goes by. Will completes his view and places it in the larger sketchbook. He sits for a while, chewing on a piece of bread given to him by the kitchen maids. It has been a dull day thus far, overcast, the sky flat and featureless. Now, though, a single coin of sunlight falls onto the sloping lawn that runs from Harewood's southern front to the boating pond in the middle of the valley. It expands, grows stronger, tinting the grass with shimmering yellow; and the clouds begin to ease apart, revealing pure blue above.

Tom stirs, sitting up, fumbling with his tail-pocket. Instead of a roll of paper, however, or a porte-crayone of his own, he takes out a pipe and tinderbox.

'You didn't wait,' he says.

'Couldn't.' Will swallows some bread. 'Work to do.'

'Suppose you did retire early. Why, it was barely dark.'

'And I'll wager you was up till it was close to light again.'

This is no wager. Will was woken in the early dawn by singing and ragged, drunken laughter, issuing from the flower garden, among which Tom's voice was plainly heard. He'd clamped his pillow over his head and made an unsuccessful attempt to swear himself back to sleep.

'Man must live, Will. Seize what he can.'

'That's living, is it, Tom? Prancing about with the Lascelles and their crowd?'

Tom grins. 'It does have its shortcomings,' he admits. 'These noble gentlemen are testing at times. Remove the carriages and the costly clothes and there's nearly always a dolt beneath.'

'Does your chum *Beau* number among the dolts, I wonder?'

Untroubled by Will's irritability, Tom opens the tinderbox and prepares the charcloth. 'You know full well what that was, Will, as you must do it yourself.' He fits his fingers in the D-shaped firesteel and strikes it against the flint. The sound is piercing, fractured; Will winces to hear it. 'God knows, they're easy enough to please. All a fellow really has to do is laugh at their damn jokes. It was Nelson last night. "Albion's foes will discover that although now *armless*, he remains far from *harmless*." From their mirth you'd think it was the sharpest line ever uttered.' Tom strikes the flint again. 'You heard of this, off on your tour?'

The news had arrived on Will's last day in York: a furious battle against the Spanish at Tenerife, a decisive defeat, England's great hero so gravely wounded. Patrons had wept openly in the snug bar of the Black Horse. Will's thoughts, as always, were of painting. It would surely make for a fine narrative subject, a scene both affecting and rousing – the enormous frigates; the perfect disc of the moon; the injured Admiral refusing all aid as he marched himself to the surgeon. But he doesn't want to discuss this now.

'What terms did he give you?'

At the third strike a minute spark flits from the flint and smoulders on a fold in the charcloth. Tom is ready with a taper, which he then pokes into the pipe's bowl, sucking on the stem as he does so. 'For my chest,' he murmurs, sucking again. 'Monro's recommendation. Damn nuisance, to tell the truth.'

Will repeats his question.

The tobacco catches, and for a minute Tom's coughing prevents all speech. Will finishes off the bread; he watches the sun spread through the valley, casting a sheet of blazing white across the pond.

'None as such,' Tom says at last, dabbing at his eyes with his coat cuff. 'Beau's idea simply seems to be that I live in the household. Spend my days out here in the park.' Sitting next to Will, his back against the rock, Tom tries the pipe again. This time is easier; he puffs twice, then exhales a coil of smoke. 'But I have to say, Will, it's a damn strange place to be. All of it is *fake*, from these woods here to the very hills they are rooted upon. It ain't nature as I know her, that's for sure.' He leans forward, gesturing with his pipe. 'And the house. Look at it. There's a hundred exactly like it elsewhere in England, damn near identical in all but size. There's no art in its construction. No history in its stones. It speaks of nothing but money.'

'You're happy enough to stay here,' Will observes, not mentioning his own similar thoughts. 'And not for the first time neither.'

Tom smokes in contemplation. 'Naturally I'm happy,' he says. 'London is hellish at present. The war goes badly still. Soldiers are everywhere. Friends of liberty, of any species of liberty, must be constantly on their guard. They'll throw you in Newgate merely for speaking out of turn – and they'll keep you in there, without charge, for as long as they damn well please. That villain Pitt wants us cowed, Will, and it's working. Why, it feels sometimes as if every decent person has fled the city.'

This picture is exaggerated. Tom has always been the sort who relishes a drama, preferably with himself playing a central part. Will pushes his sun hat to the back of his head. He waits for the other painter to continue.

'Up here, though, all that noise goes quiet. A man can rest. Order his thoughts.' Tom becomes confiding. 'And there's other advantages. This I learned well last year. Beneath the baron's roof, and toiling in the baron's farms, are many young women – and every last one of them, Will, is *bored senseless*.' He draws on his pipe. 'I mean, think of their lives. Their labours. How bleak and unending it must be. It don't take much, at any rate, to win their favour. Most of them will clutch at a chance for diversion with all they've got.'

Will smiles in dour amazement. Beside him is a raging radical prepared to bed down with arch-Tory aristocrats; a notable young artist content to travel two hundred miles and make no art; an urbane London professional eager to chase after Yorkshire chambermaids. 'You're adaptable, Tom Girtin,' he says. 'That I'll allow.'

Tom chuckles. 'Surely you can savour some of what's on offer here. Especially after the travellers' inns. What a moment it is, for one resigned to lice-ridden straw, to lie upon a goose-feather mattress! And dear God, the *peace*. No need for your cork pellets at Harewood, or a bolt on your door. Or a call for the watch.'

Will's smile disappears. This is his tour no longer. This is Maiden Lane. 'Beg pardon?'

For a short while Tom does not respond; realising his error, he fiddles with the pipe, tamping its bowl with a corner of the firesteel. 'It must be difficult,' he says. 'That's all I meant, Will. I heard about the fight, the last one, over on Southampton Street. How she broke that barrow boy's jaw. It's a damn miracle, frankly, that you're still able to work as you do.'

And then Will sees it. Tom Girtin is attempting to unnerve him, to throw off his concentration and disrupt his schedule, and thus give himself a chance to catch up. Will has managed to bar this business from his mind for the better part of six weeks – as Father had ordered him to do, in the plainest language – and he rears from it like a horse before a fire. Without speaking, without even looking Tom's way, he gathers his gear, gets up and walks west.

But now it's *there*, eclipsing everything, the memory louder and brighter than life. Mother at the height of her frenzy, spitting at Father and Will as they edge closer, trying to grab hold of her. The howl of the victim, blood spotting fast between the broken bottles. The feel of her pressed to

66

his chest, so bony and fierce, kicking backwards at his shins as Father addresses the crowd, promising grand sums if only the incident can be kept from the magistrate.

This is no use. This will accomplish nothing. *Don't you grant her a single thought*, Father had said. *The work must come first*. Will passes through a screen of slender trees, swinging at some tangled bracken with his umbrella. He rubs his brow on his sleeve, then breathes deeply and wipes the matter away. He gulps; he blinks. It's gone.

Beyond the trees is a long expanse of pasture, distant sheep drifting over its lower reaches like flecks of foam. Will strides uphill, towards an old tree-stump. The valley lies open before him, bruised by the shadows of clouds. A south-western prospect would have been best, but straight south will do. Time is growing short. He sits and prepares his materials; then he squints at the house, pulls the sun hat forward and slips gratefully into the blankness of work.

Not ten minutes have passed when a whistle makes him look up. A shepherd is moving the sheep off, funnelling them through a gate – and there, perhaps forty yards to the right, is Tom Girtin, propped against a dry-stone wall. A warm breeze sways the trees; the clouds roll back and brilliant sunlight surges across the pasture, breaking over them both, reducing Tom's face to no more than a pale blot atop his coat.

Will returns to the sketch, his resolve to complete his task and leave Harewood fortified yet further; and a detail from Tom's talk strikes him as stunningly as a pebble hurled from a sling, jogging his line by a clear half-inch.

A goose-feather mattress.

*

Things are now urgent. Will heads out onto a dandelion-spotted meadow, his boot-steps jarring his spine as he trots down the gradient towards the boating pond. He has enough for the second long view, just barely, but the afternoon is well on the wane. There are perhaps four hours of decent daylight remaining, and two more sketches to be done, of subjects he has yet to determine. The part of the commission he was least concerned by, to which he has given no real thought, suddenly looks like it may be his undoing.

All is not lost. Yesterday, while crossing a bridge in the western part of the estate, Will heard the whisper of a waterfall. He didn't pay it any mind at the time, but if there are rocks, or a picturesque arrangement of trees, it could serve his purpose. Another twenty minutes walking, a half-hour to judge the views, an hour on each sketch – he might yet make the evening mail coach.

Following the pond's bank westwards brings Will to a walled garden. He goes to the nearest door, a navy blue rectangle set into the red brick, thinking to save a few minutes by cutting through. It opens easily, revealing a grid of gravel paths laid out around plots of vegetables. Will steps inside. The air is still, heavy, scented with herbs; the only sound is the soft hum of bumblebees. Almost instantly, a gardener rises from behind a line of lettuces, a man of about his age with a downy beard and a narrow, unfriendly face. Will halts, recognising the situation: trespasser meets warden. He glances back to the doorway, wondering if he should remonstrate or simply accept ejection.

Without speaking, the gardener retreats to a nearby shed, wiping a trowel on the end of his muddy apron. Will walks on, past carrot-tops and thyme bushes; and he notices other gardeners packing up and moving away as well. He looks around him in perplexity.

Tom Girtin is strolling in through the garden door. Will considers evasion, hiding amid the beds, but sees that this would be futile. He stands in place, picking at his teeth with the scraping nail, and eyes the other painter with wary annoyance. Is there to be a discussion of their earlier rupture? Is there to be contrition, an embrace, a pledge of brotherhood?

The answer is no, thankfully, on every count. Tom appears to have excised all unpleasantness from his mind; and indeed, as he draws near, his talk is not of Maiden Lane but a herd of young deer that have wandered from the woods on the southern side of the valley.

'You should've sketched them,' Will tells him. 'Put them in a view. Just the sort of detail they like.'

Tom laughs. 'I ain't got the skill for that, Will. I didn't attend the Academy schools, if you recollect.'

No, thinks Will, you were *rejected* – and immediately feels

69

guilty. This is unjust. He knows very well what Tom can do. He says nothing.

'Besides, I ain't brought any blessed paper.' Tom is looking now at the sketchbooks; his voice grows teasing. 'I ain't so magnificently prepared as you. D'you really need *both* books out here? Scared a maid might run off with them, are you, if they was left back at the house?'

Will ignores this. 'I've two more studies to take, Tom, afore the post leaves from the village. I've got to get on.'

At once Tom is serious. 'What are you thinking?'

The question – direct, practical, genuinely interested – comes from a simpler time; from expeditions made together into the countryside around London, perhaps, when Will could stand the barber's shop no longer and Tom was truanting from the studio of Edward Dayes. Walking out to Lambeth or Putney, or the fields of Highgate, they would set themselves various artistic challenges, and deliver frank verdicts on each other's work; then talk a little of their plans, their frustrations, their common aims. It's been three years since they last did this. Three years at least.

'The waterfall. Over by that bridge.'

Tom's expression suggests approval. He offers to show Will the fastest route through the gardens. Of course – he's familiar with this place. Will looks up at the sky, at the full tones of late afternoon, and attempts to quash his aggravation. He accepts.

Another blue door admits them to a different section of the enclosure, given over in large part to a vineyard.

These voracious plants are taller than a man, their ten-
drils reaching out across the avenues, leaves blocking the
sun to such a degree that Will has an impression of being
under canvas – of proceeding through a low, yellow-green
marquee, with purple grape-clusters in place of sconces
and chandeliers. At first, this area appears to be similarly
deserted. As they approach the end of the vine plot, however, Will glimpses white up ahead – the hard white of
starched cotton. A greenhouse has been built against the
far wall, seventy feet in length, its roof angled to trap as
much light as possible. Before it, at a trestle table, Mrs
Lamb is trimming pineapples with a clasp knife. Will
slows, recalling the warmth with which she'd treated him
and how welcome it had been; and also Mr Cope's blunt
warning in the servants' hall. He decides it would be best
to slip by unnoticed.

Tom lopes past, breaking cover, and bids the still-room
maid a blithe good afternoon. Will stops and curses; then he
trails out after Tom, scanning the greenhouse and the paths
around it for the nearest blue door. Mrs Lamb turns towards
them, performing a subtle swivel that lifts her chest very
slightly. Her sun-browned cheeks are stippled with perspiration; her eyes lost in the shade beneath her bonnet brim.
With one hand, she folds up her clasp knife and puts it into
the pocket of her apron.

The conversation that follows is excruciatingly trivial: the
fine weather, the subsequent heat in the greenhouses, the
splendour of the park. Mrs Lamb responds to Tom's queries

with readiness and some wit. There's a distance to her, though, a near-imperceptible detachment; Tom no doubt imagines that he's charming yet another of Harewood's denizens, but it's plain to Will that it's he who is being handled. The still-room maid seems to recognise Will's impatience, his uncertainty, and apprehend its meaning. She looks in his direction.

'There's a rumour, Mr Turner, that you're leaving us today. Can it be true, after a stay of only two nights' duration?'

Will shifts about, feeling hot and desperately callow; his left boot sinks an inch into the gravel, briefly unbalancing him. 'I must get on, madam.'

Tom intervenes. 'Will is an object lesson to all painters, Mrs Lamb. He's forever working, forever moving. Whereas I am an idle creature, liable to sit in one place until cobwebs span my back and mice have made their nests in my pockets.'

Mrs Lamb doesn't comment on this. Instead, regarding Will evenly, she offers a farewell, voicing her sincere regret that his stay at Harewood was so short. 'You never got that reward, neither,' she adds, hefting the largest pineapple from the table. 'For your kind assistance last night.'

'No need, madam,' says Will, 'no need at all. And farewell to you also.'

Beset by awkwardness, he bows, tips the sun hat, almost drops the umbrella; then he's off through a door at the far end of the greenhouse, thinking that it must surely lead from the garden. Beyond it, however, is another huge partition – vegetable plots, fruit trees and greenhouses, and four more blue doors to choose between. He's attempting to orientate himself when Tom's boot-steps come crunching across the stones behind him.

'A *reward*, Will Turner? For your kind assistance *last night?*'

Will tries not to react. 'Which way is the damn waterfall?'

'And you played it so very coy up on the hill. Mrs Lamb ain't an entirely prudent choice, it has to be said, but I know how these things can be.'

'Damn your eyes, Tom, which way?' Will says, more loudly. Then he pauses. *'Prudent?'*

Tom grins; he pulls open his collar and nods towards one of the doors. 'A woman with enemies can be interesting. Out here, though, I honestly believe it's more likely to bite you than otherwise.'

Will thinks again of Mr Cope's warning; and of Mr Noakes, on that first afternoon, the way he'd spoken to her. 'What the devil are you on about?'

This last door opens onto a grove of oak and beech. Tom walks out in front. 'You must've seen how she is. She riles them something awful – all the senior ones, and a number of the juniors too. Too much sauce. Too much nerve. The truth of it is she's just not fitted for a house like this. There was an ally – the housekeeper, Mrs Linley – a protector, if you like; but she took her leave in the spring. You've noticed that they ain't got a replacement yet?'

Will hadn't. 'What of the husband?'

'D'you really not *know?*' asks Tom. He laughs at Will's discomfort. 'You can be at ease there. She was widowed, the others think, some time afore she came to Harewood.'

They emerge from the trees. In front of them is the boating pond, its surface aglow in the early evening light. Skating insects etch wide circles upon this golden film, while wild ducks dip among the reeds at its edge, their webbed feet batting the air. Away to the left is the wooden bridge that leads back to the house. Will can hear the waterfall, hidden in the undergrowth, whispering beneath the birdsong and the shifting of leaves.

'She's good,' Tom continues. 'Without equal, they'll tell you, in the domain of preserves, pickles and suchlike. It's the only thing that's kept her here. But it won't save her. A new housekeeper will be appointed before the summer's end, and rooting the unruly Irishwoman from the still room will be close to the top of her list.'

Will frowns. 'She's a gypsy, ain't she? Like them up on the moors?'

'Irish is what I was told. Travelling stock – came over in childhood. Started off in the kitchens of Leeds.' Tom takes out his pipe. 'And she'll be back in them soon enough.'

The frown deepens; then Will shakes his head, as if to be rid of a bothersome fly. None of this is his concern. He's been at Harewood for two days only, and in a few hours he'll be gone, off to another part of the country altogether, following his proper course. He passes the bridge, climbs down a bank thick with ivy and turns to survey the waterfall.

It is a mere trickle, fifteen feet tall at most, buried in the shadow of the bridge and the surrounding trees. Mystery and majesty are completely absent, and the picturesque also: it is *mundane*, a piece of landscape engineering, there simply to sustain the level of the pond. Will peers along the stream at the waterfall's base and sees only a spread of mean, functional farm buildings.

'This ain't no use. This won't do at all. Hell's bells, Tom, will you look at it!'

Tom is on the bridge, chewing ruefully on the stem of his unlit pipe. 'I thought it was prettier, I have to say. It's been altered since last year. Reduced, I think.'

'I can't make a sketch here. And there's no more time. Damn it all, I can't——' *I can't leave.*

'Will,' says Tom, 'you must calm yourself. I understand your wish to get back to London, honest I do. What differ-ence, though, can another day make? Your father has man-aged alone at Maiden Lane for the best part of the summer. He'd hate for you to squander this chance.'

Suddenly Will is suspicious. He glowers up at the bridge. Had this been a deliberate ploy, a trap to hinder him? Had Tom supported the idea of the waterfall knowing full well that it was no good – that Will would be obliged to stay another night and be delayed in his work?

There is no sign of this. Tom wears an affable grin; he's trying to be consolatory. 'I'll help you. We'll seek out a sub-ject together, a worthy subject. Never fear, old friend.'

Will remains doubtful. The schedule's collapse, however,

has robbed him of his energy. He jams the umbrella beneath his arm and starts to scale the ivy-covered bank.

'Very well,' he says.

*

The hall has a welcome coolness after the dim, smothering heat of the service floor. There is a hush over this level of the house; everything is in its place and newly cleaned, yet a faint charge of last night's riotousness lingers in the air. Will walks to the marble table, tugging at the sleeves of the Vandyck-brown suit. An invitation to dine with his patron had arrived not ten minutes after their return from the park. It could hardly be refused, but he's in no mind for it. The day's vicissitudes have left him spent, and damnably cross with the world. Moreover, he has a touch of sunburn on his nose and the backs of his hands; and his hair, after a second day baking beneath the sun hat, has acquired an oily immobility. Father's philosophy is that powder alone can solve such problems. Accordingly, Will made a fresh and liberal application. The result was a further stiffening – and now a single fish-hook curl rests on his forehead, the plait jutting out over his collar like the tail of a tiny dog.

Mr Cope appears at the rear of the hall, reading a note. Will clears his throat and approaches, requesting a moment of the valet's time. The note is folded and inserted into a waistcoat pocket; the greyhound face is pointed Will's way. It contains no surprise at seeing him still at Harewood, and the answer to his question is given so swiftly it is as if Mr

Cope had prepared it in advance. The hint of London streets Will heard the evening before has been smoothed away entirely.

'I would suggest the castle, sir. It stands a half-mile to the north-east, beyond the village. It is in a state of some ruination, but enjoys a commanding position over Wharfedale.'

Will gives his thanks. A ruined castle on a ridge sounds promising indeed. The valet bows, gliding back to reopen the double doors through which he entered. Beau Lascelles' voice carries into the hall, holding forth on an *objet d'art* from his collection.

'. . . those at Mennecy attempted to rival them, but Sèvres remained, in the eyes of all true connoisseurs, the only workshop for such figures. See the limbs there, the freedom of arrangement. Exquisite.'

Will goes forward, into the saloon where he saw last night's party drinking their toasts. It is the largest room he has yet seen at Harewood. Ahead, past the portico, lies the valley about which he marched so strenuously that afternoon; in the soft gloom of dusk, its distances now seem no great matter. The saloon itself is decorated with yet more half-columns and elaborate furniture, against walls of salmon pink. The grand chandelier has been left dull; beeswax candles in silver holders dot the mantelpieces and commodes, concentrated around two dozen pieces of fine porcelain. There are jugs, plates and vases, teapots and small covered bowls, painted in the sumptuous hues of the French Rococo. All feature sprays of flowers or scenes of rustic merriment; most also bear delicate patterning in gold or bronze leaf, lending a shining trim to their spouts and handles.

Beau is expounding before a figural group in glazed white – a centrepiece for a dining table. His costume is informal, a dressing gown of green silk over his shirt and breeches. He is plainly not at his best, still impaired by the excesses of the previous night; that full face is pale, lacking colour both real and artificial. Speech, however, is causing him no difficulty, and as Mr Cope announces Will he turns to crow with delight.

'Mr *Turner*,' he cries, stretching the words out to several times their normal length, with a rise in middle of the second, 'how it pleases me to see you still among us! Perhaps you found more material here at Harewood than you anticipated?'

There is a laugh. Tom is sitting off to the side, in the same plain suit as the evening before. His hair, Will notices, rests in a neat wave; and his complexion, despite his want of a sun hat, is only lightly tanned.

'I suppose we have delayed you for a day at most, though,' continues Beau with a sigh. 'Once you have made your sketches you will go.'

Absolutely correct, Will thinks. He bows. 'I'm indebted to you, sir, for your hospitality.'

Mr Cope withdraws, closing the doors behind him.

'Did I hear you and Mr Cope talking just then, Will?' enquires Tom. 'Out there in the hall?'

'I believe poor Tom is jealous,' says Beau, a trifle harshly. Tom glances over; something passes between them. 'He alone, it would seem, is permitted to befriend my servants.'

'I asked that he show me to Mr Lascelles,' Will replies, keeping his eyes on the porcelain centrepiece. 'That's all.'

Beau spots the direction of his gaze. 'Superb, Mr Turner, is it not? Come, look more closely. That devil Girtin over there is perfectly dead to anything French, but items like this deserve – nay, *demand* – appreciative study.'

Will obeys. Two nudes, a male and a female, are arranged upon a rocky bed. The recumbent poses and swan-like necks recall Michelangelo – forms imprinted forever on Will's mind by his days at the Academy schools. They are lost in an amorous trance, the fingers of the female brushing gently over the male's brow; whether this is to rouse or soothe is unclear. A gilded vine weaves around them, dark against the gleaming porcelain, flowing down to a stand of golden acanthus leaves. It is perhaps a foot high.

'The dealer,' sniffs Beau, 'grubby Israelite that he was, could not name the subject. "The Shepherd's Hour" was all he could offer. My own belief, however, is that it represents Zephyrus, the West Wind, and his bride Iris, at the—'

'Endymion,' states Will. 'Bewitched, weren't he, by the goddess of the moon.' Beau is staring; Will wonders, momentarily, if he has pronounced the name right. He nods at the figures in confirmation. 'That's who they are.'

'Why, Mr Turner,' murmurs Beau, his manner acquiring a slight chill, 'you know your Greeks.'

Tom, over on his armchair, fails to hide his smile. 'There's much about Will a fellow wouldn't guess.'

Neither accepting nor rejecting Will's identification, Beau moves on to a shallow cheese dish. The ground colour, a remarkably rich rose pink, seems almost to blush in the candlelight; it was made, he tells them, for the Duc de Richelieu.

'See here,' he says, pointing to a lozenge on the front, inside of which has been painted a bright little rustic feast. 'Peasants roasting geese, after a scene by Boucher.' He hesitates. 'They *are* peasants, aren't they, Mr Turner? I trust that is accurate enough for you?'

Frances arrives through the saloon's western door, accompanied by her husband. Tom rises from his chair and the three men bow – the artists somewhat lower than the aristocrat. This is Will's first proper audience with Lord Harewood's elder daughter. She's taller than him, as many women are; her lavender gown is cut a mite closer than is the fashion, and her powdered hair is gathered up loosely beneath a length of purple satin. She comes to rest on the back foot, her chin raised and her left hand propped upon her hip, a pose both relaxed and faintly antagonistic. It is immediately plain – unlike Beau and the equally pasty Douglas, who lurks to the rear as if trying to evade notice – that Frances was not among those who overindulged at yesterday's banquet. She is as hard and sharp as a steel pen nib, and propelled by an unnamed dissatisfaction; then she turns towards her brother and it is unnamed no longer.

'Is this an inventory, Edward, perchance?' she asks, gesturing at the porcelain. 'Are you seeking to reassure yourself that nothing else is missing?'

Will looks to his evening shoes; beside him, Tom lets out an apprehensive cough.

'You have not told your young painters, of course,' announces Frances; her natural tone is one of proclamation. 'A mishap has befallen the household, gentlemen. Two of Mr Lascelles' French pieces are gone. Broken, no doubt, by some drunken scoundrel, and then buried in a shadowy corner of the flower garden.'

Beau has gone to a window. 'It is inevitable,' he says, 'with an assembly of this size – with the state floor thrown open as it was – that there be damage, a minor depredation of—'

'My stars, so *forgiving*,' Frances cries. 'Is that the explanation you would offer to our father, if he were to enquire why his money is quite literally vanishing into the summer air?'

Beau lifts a hand to his forehead. 'Any further losses would pain me deeply.'

'Will you seek the perpetrator, then? Your darling Mr Purkiss – who still slumbers upstairs, I believe – was showing Madame de Pompadour's chocolate cup around with his usual recklessness.'

'Any further losses, Frances,' repeats Beau, 'would *pain me deeply*. For God's sake, woman, it was but two pieces. Barely a hundred guineas between them. This house has seen a good deal worse than that, I can tell you. Why, during the masquerades in the first baron's time—'

Frances laughs, saying that those days were a model for naught but moral ruin, and expressing the earnest hope that her brother would never attempt to stage a masquerade ball at Harewood himself; to which Beau replies that he would do no such thing until he is baron, and then he would do exactly as he deuced well pleased. Will and Tom stand very still. At first, Tom tries to appear amused, as if it were all good japes, but as the exchange grows more savage the smile dies on his lips.

'Must this really be thrashed out now?' Douglas interjects. 'Can't the two of you wait until after we have dined, at least?'

Frances's husband, settled by a marble table, is rubbing his eye with a long index finger; he sounds both pained and bored. Will perceives that this enmity between the heir to Harewood and his elder sister is of ancient origin. But Douglas's words prove effective. The siblings look away from one another, abruptly breaking their disputation. Beau moves out of the window, draws his dressing gown around him and calls for dinner to be brought up. A servant appears to acknowledge the order, then bows smartly and withdraws. His master stalks into the hall. Unruffled, Frances takes Douglas's arm and follows.

The artists, quite suddenly, are alone.

'Wonderful,' says Tom. 'Ain't even a question of nerve with you, Will, is it? You just can't help yourself.'

The Endymion centrepiece. Tom is correct. Will spoke without thinking. 'It was foolish,' he admits. He studies his sunburned hands. 'But Mr Lascelles was in error.'

Tom falls on Will once more, clasping him in his arms with fierce affection. He smells of soap and pipe tobacco, laced with a drop of rose water. 'You're a rare bird, Will Turner. An honest and righteous and damnably decent soul.' He lets Will go and looks across the saloon at the porcelain. 'It takes every ounce of my effort, you know, to hold my peace before this. These revolting fancies, bought for fortunes while people lay starving in the gutters of Paris. So help me, if I had but half a minute in here with a hammer, I'd show them the true meaning of *depredation*. Not a single damn chocolate cup or cheese dish would survive.'

Will can picture it clearly – the scattered, multicoloured shards; the disembodied handles and fractured lids; the glint of cracked gilding. The mere possibility is startling. Tom's embrace has twisted his coat; he shrugs it straight, unsure of what to say.

'Come.' Tom gives Will's shoulder a companionable slap. 'To dinner.'

*

The dining room is much darker tonight, lit by just nine candles: three groups of three in silver candelabras. Its windows, like all of those on the state floor, have been left open throughout the day for airing, and the advent of evening has brought in a velvet dampness. No one else joins them; Mary

Ann, it appears, is in some degree of disgrace, on top of the delicate circumstance explained by Mrs Lamb. Allowed a measure of freedom for the banquet, the younger sister proceeded to defy all good sense and dignity, larking about in the flower garden until early morning, and as a result is confined to her rooms.

'Where she will remain,' Will hears Frances murmur to her husband, 'until she can demonstrate even the smallest understanding of her situation here.'

This is another disappointment. Amid the various frustrations of his delay, Will was looking forward to encountering Mary Ann again. He was keen to discover if the still-room maid's revelations would alter her at all in his eyes – if he could detect any sign of scandal or dishonour. Lord Harewood's second daughter has been in his thoughts, he can't deny it, despite her hostility towards him; the white curve of her neck, and the fall of her lower lip; the intense, wordless exasperation with which she bore the barbs of her brother and Mr Purkiss. Further experience of her siblings has only increased this sympathy.

A thin broth is brought out. Will hasn't eaten since that piece of bread in the valley. He tries it. Game, partridge perhaps; good enough, at any rate. He starts to spoon it in.

Beau pushes his away untasted. 'You younger gentlemen may be wondering,' he says, 'what precisely happened at those masquerade balls I mentioned in the saloon.'

Will's spoon stops in his mouth. He looks at Tom and then at Frances, who carries on eating her broth with calm application. Beau, it seems, is purposely initiating a second bout. Will slowly draws the spoon back out and lays it on the tablecloth.

'*Worsley* is the crucial name. See how my poor sister flinches just to hear me say it. Lady Seymour Worsley, to be more precise: a stepdaughter of the first baron and a perfect hellion, married off to a baronet who could not begin to control her. John Douglas over there will remember the stories.'

Douglas's lean features are pinched by something that is more a wince than a smile. 'Is it really the moment, Edward?'

Beau pays no notice, going on to tell of one Christmas masquerade twenty years previously, when this rampant noblewoman sought out the gentlemen's ordinary clothes and then hurled them, in vast armfuls, from the state windows. Wigs were left perched on hedges; waistcoats were lost among the rose bushes; breeches trailed from the boughs of trees.

'This single night – as well as the harm to his reputation, which was considerable – cost the baron over eight hundred pounds in damages.' Beau sips his wine, letting this figure hang before them, dwarfing that of his own misplaced porcelain. 'We still have her portrait,' he adds carelessly, 'a rather splendid piece by Sir Joshua Reynolds. The young lady's spirit positively glares from the canvas.'

There is a silence. Frances makes no deliberate reaction, but her movements strain with displeasure. Douglas shifts in his chair, bracing himself for a renewal of battle. Will looks regretfully at the broth cooling in his bowl.

Then Tom speaks. 'Will here knew Sir Joshua. In fact, during his last days, that great painter came to rely on young Master Turner – to retrieve his escaped canaries, you understand, from the branches of Leicester Fields.'

This is a route away from Lady Worsley and Frances takes it readily. She sets down her spoon and fixes Will with a firm, enquiring stare. 'How extraordinary, Mr Turner, to have experienced such an august connection. Were you attached to Sir Joshua's studio?'

Will has that which eluded him so completely on his first night: the attention of the room. He plumbs his memories of the old man – the frilled shirts and brass ear trumpet, the scarred lip and the snuff-dusted waistcoats, all those damn little birds – trying to craft them into a diverting tale, as Tom might do. He uncovers only a strong, contrary desire *not* to talk: to cross his arms, sit there in dogged silence and thumb his nose at the lot of them.

'I was not, madam.' He pauses. 'I heard his discourses, like any student of the Academy, and would call on him from time to time. I held Sir Joshua in the highest regard.'

Frances isn't about to release him. 'Did you ever consider a career in portraiture yourself? It is one of the more useful branches of your art, I always feel.'

'No, madam. I did not.'

Tom comes to Will's aid. 'Landscape has been our sole object, madam,' he says, 'from our early boyhood. Neither of us ever thought of anything else. It bonded us. We'd roam the borders of London together, sailing out far along the

86

river in search of scenic effects. We'd immerse ourselves in the beauty of the world.'

'And yet ...' Frances stops. She turns to Tom; her smile is slight and merciless. 'You will forgive me, Mr Girtin, if I speak plainly. My brother likes your productions very well and that is his business, but to me this new approach of yours seems decidedly coarse. The pigment is applied so thickly, so haphazardly, and you scratch it and smear it about in a manner that defies my understanding. I confess that I see scarcely any beauty in it at all.'

This is reprisal, obviously: a blow struck back at Beau, who sighs loudly and waves for more wine. Will catches something else in Frances's voice, though, as she details her complaints to Tom —flirtation, almost. She certainly sounds more entertained than she has so far that evening.

Will fares badly with criticism. He's known for it – the muttered profanities, the black looks, the unexpected departures – and he's squirming now, impatience nibbling at his innards. Tom, however, appears untroubled by Frances's words. After the soup dishes have been removed, he offers a riposte, pontificating about the elevation to be found in Nature; the finer sentiments it can stir in the soul; the ways in which it can identify us with what he terms 'our more permanent existences'.

'Think, for instance, of when you stand alone before a range of hills – or see the clouds piled in the sky, towering up to Heaven, afire with sunlight. That is the sensation we seek. The Sublime mysteries of Creation, distilled into art.'

87

The entrée is served: rare beef, thinly sliced, rolled up and laid atop a lettuce leaf. Will has been listening to Tom's deft paraphrasing of wiser men, his feelings somewhat mixed; but at the sight of food, hunger usurps all other considerations. He cuts off a large piece of the rolled beef, almost half the quantity on his plate, and works it into his mouth.

'This can make us impulsive in our technique,' Tom continues. 'We admit it. We're all in a rush at times, Will and I, and for that we can only apologise. But isn't there hope in honest imperfection – in a striving that has yet to attain?'

Beau clearly judges his sister's latest attack to have been thwarted. He growls in appreciation, banging the end of his knife against the table. 'Quite right.'

Frances, if not actually impressed or convinced by Tom's reply, has at least been drained of some of her venom. 'And would you agree with that account, Mr Turner? Do you also seek to communicate the mysteries of Creation in your paintings?'

Will looks back at her in alarm. His mouthful was far too ambitious: there's almost more than he can chew. He can't speak, not with any decorum, but neither can he stay silent. Spitting the meat into a napkin is out of the question. Only one course is open to him. He grips his cutlery and swallows.

The beef's passage is agonisingly slow. It seems to stretch Will's throat to tearing point; to press hard against his collarbone; to halt at the top of his chest, blocking both blood and air. Tears edge from his eyes. He can feel the skin flaming from his temples to his neck, reaching the extremes of colouration. His vision dims and he wonders if he is to choke to death, right there at Lord Harewood's dinner table, just because Tom Girtin has delayed him with his chatter and his misinformation, and prevented him from keeping to his schedule; and suddenly the beef is gone, worming into the lower chambers of his body, leaving him blinking and gasping atop his chair like a drunk hauled from a river.

'I do,' he whispers.

*

The party breaks up after dessert, too fatigued and fractious to contemplate any further entertainment. Mr and Mrs Douglas retire straight away. Beau remains a while longer, leading his painters through to the music room so that he can rattle on about some topic or other, but tiredness soon gets the better of him and he withdraws also. A minute later servants are drifting about, removing glasses and extinguishing candles.

Will rises from his chair and looks towards the hall, plotting a course back to the casket chamber that will give the still room the widest possible berth. Mrs Lamb doesn't need to know that he's been obliged to remain at Harewood. This has to be kept simple. He bids Tom good night.

'Tomorrow morning.' Tom stays seated, leaning back, his hands behind his head. 'Tomorrow morning, Will, you and I will put all this nonsense aside and apply ourselves properly to the pursuit of art.'

'Pretty speech you made back there.'

Tom grins; he lowers his voice. 'She's a nasty old trout, that one, but it don't take too much to throw her off. As you saw.' He sits forward. 'We'll talk to the gardeners. One of them will be able to advise us, I'm sure of it. It'll be a good day.'

Will has already devised a new schedule. Out alone at dawn with books, bundle and umbrella, having left a note of gratitude for his patron; sketches of this castle, two separate views, done by noon; then off to find a carrier in the village. Tom's determined camaraderie prompts a ripple of guilt, but he reminds himself that this is still, at heart, a contest. He must play to his strengths, just as Tom does. Besides, he's certain that whatever sadness Tom might feel at discovering he has gone will last an hour at most, and that he'll be forgiven immediately when next they meet in London; by which time Will's Harewood drawings will be close to complete.

'Could hardly be worse.'

At this Tom is up, taking Will's arm, predicting great successes as they walk towards the hall. Once they are through the doorway, however, the two painters begin to pull apart. They stop, for a second equally surprised; then both see the reason. They are bound for different floors.

'Of course,' says Tom. 'You'll be wanting to call on the still-room maid. Inform her of your continued residence.'

Will ignores him. That odd note from their earlier conversation, forgotten in the dash for the waterfall, sounds again in his mind. 'So there it is,' he says.

'What d'you mean?'

'The *goose feather mattress*.' Will's nose twitches with anger. 'You mentioned it out in the valley. I wondered how such a fine thing could fit in a basement room – a damn closet such as the one I've been shoved into – and here's how. You're upstairs with them. An *honoured guest*.'

A door opens in the shadows, off towards the saloon. Someone is listening.

Tom is shaking his head. 'I'm up there, yes,' he concedes, 'but the room is small enough, you can be sure of that. For a valet, I think, or a ladies' maid. Someone who has to be on hand night and day. They told me it was the only place left.' He attempts a laugh. 'If it's the *mattress* that's upsetting you, then I'll drag it down to you now, this very minute, and sleep on the damn floor. Give the word, Will, and I'll do it.'

None of this signifies, Will tells himself. It just proves what you knew already. He starts quickly across the hall, towards the door that leads to the central service staircase. It is all but dark; only the blackness of the mahogany against the grey walls enables him to find it. He hears Tom following him and imagines his remorseful pose – the embrace that would surely follow.

'You stop there, Tom Girtin,' he says, without looking around. 'You leave me be.'

Will feels his way onto the staircase. Halfway down he stumbles, stubbing a toe through his flimsy evening shoes, triggering a flow of curses that continues until he is back in the casket chamber. He sits heavily on the bed, on the mean mattress stuffed with Lord knows what; then he turns to check the sketchbooks.

A parcel rests in the middle of his pillow. The paper is familiar, cheap and thin, wrapped around a half-dozen hard, tubular objects. At once Will realises what it is and who it is from. He lights a taper in the hall, coaxes a tallow stub to life and unties the string. The parcel contains beeswax candles, identical to those burning upstairs, forbidden on the service floor. He stares at them; the white sticks seem to glow against his breeches, to hold a trace of the radiance they will cast. This is his reward. Mrs Lamb knows he is still at Harewood.

Again, there is print on the inside of the paper – an illustration this time, set in a rectangle in the top half of the page, with two columns of dense text beneath. The candles clack together as Will sets them on the bed; on impulse, he picks one up and touches it to the tallow stub. It flares immediately, smothering the tallow, filling the casket chamber as a flame fills a lantern.

Will flattens out the sheet. It is headed *The British Slave Ship Zong Throwing Overboard the Dead and Dying*. The drawing, although inexpert, is unsparing in its confrontation of this notorious incident. Negro bodies cover a ship's deck, clad only in loincloths and irons. A number are being heaved up by sailors, by British tars, and tipped into the ocean. Most, despite the title, plainly live still. Some pray; some try feebly to resist and are lashed; all are surely doomed.

Will is dimly aware of this case. A decade or more old, it

has long been employed by the Abolition movement as the ultimate symbol of the slave trade's turpitude. As with the *Brookes*, his mind begins to roam around the image before him, to search out its possibilities – and again, there is a shock of revulsion at what he envisages. This time, however, he forces himself to persist. He dwells on the moments after the throw; what it would be to plunge into the limitless ocean, your limbs weighted and your body weakened by hunger and disease; the drag of the waves and the black chasm yawning beneath; the sun overhead, a drop of blinding fire, awful in its unconcern; and the despised prison ship, so cruelly transformed into your last chance for life, rolling off towards the horizon, forever beyond reach.

A voice passes in the distance. 'It's this, then it's that, then it's summat else. I swear, if he tells me once more, I'll take that kettle and—'

Will looks up. His door is ajar. The blaze of the beeswax candle – this prohibited item, very probably lifted from a pantry or the steward's room – would be visible some way along the corridor. He cups a hand around the flame and blows it out.

Friday

Harewood Castle is one for the books. Will knows it as soon as he clears the village. The ruin stands alone in a stretch of rough, sloping grassland, built into the valley's side to shelter it from the worst of the weather. The two lower storeys have been hollowed out but are intact, more or less; much of the third, however, has been knocked away, with only two juts of stone remaining at the southern corners. It has the look of a huge, heavy armchair, placed on the edge of Wharfedale for the repose of a weary northern giant.

Drawing closer, Will notes the details – the pointed arches of the doorways, the arrow-slits and carved stone-work, the climbing ivy – and his satisfaction grows. Here is a subject he can make use of. His notion is that prospective patrons, calling on him in the airy studio he'll soon occupy, will be able to peruse an expanding library of sketchbooks, selecting the scenes they would have worked up into draw-ings. An ancient place like this fires the imagination in all the necessary ways and will have a strong chance of attracting custom.

Past the castle, furthermore, lies a fine Yorkshire prospect: a winding river, several miles of tranquil farmland and a horizon of gentle hills, coloured in the cool tones of a summer dawn. The sun is just beginning to rise, the orb itself hidden in luminescent vapour. Will studies the sky as he trudges along. Yellow lake, he reckons, washed very thin, with a smoky hint towards the top, up in the firmament proper; ultramarine would serve best, with possibly the smallest speck of madder brown.

The first composition is found to the east: the ruin, angled slightly, set off centre to allow for a decent sweep of the landscape beyond. Will settles on a mossy bank and unclasps the smaller of his sketchbooks. Although well stocked with abbeys, cathedrals and castles, this book still has perhaps twenty blank pages left. The sketch is made intently, without further thought, and it is finished before the sun has moved through a quarter of its course. Well pleased, Will collects his equipment and walks around the building, moving downhill in order to take it from the opposite diagonal.

This view is not so successful. The absence of a landscape behind makes the ruin seem too tall; it cannot be fitted properly on the page. Will continues working, but his concentration begins to ebb. He thinks of the stairs at Maiden Lane, the flight up to his painting room with the bulging wall, and a bruising altercation that once occurred there; a ballad about a knife-grinder, heard in a Cumbrian tavern the month before; the slave ship *Zong*, sails unfurled, a multitude of bodies floundering in her wake.

A twig strikes the page at a top corner, skittering into the crease. Will brushes it away and turns – and a man is rushing at him, leaping atop him, barging him over. Something flutters against his calf, light as a moth, and gives him a vicious bite. He struggles towards it, swearing; and this other person moves off, twists back, hopping across the grass.

Will claps at his stinging skin, perceiving several things together. His assailant, of course, is Tom Girtin; he has not been bitten but burned, the contents of Tom's pipe bowl having dropped onto his leg and scorched a hole in his stocking; and Tom has the smaller sketchbook – is flicking through it with mounting amusement.

'By God,' he says, 'you did stick rather closely to my own progress, didn't you Will? Jedburgh. Kirkstall. St Cuthbert's at Lindisfarne. Why, there's hardly a ruin in here that I didn't sketch myself last year.' He nods at Harewood Castle. 'Not this one, though. I had no idea that it even existed. Small beer, ain't it, by comparison?'

Will gets up, wondering how Tom found him. Could Mr Cope have talked? He eyes the book, which the other painter is swinging about in a nonchalant manner, and is glad that he opted to stow the loose leaves in the larger one. He doesn't move. The Academy schools, various menial office posts and rowdy nights in London taverns have seasoned him in horseplay. He has his own way of meeting it.

'It'll sell,' he replies. 'To Lascelles, and others too.'

This is deliberate provocation. Tom snorts; he bridles as if confronted by something disgusting. There's a change in him today. That dash of languor has gone. In its place is an aggressive exuberance – the high spirits of one filled with a renewed sense of himself, of who and what he was. The cause of this is unclear.

'A mound of old stones. A commonplace landscape. A horse, a sheep, perhaps a couple of peasants to add some life. Ain't you growing so damnably *tired* of it?'

Will has been asked this before, numerous times, and lectured on the need for modern subjects taken from the world, for a whole new approach. He's seen Tom out on Dr Monro's balcony at Adelphi Terrace, sketching the dome of St Paul's, the lighters on the Thames, the long jumble of buildings on the south bank – a great span of London spread out across five or six pages. He slides the porte-crayone in his tail-pocket.

'Any commissions, then, for your views of Blackfriars? What terms have you got?'

Another calculated remark. Much as he affects to scorn money and those men who make no secret of their desire to earn it, Tom's financial requirements are as pressing as any-one's. As he begins his answer – speaking of the possibility of *a different model*, as he phrases it, a way of funding their art that has been freed from the narrow tastes of the rich – Will darts forward and grabs for his sketchbook. Caught unawares, Tom tightens his grip on the spine; so Will lands a punch against his chest, just above the heart. The effect of this blow exceeds his expectations by some measure. Tom is brought down; at once he is coughing, convulsing, burying his face in his sleeve. The sound is harsh, raw barks forced from deep within his body – worse than any Will has heard from him. He stands by uneasily, waiting for his victim to recover. The sketchbook feels heavy, the leather cover slipping in his sweaty hands.

After a minute Tom rises onto an elbow; he spits and wipes his eyes, then pats the grass to his left and right, searching for something. There is laughter between his short, snatched breaths. What exactly has prompted this Will cannot tell, but relief nevertheless brings a hesitant half-smile to his lips. He sits and examines his calf again, poking his scraping nail through the tiny hole that has been scorched in the stocking.

'Best cotton,' he says. 'That's fourpence you owe me, Tom Girtin.'

Tom's mirth increases. He rolls onto his back. 'I've no damn fourpence, Will,' he replies, gravel-voiced, 'but I'll make you a gift of my artistic opinion. If you honestly want a second view of this heap here, your best bet lies down the ridge.' He throws out an arm, pointing vaguely. 'By that river yonder, I'd say, facing back up.'

Will sees it straight away. This will give him what he needs. The schedule is revised: he'll remain until sunset and catch the evening mail coach, as he'd planned to do the day before.

But Tom is with him now. The empty pipe – the item for which he'd been hunting, mislaid when he fell – is located and stuck back in his mouth. That Will had ignored his offer of help, that he'd made secret plans and had plainly been intending to quit Harewood without a farewell, doesn't even appear to have registered in his mind. He insists on carrying the bundle and the umbrella, in fact, as if to demonstrate his vigour after the coughing fit. They head downhill, moving through a row of trees and along the edge of an undulating hayfield, crossing the river at a plain stone bridge.

Will turns to make his survey. Everything is right. The sun to the west, declining slightly, illuminating the trees and scattered clouds; the dark river passing in the foreground, below a bank of crumbling clay; the yellow hayfield, labourers scything channels in the dry grass; and the castle, planted to the rear, a weathered rock rising against the sky. He looks for somewhere to sit.

Tom stops to drink from the river, then returns to Will's side. He drops the bundle and umbrella, lowers himself to the ground and reopens their debate. The next stage is always the same – Tom casting stones at Will's conventionality. Will listens in silence; penance, he tells himself, for that intemperate punch.

'You don't care for any of my talk, do you, Will? Art for you is a straight road that simply has to be followed. More ruins and cathedrals and mountains. More maritime pieces. Perhaps, one day soon, a famous battle, then something from Milton, or Shakespeare, or one of your Greeks. Eight-foot oils in golden frames, hung on the line at Somerset House.' Tom's manner is lightly mocking, sincerely concerned, faintly frustrated; a typical mix for him. 'I'll wager that you'll have bargained yourself a place among the Academicians before this century is ended, and will set about wagging your finger at younger men.'

Will remains impassive. He sketches in a fringe of river reeds, thirty close strokes of the porte-crayone, made with the unerring swiftness of a chef slicing an onion. There's truth to Tom's conjectures. He does indeed aim to join the Royal Academy at the earliest opportunity – to have those letters, so reassuring to patrons, appended to his name – and to paint in oil on the grand scale. He can see no advantage at all in remaining outside the room, kicking and swearing at the door.

Tom, meanwhile, is running on, moving from castigation of Will to the usual fantasies about an art without academies or aristocrats, popular and universal in character, available to the people of England as a whole. Will's sense of contrition, weak enough to start with, abruptly expires.

'Have you paper today, Tom?'

Tom stares back at him. 'I have,' he replies, slightly indignant, reaching into his tail-pocket. He takes out a painting kit – a roll of worn leather wrapped around a ceramic pallet the size of a saucer, and a small water flask – and nothing else. He checks the pocket again.

Will has already unclasped the larger sketchbook. He retrieves a single sheet of Whatman paper, the very best, bought in York for his studies of the house. The price for quiet, he thinks, handing it over.

Tom accepts the paper with a sigh. He clearly wants to expound further, to argue down the sun, but even in his present mood he can tell that his mule-like companion means to work and nothing else. For a while he gazes at the river, filling his pipe, smiling at a private recollection; then he unrolls his painting kit and selects a short-handled watercolour pencil with a well-chewed end.

'So be it,' he says.

*

The two artists separate soon after. Determined to capture everything, Will moves back from the river, then off to the east, setting down three good studies in as many hours. The last one is perhaps the finest of the day: a perfect triangle with the river as its base, the sunlit castle at its apex and the hayfield enclosed in its centre. After it is complete, Will feels his body flag. The afternoon is growing cool and overcast, the metallic taste of moisture seeping into the air; unexpectedly, he begins to hope that Tom might come over to propose a well-earned supper in the village tavern before his departure. He looks along the riverbank.

Tom Girtin is nowhere to be seen. Will is both disappointed and peevishly unsurprised. The fellow has most probably returned to the house to seek some inane diversion with Beau Lascelles. Shrugging off his hunger and his fatigue, Will resolves to keep working. He glances skywards. The clouds are turning rapidly from white wool to wet slate; away to the south, several of the largest have sunk so close to the earth that they seem ready to land upon it. One more exterior view, he decides, looking uphill from the north east, and then a foray inside. Interior scenes of ancient ruins – shattered columns, cloisters littered with rubble, fragments of carvings or statuary – have an established appeal, particularly to patrons of an antiquarian bent. He reproaches himself for not thinking of this sooner.

Five minutes later Will is back across the river, perched on a stile, commencing his sixth impression of the castle. He feels righteous and dutiful, yet also a touch disconsolate. He could draw this ruin from memory by now. Tom's words return. *A mound of old stones. A commonplace landscape. Ain't you tired of it?*

The sketch is well advanced when a violent wind drives through the valley, sending the trees flailing this way and that, and whipping up a spiral of golden strands from the surface of the hayfield. Will holds down the page with his left hand, finishing off the gnarled trunk of an oak as the first raindrops tap on the brim of his sun hat. The umbrella is opened and propped against his shoulder; a number of Will's best studies have been done beneath its black canopy. Within a minute, however, it has been knocked over and blown almost inside out. Will closes and clasps up the sketchbook, presses the hat onto his head and wrestles the umbrella towards the wind. Past the trees, a final sunbeam strikes through the approaching downpour, forming a trailing silver curtain that shimmers and billows across the hayfield. There are cries from the labourers as they scramble for cover, pulling shawls and jackets over their heads. The umbrella snaps into shape like a dislocated joint finding its socket. Awkwardly, Will scoops up the other sketchbook and fastens both beneath his coat. He swivels on the stile, facing the ruin. It's time for that interior scene.

After the turbulent valley, the inside of Harewood Castle has the gloomy calm of a coastal cave. Beyond the arch of the eastern doorway lies what must once have been a hall. The wind disappears; Will's hold on the umbrella relaxes. No roof survives, but the remnants of the upper levels are keeping out most of the rain. A stale smell hangs about, as if creatures have died there and rotted into the rough earthen floor. Will positions himself on a ledge in the outer wall and sets to work. He's careful to keep his study economic, detailing only one especially well-preserved alcove; afternoon is edging into evening, and he is not going to miss that mail coach. Squinting in the sepulchral murk, he starts to think of Milton, mentioned so dismissively by Tom, isolated phrases and half-remembered lines looming large in his mind. Before very long he's uttering them aloud.

'Now still evening came on, and twilight grey had in her sober livery all things clad; silence accompanied, for bird and beast; all but—'

The laugh is quiet, yet clearly audible over the rainfall outside. Will halts his recitation, lifting the porte-crayone smartly from the page. Someone, a woman, is listening in. His ears grow hot beneath his hat; he is sorely self-conscious about his poetry, both what he reads and the scraps he has begun

to write. There is a second laugh, slightly harder, a smothered giggle. He realises that it comes from the far side of the
ruin, a chamber beyond the area he occupies, too far from his
ledge for him to have been overheard. This brings little com-
fort. It must be labourers, come in from the hayfield in search
of shelter. The ruin would serve this purpose well. Are they
about to pour in by the dozen, jostling and spitting, filling the
castle with their incomprehensible conversation – spoiling his
sanctuary completely and obliging him to flee?

No others come. The laughter tails off into a moaning
sigh. Will rolls the porte-crayone against his palm. It is
lovers. The castle is a good place for this also, he supposes:
secluded, a distance from the village, with many points of
entry or escape. They're no doubt taking advantage of the
storm to slip away from their duties on the estate. He's considering going back out, braving the rain to walk back up
the ridge, when a man speaks, his voice low and light and
tinged with hoarseness.

'Did they warn you against that as well?'

Tom Girtin.

Will is amazed, then immediately annoyed by his amazement. It was *obvious*. The change in him earlier, that bullish
swagger: here is the reason. He found himself a girl in the
village or the fields while Will was making his first sketches
of the castle. They arranged to meet after he'd paid a couple
of hours' perfunctory attention to his art. And now they are
laughing together, the sound intimate and conspiratorial as
they trade their caresses. Will is angered by Tom's continued

lack of seriousness, grudgingly impressed by the speed at which he has operated and achingly jealous of his success. That such a thing is even possible staggers him. He simply does not understand what a man must do to bring it about. His own sporadic, tentative attempts at courtship have met only with ridicule or chilling indifference. What knowledge he has gained thus far has been the result of transaction rather than skill, and he honestly can't imagine any other way of accomplishing it.

As soundlessly as he can, Will steps over his umbrella and bundle and sneaks forward. He must see her. He must see what Tom has achieved out here. Past the hall is a narrow corridor holding three dim doorways. Tom and his farm girl are through the furthermost, their murmurs amplified by the empty stone. The sketchbooks are still in Will's hands, his left index finger marking his place in the smaller one. It occurs to him that he could take a study, should he remain undetected. The notion has a powerful, clandestine appeal that he can't quite explain; and of course it would also be a fine joke, back in the taverns of Covent Garden. 'Here's how *Tom* occupied himself in Yorkshire . . .'

Will spies a naked knee, creamy white in the surrounding dullness. Bathsheba, he thinks. Danae visited by Jupiter. Diana discovered by Acteon. It is smooth, pleasingly plump, hardly that of a milkmaid or field worker — and suddenly Will knows what awaits him. Unable to stop or retreat, he covers the last few feet to the doorway with rather less care than before.

The lovers are lying in a wide fireplace, upon a bed made of Tom's brown coat and a ladies' riding habit. They are undressed, in part at least, various items of clothing removed or unfastened to enable their coupling. Will sees Tom's buttocks, moving between her thighs; he sees her feet and ankles snake across Tom's long calves. They shift about, picking up their pace, Tom bracing himself against the edge of the fireplace; and there she is, Lord Harewood's youngest daughter, staring off at the rain that hisses on the window sill, her pale skin reddening as she bites at the collar of Tom's shirt.

Will draws back from the doorway, as if dodging the swing of an axe. Mary Ann looks over, her eyes going directly to his. She shows no trace of alarm or shame. The connection lasts perhaps three seconds; then she releases Tom's collar from her teeth and gathers him closer, hooking her arms around his shoulders, squeezing hard with her legs.

'They did, Mr Girtin,' she says, her voice tightening. 'Exactly that.'

*

The sketchbooks are Will's first concern. The umbrella is collapsed and tossed on the floor; the sodden bundle kicked beneath a chair; the sun hat prised off his damp, greasy head and set at a far corner of the table. Laying the leather-bound volumes side by side, he goes through every page, making a meticulous search for the creep of rainwater. There is nothing.

Will closes the books, stacks them by his elbow and gazes at the table. The wood is crisp, unstained; a new table in a new tavern, built at the crossroads in the middle of Harewood village. Farm hands pack the bar, released early by the storm, but the three other chairs at Will's table remain empty. He looks up, into the room. Several heads promptly turn away.

Supper arrives: a gristly, overcooked chop and a pile of boiled beans, shaken from a pan somewhere out back. Will hasn't eaten all day, yet he doesn't now. Thoughts crowd his head; fear knots his guts and numbs his muscles.

Catastrophe has struck.

This isn't a daring, misguided adventure, or an unfortunate scrape, or a regrettable lapse in judgement. This is a *catastrophe*. Tom Girtin is a child, a mere *child* in his understanding. Because he has no respect for the boundaries of rank and wealth, he believes that they do not apply to him. The woman with whom he was frolicking so unrestrainedly is a nobleman's daughter. A nobleman's *unmarried* daughter. Far from immaculate, of course – Will briefly recalls her arranged there on the hearth and experiences a flicker of envious desire – but the baron has thirty thousand a year, and a seat in the Lords, and ambitions to rise still further. There would be a plan in place for Mary Ann.

Will gives the chop a distracted prod with his knife. Any reprisal is bound to be severe. Stories are told among the artists and fine craftsmen of London regarding the vengeance of patrons – the dire punishments visited upon those deemed guilty of transgressions like this one. All know of Daniel Lofthouse, for instance, a master carver who returned from Sedley with his right arm badly broken, following a mysterious incident said to have involved the teenage countess; of the gilder Carr, who would neither speak of his engagement at Wedderburn Hall nor show the wound he received there, and who died penniless not long after; and most notoriously of Anthony Neville, noted architectural draughtsman and rogue, who seven years earlier had vanished, vanished *entirely*, while executing a commission at Groombridge. These estates are fiefdoms, in essence, under absolute rule. There's no town watch out here, no magistrate or officers of the court. Only the baron's men.

For discovery is inevitable. Will hasn't the slightest doubt of this. Tom is unable to be secretive. It is simply not in his nature. Anyone could have come across them as Will did – anyone at all. Hadn't he thought that the ruin was well suited to sheltering labourers from the rain? They could easily have had a damn *audience* as they panted there in that fireplace.

And the taint of it, the blame for it, would surely extend to Will. Of this he is also quite convinced. Beau Lascelles knows that his association with Tom goes back to their child-hood. He'd assume that Will is an accessory, acting as a look-out perhaps; it could reasonably be claimed that he'd been standing guard that afternoon, in fact, over at the castle. Even if they were spared a beating, or a more enduring mishap somewhere in the grounds, Beau would see them both blacklisted. They would be branded, in effect: Girtin and Turner, depraved corrupters devoid of decency, not to be trusted for a second by any conscientious gentleman. All patronage would cease. They would be finished.

Will rubs a patch clear on the misted window and looks at the rainy lane outside. Villagers dash from cottage to cottage, hopping across the puddles in the rutted road; a gang of children crouch beneath a haywain; and there, before a short parade of shops, is the mail coach, its lamps lit and crimson panels gleaming. This is a difficult sight – a route out of Harewood that he can no longer use. How could he possibly take flight now and leave his fate in the unsteady hands of Tom Girtin? His course is plain: he must return to the house, locate Tom and convince him to end this affair right away. They'd depart together at dawn, on the first coach to anywhere. A proper explanation could be spun for Beau at a later date – a collaborative project maybe, inspired by Harewood, that had compelled immediate action. It would just have to be hoped that Mary Ann was fond enough of Tom, and had enough understanding of their situation, to stay silent.

Ignoring his lack of appetite, Will applies himself ill-temperedly to his supper. It is a fragile, unsatisfactory scheme, liable to all kinds of upset. Should it work, should they actually manage to escape this place, he vows to pluck that pipe from Tom's idiot lips and stamp on it.

The chop and beans are soon gone. Will rises, takes three pennies from his waistcoat pocket and lines them up next to the tin plate. As he gathers his possessions a path opens through the busy tavern, running from his table to the front door. He stands for a second, thoroughly confounded. I am no damn *lord*, he wants to say: look at me, for God's sake! Nothing to be mindful of here! But every face avoids his; bodies shuffle further aside, urging him on his way.

There's no time to ponder this. Will crosses the tavern, opens his umbrella and pushes out into the rain.

*

Halfway up the drive the deluge eases to a drizzle, pattering against the umbrella and the leaves of the surrounding trees. The storm winds have subsided; the air smarts a little against the skin, as it does after a hot bath. Grey-blue mists blend together woods and pasture, horizon and sky, sinking Harewood into premature night. Will walks quickly, but he is afraid – disturbed by an unfamiliar sense of vulnerability, even of insignificance. Artistic prowess no longer seems important. Tom and himself are humble men, of neither breeding nor means, and they are trapped in the lap of one of England's most powerful families. As usual, he shores up his courage with consideration of method, carefully mapping out the steps that must be taken to reach the necessary end.

Three problems lie before him.

First, and most imperative, is the state of things within the house. Part of Will is certain that they'll already have been exposed; that someone else will have found Tom and Mary Ann in the castle, or noticed them leave it, and run directly to the baron's son. He strides off the drive, circling

the spot where he made his first close study two days earlier, and stops to survey the northern façade. The library
windows are shining with beeswax candlelight. Will moves
closer, his boots splashing through the waterlogged grass;
Beau Lascelles can clearly be seen, playing at billiards with a
handful of other gentlemen. As Will watches they all laugh
together, most heartily – not what you'd expect had the
household just been shaken by disgrace. Somewhat reas-
sured, he cuts across the wide lawn towards the eastern
entrance.

Second is the note, written that morning in Will's best
hand and propped on the ledge outside Mr Noakes's office.
It explained how pressing business had obliged his departure; how he was grateful for Mr Lascelles' hospitality, the
kind opportunity et cetera, and how he would be delivering
the six watercolour drawings to Hanover Square as agreed.
And yet here he is, back at Harewood House that same day.
Having gained entrance – a footman recognises him and
opens the service door – Will goes straight to the steward.
Noakes isn't required to supervise dinner tonight; he's at his
desk, scowling over account papers, the tie-wig on its stand.
He doesn't look up as Will enters.

'You left us, Mr Turner.'

His tone is flat, uninterested; Will knows at once that
there will be no trouble here. 'An error, Mr Noakes. I find
that I've more to do. Mr Lascelles will understand.'

The diminutive steward strikes something through with
his quill. 'Instruct a maid to bring you fresh bed sheets.'

The third problem, and definitely the thorniest, is that of Tom Girtin himself. Will leaves his belongings in the casket chamber and heads upstairs, hoping to find Tom's bedroom before he comes down to dine. It's too late for this, though; as he enters the hall, a dinner party emerges from the library, on its way to the table. Will is not fit to be seen. His hair is grease-spiked and wild, his face is unwashed and his outdoor clothes are in high odour – a mixture of sweat, tobacco smoke from the tavern and the earthy smell of the castle. He has no wish, furthermore, to talk to Beau, whose questions about his decision to stay will certainly be more probing than those of Mr Noakes; so he hides behind the bronze Minerva.

The party is discussing an entertainment, a last-minute affair being urged upon the Lascelles by their guests – two couples, well if rather loudly dressed, who may or may not have been at the riotous banquet two days earlier. Beau and Frances are arm-in-arm, their animosity forgotten; or suspended, perhaps, for the sake of polite company.

'Maxwell, you hound,' Beau declares, 'our intention was a *quiet interlude*. How can you be so cruel as to tempt my sisters with your talk of the cotillion?'

This meets with a genteel laugh. 'My dear Mr Lascelles,' someone says, 'ladies of such distinction should always heed the call of Terpsichore.'

Will peers past the Minerva's elbow. Mary Ann, her privileges apparently restored, is clad in a gown of pale rose. Paired with her brother-in-law, she is behaving tonight, her bearing almost demure as she moves across the polished stone. Despite everything, Will's admiration is revived. A living Juno, he thinks, gliding among the antique bronzes; then she lifts her chin and he detects a faint gloss of irony, as if she considers all of this a rather sorry charade.

Tom is at the rear of the company, walking alone, dressed in his cheap evening suit. Mary Ann turns to him; loosening her hold on Douglas, she goes out almost to her arm's length, laying her fingers against Tom's shoulder as she shares an observation. They smile together for a few seconds, virtually purring with delight at their secret attachment. Will shifts behind the statue; he presses the scraping nail hard against his lower lip. The indiscretion is dumbfounding. Anyone who so much as glances their way will surely realise what is afoot.

No one does. The party leaves the hall, proceeding to dinner. Will watches the door close behind them. What can he do now but wait for the evening to end and Tom to retire? Withdrawing to the casket chamber, he drops to his knees, pulls his blue coat over his head and bellows against the mattress until he is quite breathless.

Afterwards, slumped on the floor, he feels a fresh, stinging slap of disbelief. How the *devil* can he be caught up in this? He should have left the instant he discovered that Tom Girtin was at Harewood. What kind of a painter *is* this fellow? Why isn't he working upstairs, where Will might be able to get to him? Why is he among the Lascelles yet again – these people he affects to despise? Why is he risking his livelihood, his prospects, even his *safety*, to fornicate with one of them? Will thinks of Father, whose opinion of Tom has always been qualified. *Talent there, to be sure,* he'd say, *but I wouldn't trust that jackanapes to heat the curling tongs.* The old man would disapprove strongly of the course Will has chosen. He'd have had his son on that mail coach – or reporting Tom to Beau himself. Tom's fate wouldn't concern him, not if there was a chance for Will's acquittal; he has a pitiless streak, does Father, and an innate regard for the authority of lords and gentlemen. Will wonders for a second how that conversation might begin. *Beg pardon, Mr Lascelles, but while I was out by the castle today I happened upon a most disturbing sight . . .*

Here his imagination fails. It can't be done. He can't feed another man to the dogs, a man he knows well, in order to win his own freedom. A thread runs between him and Tom, gossamer thin yet irksomely resilient, the result of a shared trajectory that has put them in many of the same places, and burdened them with many of the same concerns. It resists easy definition – he's unable to think of it as friendship or fellow feeling, and recoils from the idea that it might be some form of respect – but it's there. This cannot, in good conscience, be denied.

And in any case, going to Beau would save neither Will's career nor his reputation. For all his wrong-headed opinions, Tom is widely liked. At least half the artists in London would abjure Will as a louse and a coward should he bring about Tom's trampling by the Lascelles. Backs would turn at tavern tables. Studio doors would be shut and bolted. The Academy would become unassailable. The upper levels of art, his life's one goal, would be raised forever beyond his grasp.

Will fights off his twisted coat and throws it into a corner. He is not a louse. He is not a coward. There is hope still. He sits against the bed and waits.

*

Two chambermaids stand at the pinnacle of the central service staircase, on the upper floor where the family and their guests are accommodated. One holds an armful of linen and the other a silver tray, upon which a beeswax candle burns in a dainty ceramic holder. They are engaged in whispered discussion of a recent household drama: a David and Goliath clash in which Goliath had apparently prevailed.

'Square in the eye, that bitch socked our Gem. She got a scratch in herself, a good 'un, but the bruise's bad enough to keep her in 't scullery for a week at least.'

'It's a blessed mystery to me how the wicked old doxy still has her place.'

'Aye, well, Lord Harewood will be certain to see to it when he gets up here. There's to be changes, my love, and not to the bloomin' wallpaper neither.'

Lord Harewood.

Will, tucked in the shadows below, attempts stoicism. This is an unwelcome development – the further curdling of a circumstance already pretty well soured. These maids are being maddeningly vague: from their talk, the baron could be arriving the very next morning, or at any time afterwards. With him will come order and stern patriarchal sense. He'll perceive immediately what is eluding his two eldest children. Tom will be doomed, and Will Turner along with him. Lord Harewood will grind them both to powder, and then cast it across his boating pond in great angry handfuls. They have to act. They have to run.

The two chambermaids have moved on to the new house-keeper that the baron is said to be bringing with him, running through rumours heard from contacts at Hanover Square and sharing grim predictions concerning the regimen she will impose. Will considers ascending, cutting between them, perhaps even asking directions to Mr Girtin's room. What could be thought untoward about two brother artists conversing a little before bed? But he stays where he is. The encounter might be mentioned in the servants' hall; then someone would tell Mr Noakes, who in turn would inform Mr Cope; who would file it away, producing it later as evidence in a case against them.

They spoke together in their rooms, late at night. We can only guess as to the topics that might have dictated such confidentiality.

Far better to remain unobserved. Besides which, Will is dressed for stealth, in his Vandyck-brown coat, which is rather darker than the blue, and a pair of black breeches. He'd been wearing his evening shoes, due to their lightness, but at the base of the stairs they let out a plaintive squeak, obliging him to stuff them in a pocket and continue in his stockings. He steps onto the state floor and heads for the hall, intending to cross over it to the main staircase. Candles still burn there, however — a footman is dismantling a flower arrangement on the marble table — so he plots an alternative route through the reception rooms that line the southern front. They'll be empty at this hour. They must be. He decides to chance it.

The first room is vast and quiet. Will feels the bumps and seams of the carpet pattern sliding beneath his toes. Watery moonlight spills across gilt and damask; and portions of several canvases, portraits on the grand scale, from the hand of Sir Joshua Reynolds. One stands out, almost fully illuminated against the western wall. It shows an arresting lady of no more than twenty-five, dressed for the outdoors in a black feather hat, tight jacket and skirts. This suit is the colour of port wine; in daylight it must be a bright, military scarlet. She is arranged in a dueller's pose, her left arm brought back behind her waist; and in her right hand, in place of a rapier, is a riding crop, as if to whip at the calves of any gentleman who displeased her.

Lady Worsley, Will thinks, the wild stepdaughter of the first baron, who so misused the great house and its guests. What Beau said of this portrait is true; Sir Joshua has certainly captured the lady's wilfulness, and her youthful vigour. Will had known the name. There had been a divorce in the early eighties, when he was but a young boy, with all manner of lurid public revelations — a scandal of such enormity that it was still cited in Father's shop as one of the perils that could befall a marrying man. She'd been ruined, of course, jettisoned in disgrace; and although her portrait hung in this majestic chamber, receiving the admiration of connoisseurs, if she were actually to appear at the door of Harewood House – and she couldn't yet, by Will's reckoning, be so very old – the Lascelles would no doubt have her chased off without delay.

From further along the southern front comes a swell of masculine conversation, several voices raising good-humouredly to contest a point. The gentlemen have not yet retired. Will's self-possession falters. He knows what this will mean. Leaving Lady Worsley, he eases open the heavy door that leads to the saloon, where Beau showed off his French porcelain. There is less moonlight in here, but a greater sense of occupancy; he smells scent, liquor and the oniony whiff of overheated bodies. The door opposite, perhaps forty feet away, has been left ajar. The room on its other side is empty, unlit; the gentlemen are installed in the one beyond. Will steals into the saloon, convinced that Tom will be among them, lounging about in the lions' den, laying himself bare in a hundred tiny ways. Before he can confirm it, however, the door to this distant room opens, admitting a blast of noise and light that is swiftly sealed off again.

Mr Cope has come through, bearing a candle holder. Will tenses, poised to retreat; but the valet is not headed for the saloon. Setting the candle on a sideboard, Mr Cope walks to the room's rear. He is talking now, addressing an unseen companion. His voice is too low for the words to be discerned but his tone is strangely tender. Will edges forward, keeping to the shadows, curious to see who warrants such uncharacteristic warmth.

It is Beau Lascelles. The baron's eldest son is packed skilfully inside a patterned waistcoat, his complexion flushed once more by the evening's indulgences. Mr Cope appears to be running down a list, stressing certain details. Their entire demeanour is altered; they are like confidantes, Will thinks, the most intimate of friends. Then Beau, who has been nodding with the weary air of one very familiar with what he is being told, lays his rosy face on Mr Cope's chest. The valet responds with an embrace, his head bending down towards his master's. Will can hear them laughing softly together.

There is another sound, far closer: that of a large person pushing past a chair. Someone else is in the saloon. Will's fear buffets against him, makes him catch his balance as if the carpet were being wrenched from under his feet. It is a trap. Men have been placed around the house, ready to spring out, to seize him in the act of reaching Tom. The Lascelles know everything – and their vengeance would surely follow.

'Be easy, sir. Why, I can hear your little heart from over here.'

Mrs Lamb is in an alcove, a black shape only, positioned behind a column that does almost nothing to hide her. Will starts, then sags with relief. He is baffled, utterly mystified, as to why the still-room maid would be up here, padding about in the darkness. The plain note of sarcasm in her voice is vexing. It suggests a grievance, as if he has disappointed her somehow — as if those obscure manipulations of hers, the rumours so carefully shared, the candle packages and the pamphlets that had wrapped them, had a result in mind that he has failed to supply.

'Madam,' he hisses, 'what the devil is this?'

Mrs Lamb does not reply. Leaving her alcove, she passes through a narrow band of light cast across the saloon by Mr Cope's candle. Her expression is deadly: mocking, contemptuous even, an unpleasant contrast indeed with the favour she has shown Will up until now. As she turns towards the hall doors, he notices a scratch, angry red and quite straight, running diagonally around her forearm.

One of the double doors opens. Footman and flower arrangement are gone; the hallway beyond is clear. Mrs Lamb walks out. She stops, shifting her shoulders slightly, a hand still on the door. Will realises that she is mustering her strength.

The slam resounds through the state floor, a firework bursting in an empty church. Will stands dazed in the deep hush that follows. He knows that he must flee, get to the portrait room, to the service staircase, to the casket chamber, as speedily and surreptitiously as he is able; but his limbs are insensible to the frantic urgings of his brain, seeming at once impossibly heavy and weightless. Light breaks over him, wobbles around him, lapping against a pair of gold-green chairs. Mr Cope is at the doorway on the opposite side of the saloon, the flame of his candle swaying atop the wick. There's no sign of Beau or anyone else. All laughter, all tenderness are gone from the valet; he has reverted so absolutely to his regular self that it makes Will doubt what he just saw.

'Mr Turner.'

Will is caught. He looks down at the carpet – at his stockings, nestled in the loop of a huge silvery leaf. He wriggles his toes inside the grubby cotton. 'Shoes was pinching,' he says.

Mr Cope seems to accept this. 'Did the castle meet your requirements?'

'I took studies.'

'And yet you remain at Harewood. Forgive me, sir, but my impression was that you were eager to depart. May I ask what altered your plans?'

The explanation arrives in Will's mind fully formed, miraculously almost; he only has to voice it. 'A natural subject,' he says, a touch too quickly. 'I have ruins, Mr Cope, and I have the house. But I need nature. Something with ... with scale. Something outside of man.'

Something outside of man. These sound like Tom's words. No matter: Mr Cope appears to believe them. He walks into the saloon and closes the door. Will detects the same dry sympathy the valet had shown him in the servants' hall, when he delivered his warning about Mrs Lamb. Did it arise from a sense of kinship, perhaps? Might Mr Cope feel that they were on similar paths – low-born, industrious men trying to advance themselves in the world of the rich? He calms a fraction. There's no trap here; not now, at least.

'I'll talk to the groundsmen and see what they recommend. I'm afraid, however, that Mr Lascelles has retired. You cannot speak with him today.' Mr Cope hesitates. 'I assume this was your purpose in coming up here?'

Will swallows; he feigns regret. 'Indeed it was. A shame. Much to report.'

'He will be in the flower garden tomorrow afternoon, with a party from Harrogate.' Mr Cope and his candle cross to the double doors. 'Would you have me escort you to your chamber?'

This isn't a question. Will, in truth, is desperately tired, sustained chiefly by his fear. Two hours' rest, he tells himself, then back up to find Tom, after everyone else in this damn house is in bed.

'Too kind, Mr Cope. Too kind.'

Saturday

The knocks sound barely three feet from Will's head. He throws back the sheet, squinting at his window: the sky is pearl grey, the colour of early dawn. He's been asleep for longer than he intended. The house will be rising. It's too late. His chance is gone.

The knocks sound again, louder this time. Will climbs from his pallet and opens the door. One of Harewood's gardeners is leaning against the frame, the large, bearded man who'd been in Mr Noakes's office on Will's first afternoon – Stephen. His eyes are directed firmly along the corridor; his voice is empty of interest or civility.

'I'm 'ere to take ye to Plumpton. Wi' Mr Cope's compliments.'

Will stiffens; his heart drums beneath his shirt. 'What's that, then?'

'Plumpton?' Stephen grants him a second's scrutiny, of the kind one might give a hopeless dunce. 'It's rocks.'

Will is led out into the morning; like a man brought to execution, he thinks. Has it happened? The series of events is easily reconstructed. Tom's been found in a corridor, or even within the curtains of Mary Ann's bed. Judgement has been pronounced and Tom himself already dealt with. And now Will, his presumed accessory, is to be dispatched as well. This gardener has not been ordered to escort him to the rocks at Plumpton, but something altogether more sinister. Will looks at the broad back ahead. The fellow could crush his skull in the palm of his hand if he had a mind to. His doom would be assured.

They go downhill, following the curve of the driveway to the stable block. It is a two-storey quadrangle, built simply in the Doric order, but larger than many London mansion houses. Horses are brought through the gates, a pair of bay mares, finer than any Will has ridden before. He is not, in truth, a natural equestrian; and as he mounts he is trembling so hard that it takes him four attempts to get his boot in the stirrup.

The two men ride north, soon leaving the Harewood estate. Will wonders whether an accident is to be engineered, out on some remote lane or bridle path. Would his horse rear on that bridge there, dumping him into the river below? Would a branch whip round, dragging him from his saddle? Or would his so-called guide just slip a blackjack from his sleeve, crack Will's pate and blame it on a fall?

There's little indication of any of this. The gardener, riding in front, seems to go to sleep, his head dipping forward, his shoulders rocking with his horse's steps. Will's apprehension for his wellbeing is coupled with the more immediate worry that they are travelling blind, wandering out into the raw Yorkshire countryside. This scenery would have pleased him on a different day, at dawn especially: a landscape of ridges and sweeping banks, mist lingering in its hollows; of undulating pasture and narrow clusters of pine, the trees black in the low light; of reddish rock formations, poking through folds in the turf like knees from a robe. Now, though, he pays it only cursory attention, occupied mainly with arranging and rearranging his drawing equipment, in case a rapid dismount is required.

After half an hour the horses stop to drink at a stream. The water ripples over a shallow, stony bed, winking in the first rays of the sun. Stephen is roused, by the noise perhaps; he speaks without looking around.

'Spofforth.' He nods downstream, to where chimney smoke stripes the pink sky. 'Castle there. Mr Cope said ye'd want to see.'

The ruin is at the edge of a quiet village, a long, roofless hall sunk into a hill in a similar manner to the one at Harewood. Will's only course is compliance. As he selects his spot, he finds that he recognises the style: this is a Percy castle, like several he's sketched before, and certainly worth a page from the smaller book. He fits together a composition. The lone surviving tower, just off-centre; a stretch of wall to its right, including a double row of fine arched windows; and to its left, a short distance away, a huddle of farm buildings that have been thrown up in the ruin's shadow.

Three minutes into the study, it occurs to Will that Spofforth Castle might in fact be the site of his demise. A gang of the Lascelles' men could be hiding in a barn, planning to come at him while he's working. He'd have to notice their approach, get to his feet, decide which way to flee – by which time they could be on him, pounding out his brains with stout sticks. The village is stirring, it's true, but its inhabitants wouldn't be in any hurry to oppose Lord Harewood. Will could count on no rescue from that quarter. Stephen is nearby, his cloth cap pulled down, smoking a clay pipe. He could be standing guard, waiting until the young painter is fully absorbed in his task before making a signal . . .

Will shivers; he squeezes the porte-crayone until the metal screws bite into his skin. This is *nonsense*. The Lascelles would hardly go to such lengths if they meant to end him now. It would have been done back in the casket chamber, or somewhere in the park. The affair hasn't yet been uncovered, or at least it hadn't when they left – and here lay the morning's real hazard. Every hour that Will is away from the house is one in which Tom Girtin could destroy them both. Mr Cope's willingness to help him may prove his undoing. He regrets that lie in the saloon, so God-given it had seemed; why hadn't he just said that he needed another day on the estate? The sketch is finished as quickly as he can manage. He closes the book and waves to Stephen, announcing his readiness to move on.

The second leg is shorter, less than half the distance between Harewood and Spofforth, leading them from the fields into a band of wooded hills. Morning breaks bright and warm; the net of branches overhead dissolves in the white sunlight. They round a summit and start to descend. Will glimpses a body of water between the trees, reflecting the drifting pattern of the clouds. Soon afterwards, Stephen dismounts and tethers the horses to the bough of an oak.

'Plumpton,' he says.

The gardener disappears down a slope. Will follows, the umbrella held out for balance, his boots skidding on leaves and the loose red earth beneath. At the slope's base is a lake, a dark oblong hemmed in by woodland; man-made, he notices, dammed at one end with a footpath laid out around its banks. On the southern side are the rocks – a few close, squashed-looking stacks, maybe three storeys high, their contours softened by time and a crust of pale moss. It's a pleasure park, essentially, not so very different from Harewood itself – fake, Tom would call it. There's no power here. Again, though, Will has no choice. He can't very well rush back from this outing with nothing to show. Two studies should do it, on the Whatman paper, taken at facing points around the lake; an hour or so on each and he could reasonably ask Stephen to return him to the house. A small rowing boat has been left upturned on the black mud. He settles on its flank.

Sketching the rocks proves surprisingly difficult. The rich, decaying smell of a lake in high summer is close to overwhelming. Insects of every description crowd the air. Worse still, Will's mind simply will not clear. He cannot locate that condition of absence that attends on his better days. At first, his thoughts are dominated by escape. He plays out the afternoon to come, rehearsing it minutely: every line of the talk he'll have with Tom, the precise sequence in which he'll pack his possessions, the combination of coins he'll hand to the coachman. Yet as the hours begin to mount, he finds himself dwelling instead upon the sheer damnable oddity of this whole business. Mrs Lamb's presence in the saloon causes particular bewilderment. Had she been eavesdropping in that shadowy alcove? Is this how she knows so much about the Lascelles family and the various rumours that hover around it? Recollection of the look she gave him makes Will quail, unaccountably ashamed; and bristle the next instant with hot resentment. Should he assume that she is now his adversary? But what has he *done*, exactly, to earn such ire?

When Tom appears Will is at the far end of the lake, hunched atop a knoll of sun-baked earth. The second study has slowed to a standstill; he's watching a dragonfly cruise amid the water weeds, occupied entirely by an imaginary confrontation across the still-room table. He sits up, greeting the sight of the other painter as coolly as he can. Tom is changed again. Gone is the ebullience of the previous day. The fellow has not tracked him to Plumpton for more foolish japes and argumentation. He knows, Will thinks; he knows that I know.

Tom halts before the knoll, standing with the discomfort of a guilty man called into the dock. 'My God, Will, how the devil did you ever find your way out here? I've been roaming in circles all morning.' His chuckle is uncertain; he presses his palms together, rotating them in opposite directions. 'Who'd have guessed that the countryside could be so damn muddling?'

Will realises that he hasn't seen Stephen since their arrival. He looks around the lake. The gardener is half-concealed beneath a shady beech, a fishing line trailing in the shallows before him. He has a clear view of them both. Will appraises the unfinished sketch, dashing in a few lines that could be filled in later if needs be; then he puts the page away, inside the larger sketchbook, and rises to his feet.

'The rocks,' he says. 'Now.'

*

'Gritstone,' murmurs Tom, peering up at a massy overhang. 'Burnt umber and gamboge, wouldn't you say? A wash of yellow lake for that pinkness there?'

'What d'you want, Tom?'

Plumpton's outcrops lean around them, creased and gnarly like the carcass of an ancient, outsized elephant. The ground is the colour of rust and rutted with exposed roots; it slopes back sharply towards the lake, whose waters have crept among the rocks to form black, brackish pools.

Tom lowers his head. 'She told me you was there. At the ruin yesterday. That you may have seen us.'

Will pictures Mary Ann lying in the castle hearth; their eyes meeting over Tom's back. 'May have, Tom? *May have?*' He stops, urging himself to remain steady, to remember his rehearsals of this conversation. 'You two was laid out for the inspection of every man-jack who happened to be passing.'

Tom nods, as if accepting fault. He wants to talk, to make sense of this dangerous circumstance he has created, and in the minutes that follow he delivers a full confession. The story is predictable enough. Mary Ann and Tom had been on amiable terms since his visit the previous summer, and were most pleasurably reunited at the dinner held on the night of his arrival. The next evening, after Will and he parted in the hall, they met by chance in an upstairs corridor. She made a declaration, impulsively it seemed, and conquered him at once. There was a kiss, and vague promises; and an interruption, someone mounting the stairs behind, which obliged them to flee to their separate rooms. And the day afterwards, as Tom sat sketching near the castle, she wafted into his line of sight, dressed for riding, strolling idly along the borders of a wood.

'The castle was her suggestion. I didn't think that it might rain. The morning had been so fine.' Tom sets a hand on a pocked hump in the rock face. 'She spoke of her suffering. The miserable conditions in which the baron keeps her, while treating his sons generously. That elder sister, who confines her and condescends to her like she's an idiot child, and sees fit to punish her like one as well. And Beau. Good God. I mean to say, I had my suspicions. No one who spends any time with them could not. But the facts of it, the peculiar delight he takes in humiliating her – it damn near defies belief.'

Will has been simmering in silence, frowning so hard that his features were beginning to ache; these last revelations, however, succeed in winning a measure of his sympathy. 'This I've seen,' he admits.

Tom looks back at him. 'What of the portrait in the gallery, then? Ain't he shown it to you yet? That's the thing he's most pleased with.'

'Beg pardon?'

'One of your pals from the Academy painted it. That lickspittle John Hoppner. Beau had used him before, for himself and the baron mostly, but last year he ordered one to be taken from Mary Ann as well. Unknown to her, though, the artist and his patron had agreed on a few special terms first.' Tom smiles bitterly. 'See it and you'll understand why she longs for release.'

Not all she longs for, thinks Will; and he wonders for a moment how the lovers progressed from an earnest discussion of her woes to the scene he discovered. He steps closer. 'Do *you* understand, Tom, what'll happen if they catch you? Word is that Lord Harewood will soon be back at the estate. What d'you reckon he might do about this?'

Tom's blood is up now, his rebellious spirits roused, any penitence forgotten. He crosses his arms, glowering happily. 'But we ain't been caught. And we won't be.'

Will stays calm; he speaks firmly. 'He'd set his men

on you, for starters. Men like the brute who brought me here. Who watches us right this minute from over yonder.'

'Stephen, you mean? He ain't no *brute*, Will. Why, his whole life is given to the growing of peaches.'

'I should think Anthony Neville said similar things, afore they did for him.'

Tom doesn't respond.

'Draughtsman from Long Acre,' Will enlarges. 'Disap-peared a few years back, while at Groombridge. That were the lord's daughter too, or so they think. It's claimed—'

'Will,' says Tom, 'that's tavern gossip. That's the guess-work of drunks and liars. As I recall, as *I* was told, this Neville of yours fled his debts. Ran off to Ireland, that's all.' He laughs in exasperation. 'These daft stories stick to you like tar, don't they? Always have. You let yourself be steered by the lowest claptrap, the most moonstruck notions. I've never understood it.'

'Don't be a fool. The baron would have you flogged. Very probably worse.'

Tom won't listen. 'The only floggings done in Lord Harewood's name,' he says, 'are served out on black backs and shackled black limbs, many hundreds of miles from Yorkshire. I'm sure he wouldn't care at all for such unpleas-antness to reach his home soil.'

Will blinks; he sees the deck of the *Zong*, the slavers' whips curling and snapping in the ocean air. 'That don't ... you can't—' He stops. Draws breath. Changes tack. 'Your art. These new strategies you talk of. It'll never come to pass if Beau Lascelles takes against you. You'd be lucky to find work painting barges on the river. You know what can happen. You've damn well *seen* it happen. Destitution, Tom. Beggary. We ain't got so very far to fall, God knows. Neither of us.'

And there it is, that pitying expression of Tom's, excusing Will once again for the limitations of his mind. 'But the goal, Will, the whole *point*, is to liberate ourselves from these nobles and gentlemen. To make a stage for our work – ways of earning that'll free us from their patronage.'

More is said, but Will hears only that he is being denied; his careful solutions rejected, his plan for their salvation cancelled out. His fingers tighten around the sketchbooks. 'So you're going to *rescue her*, that it?' he interrupts. 'This precious young miss, reared in luxury, is ready to run off with a penniless watercolour painter, and bed down with him above his mother's shop on St Martin's Le Grand? Stand by him as he chances everything with his hare-brained schemes, and condemns them both to the gutter? Is that what's to happen?'

This scenario pokes hard at a tender part of Tom – very possibly because he has yet to give any thought to the matters it raises. He spits out a sound, disgusted and impatient, and starts to stride away, past a spur of gritstone; then he turns back.

'Why, I wonder, are you still here? If I'm as blockheaded as you say, and my prospects as dire, then why the *devil* are

you still here? Why d'you not just take your damn leave?'
Tom is pointing, his arm bent and index finger straight, the
thumb sticking up like the hammer on a pistol; those fine
brown eyes bulge a little in their sockets. 'You're a *canker*,
Will Turner, a strange and dark and ... and *bilious* soul.
Many in London say so. They marvel at my long association
with you. I tell them that they're wrong, that they run you
down most unfairly. Yet here you are, trying your best to
prove that it's *me* who's in error. That it's your detractors
who see the truth.' The pointing ceases and Tom is off again,
around the spur; and again he halts. '*Go*. Go on, return to
Maiden Lane. Christ alive, it ain't even like you're actually
involved.'

Will allows himself no reaction. 'The baron'll reckon I
was a party to it. You can bet on that. Keeping watch and so
forth. Or at least that I knew of it and said nothing.' Which
is now the case. 'We both must leave, Tom. Get to the closest town and find ourselves a stage-post. You must write to
Miss Lascelles and ask her to remain quiet. And then we
must wait. It's our only course.'

Tom's anger is briefly overtaken by his disbelief. 'Your view
of all this,' he declares, 'is warped beyond reason. Fleeing
won't do no good. It'd be the surest path to discovery.'

'How in blazes can—'

'What you overlook, Will, what you damn well overlook
is that Miss Lascelles is taking this risk also, along with me.
If I go she'll be left to endure them alone. So I won't do it.
D'you hear me?'

Tom walks uphill, away from the lake – to a horse, presumably, on which he'll ride straight back to Mary Ann. Famed for his intractability, Will absolutely cannot abide it in others. He begins a pursuit, shifting his hold on the umbrella, pinching at the cuff of Tom's jacket, to secure him for further remonstration. Tom shakes him off; he grabs out a second time, rather less gently, and they are grappling, Tom pushing at his head, dislodging the sun hat and crunching his grease-and-powder-caked hair up into a ragged fin. Toppling backwards, Will glances against the gritstone spur and reels on towards one of those grimy pools, knowing with certain horror that his momentum is enough to carry him in.

The pool is deeper than it appears. After a few splashing steps, Will is in up to his knees, warm, soupy water filling his boots. The silt bed has a dreadful softness, almost without form. He treads about frantically, struggling to find purchase, sinking to the tops of his thighs. The umbrella, the quality piece from Oxford Street, which has given so much good service on the tour, is abandoned for the sake of equilibrium; the sketchbooks are taken from under his arm and thrust above his head. Once they are aloft, however, the loose leaves start to slide out. Will slams the books against his crown with such force that he staggers, bright beads of light twining across his vision, and sinks a few inches further; but one sheet still gets free, slithering over his face and chest. A corner touches the surface of the pool and moisture rushes in. Weighed down, the sketch flops over like a flatfish and spins slowly away – a close view, he sees, from his first day in the park – the saturated paper darkening, blending with the black water.

'Pass them to me.' It's Tom, back on the shore. His voice is level, all anger set aside; his hand is extended. 'The books, Will. I think I can reach.'

With some difficulty, Will turns around. He is now submerged past his waist, the pool lapping into his navel. Its thick reek blocks his nostrils and coats his throat. Tom's suggestion is stupid: even if he could reach the sketchbooks, which is highly doubtful, moving them about would surely result in more sheets falling. Will makes no reply but gathers his strength and his resolve and wades very carefully to land – concentrating on keeping the bundle of paper pressed against his head and the boots from being yanked off his feet by the sucking silt. Arriving without further accident, he drops to a crouch, lays the books and pages on the ground and commences a thorough examination. Tom, just wise enough to leave him be, finds a stick and attempts to salvage the umbrella – which is speared in the mud about six feet out, tilting like an old mooring pole.

The lost sketch is an important one, the close north-eastern view, and a decent piece of work as well. Will shuts the books and sits nearby, a short way downhill. His breeches, his shirt, the tails of his blue coat are all heavy with water; his boots, once kicked off and shaken, release several handfuls of pungent sludge. Taking the porte-crayone from his tail-pocket, he tests the point against his fingertip. The damp graphite crumbles to grey grit. He looks at his muddy stockings. His frustration and his urgency have departed. In their place is a profound sense of defeat.

Tom gives up on the umbrella. 'It's gone,' he says. 'Another thing that I owe you.' He walks to Will's side. 'I see what you're doing, you know. What your aim is in this.'

'You do?'

Tom sits close, indifferent to Will's soggy clothes. 'You're trying to help me. That's why you've stayed. You're behaving as a true friend should. And I reward you with harsh words.' He pauses, grimacing with self-reproof. 'A plunge in the damn waters. The loss of your work, for God's sake.'

Will says nothing.

'You could've given me up. Others would have, immediately, in hope of favour from the Lascelles. And yet you've kept our secret. Heavens, Will, I don't believe the thought of betrayal has even entered your mind. For that you have my thanks, and my love.'

Tom stands again and takes a piece of quality paper, folded in two, from his tail-pocket. On it is a watercolour drawing, done on a half-scale with perhaps five grades in the tone. He turns this sheet in his hands, altering his hold; then he wheels about and casts it towards the pool with an almost contemptuous flourish. The drawing's rough 'V' shape causes it to twist skyward, spiralling off to one side, landing instead in a knot of waterside ferns. Will is about to exclaim, to ask why on earth he would do such a thing, when he sees it: Tom is seeking atonement by destroying the one piece of art he's produced since his arrival from London. He faces Will and makes a frank appeal.

'I ask that you return to Harewood with me, for tonight at least. They'll think it odd if you leave without explaining yourself, or claiming your bundle. We could have your clothes laundered. Drink some more of Beau's brandy. Talk of art, and of London. And I swear to you that I won't be discovered. I swear it, Will. On the lives of my mother and brother.'

Quite the reversal, thinks Will, for a man who was commanding me away not two minutes earlier. Such turnarounds are common in Tom, though, and his request is not unexpected. It's already plain to Will that he'll have to go back. Even if he could bring himself to trust Tom with this insane liaison – which he emphatically *cannot* – and continue the northern tour without his usual provisions, he's now one sketch short. The commission can't be fulfilled with what he has. That close view has to be retaken. So, rather numbly, he nods.

Tom interprets this as a further demonstration of loyalty and friendship. Grinning, offering again his sincerest thanks, he leans in to grip Will's shoulder; then he strides around the outcrops to hail Stephen across the lake.

Once Tom is out of sight, Will goes over to retrieve the drawing. As he thought, it is the Whatman page he gave Tom out by the castle, upon which he'd appeared to begin a colour study. There are a number of such studies in Will's sketchbooks – supplements to the porte-crayone sketches, made quickly with a limited palette to record precise effects of light and atmosphere. This page, however, holds a considered work, an end in itself, despite the readiness with which Tom disposed of it. The view, perversely enough, is not of Harewood Castle, but the bridge they'd crossed on their way to the valley floor, a modest dry-stone structure, its arches mirrored in the water flowing beneath. Past it, to the right, is a sunny meadow, and a wood – and an indistinct female figure, clad in a pale riding habit, floating like raw cotton in the shadows of the treeline.

Tom's style, like Will's own, has its critics in the more conventional Academy circles. Too rough, they say. Uncouth, unprofessional, unfinished: a whole host of *uns*. There are blots on this drawing, it must be admitted, and a thumb-print, and the palette is constricted by the circumstances of its creation; but the *grasp of light*, of the effects of light as it falls upon and defines the world, is truly expert, and expressed with a simplicity and a purity that Will suspects his own productions cannot match.

Indeed, the drawing's brilliance, its *offhandedness*, makes it painful to behold. All at once it causes Will to doubt his own ability and the direction he has given his labours, not to mention his future prospects – to picture himself as a failure, rejected by the Academy, forever poor and unnoticed. Tears sting his eyes; one slips out, darting across his cheek and jaw. It has happened before, this inopportune blubbing – normally in the houses of patrons, when encountering the canvases of Claude or one of the finer Dutchmen, and overwhelmed by his feelings of personal deficiency. Father has no patience with it.

What use is there in pitying yourself? the old man would ask. *You've got to heed their virtues, boy, and add them to your own. How else will they be bettered?*

Will recovers his determination. Tom is still occupied, talking to Stephen about pike; so he wipes his eyes, opens the larger sketchbook and places the drawing inside. Then, having fastened the clasps, he plucks his sodden boots from the ground and begins a squelching passage back to the horses.

*

The painters are seen soon after they clear the south-western end of the house. A murmur runs through the gathering in the flower garden, and costly hats turn; and Beau Lascelles is up, teetering atop a chair, hailing them enthusiastically over an immaculate hedgerow.

'My Michelangelo, my Raffaelo! Join us, I insist!'

Tom halts his horse and dismounts, passing the reins to Stephen. Will sits rigid in his saddle, staring towards the stable block.

'Come,' says Tom quietly, moving to his side. 'We must.'

The two painters stop behind the hedgerow to make their preparations. Will has been riding in his stockings, with the boots strung over his horse's rump; now he bashes them together, knocking off as much mud as he can before working his feet reluctantly into their slimy confines. Tom, meanwhile, is pulling his jacket straight across his shoulders,

brushing his waistcoat front, coughing against his hand —
collecting himself, Will thinks, like an actor about to step
from the wings. As they walk out between the flower beds,
he becomes uncomfortably aware of the performance he
too will have to deliver. The family and their guests must
be convinced that all is perfectly ordinary. That his commission proceeds as normal, notwithstanding a couple of minor
delays. That he hasn't spent the past day striving to escape.

The party in the flower garden is close to its conclusion.
The outer tables are being cleared discreetly; gentlemen and
ladies are partaking of a final glass of cordial or champagne
as the sun begins its decline. Beau, clad in a Prussian blue
hunting coat and glossy black hat, works his way towards
Will and Tom with impatience and no little pride, still eager
to draw attention to the two young artists he has brought
up from London — and plainly ignorant, as yet, of the full
extent of their activities.

Tom returns Beau's lively greeting, accepts a glass from
a footman and resurrects some great joke from the night
before. Will stays to the rear, scanning the company, hoping
to locate Mary Ann and gauge whether she means to come
over to greet them or maintain a sensible distance; and he
realises that he's filling the very role that he'd feared the
Lascelles would assume was his. He is their lookout.

'What's this, then? A filthy little troll, come out from
under his damned bridge?'

Mr Purkiss skulks nearby, beside a bed of white roses. He
holds one of the choicest blooms in his hand, bending it out

from the bush, and is carelessly tearing off the petals. His costume is smart enough, but has been loosed and unbuttoned in several places. A scowl is etched upon his pocked, puffy face.

'Look at yourself, sir. Heaven preserve us. Have you been paddling in a sewer?'

'A fall's what it was. At Plumpton.'

Purkiss isn't listening. 'You're a queer fish, ain't you. A damned queer fish. I can see you in a hermit's hovel, y'know, twenty years from now, buried beneath a hoard of bottled piss and cat bones. Scribbling on the walls like a damned lunatic.'

A lunatic. This can't be chance. What has this gentleman learned? What might Tom have revealed while he swilled down Beau Lascelles' liquor? Will looks off to the treetops, feeling his colour rise, with no clue of what to do or say; his clothes seem to shrink, tightening around his limbs and impeding his breaths.

Spotting his predicament, Tom starts to spin the tale of their meeting at Plumpton Rocks. It's a fanciful account, disregarding truth to supply amusement, and it soon wins the attention of the company at large. The mulish Will Turner so set on a view, on his pursuit of natural beauty and picturesque effect, that he clambered atop a steep rock and lost his footing; the tumble, the splashing about, and Tom's own comically inept efforts to rescue him; the supposed attempts of both to save Will's sketchbooks ahead of Will's life, such is their dedication to art. There is laughter and a general lightening of spirits, even Mr Purkiss growing a shade less loathsome; and Will notices Mary Ann, off among a group of young ladies on one of the garden's upper tiers. Lord Harewood's younger daughter wears a dove-grey bonnet and holds a painted parasol. She is watching her paramour closely, with an expression he can't quite construe.

Will too watches Tom, so at ease with centre stage, his accent and demeanour having undergone their usual adaptation – and he decides that charm, be it that of Tom Girtin or anyone else, is but a fine polish applied to deceit. The fellow is betraying the Lascelles' trust in a manner most intimate and profound, and he is making them love him as he does it. Will remembers his remarks on the house and grounds, on the French china, on Beau and Frances and the West Indian origins of the family's astounding wealth; and he sees that this affair with Mary Ann, conducted so brazenly, with so little fear of the baron or his heir, is an act of defiance. An expression of his contempt.

Beau guffaws and lays an affectionate hand upon Tom's shoulder. 'These mishaps must be common enough, Mr Turner. An occupational hazard, one might venture, for the committed landscapist.'

'No,' replies Will. 'They ain't.'

Beau blinks, his broad beam narrowing a little. 'Still, you are with us for yet another night, despite your best efforts to be gone. The fates are conspiring to keep you at Harewood. My artistical partnership has come to pass after all.' He turns towards the house and says his valet's name.

There is no sense of Mr Cope's arrival, or of him having been absent before. He seems merely to have become visible. Master looks coolly at servant, and Will recalls the glimpse he caught of them the previous night, entwined like swans in that dark corner of the state floor. Such relations between men are known in London, as everything is; Mrs Wadsworth's molly house, said to be popular with all ranks of society, stands only fifty yards from Father's shop. Will finds the notion unfathomable. It may account for the valet's ubiquity, though, and the singular position he has been allowed in the household.

'Would it be possible, do you think, for Mr Turner to be included in this evening's outing?' Without waiting for Mr Cope's reply – which is, in any case, a neat affirmative – Beau launches into an explanation, as much for the company as Will himself. 'It is a late arrangement, you understand, agreed upon only yesterday. My dear sister Frances has an unshakeable preference for *private balls*, but I have assured her that a public assembly in a smart little town such as Harrogate shall furnish us with diversion both plentiful and refined – and *variety*, of course, that vital quality, which can so enliven an occasion. You, young sir, shall help me to demonstrate all this.' Beau's voice grows louder still, his eyes acquiring a sheen of cruelty. 'Mr Turner, you shall join our party tonight. You shall dance at the Crown Hotel.'

The thought of this squat, grubby person parading about a ballroom, public or private, draws sniggers from Beau's guests. Will looks over at Tom, who is wearing a glassy

smile. It's difficult to tell if he purposefully omitted to mention this expedition, in order to ensure compliance, or if it
just slipped from his mind.

The ball is a punishment. This much is plain. Will's
behaviour – his stated desire to leave Harewood, and his
repeated failure to do so – has affronted his patron. Now,
thanks entirely to Tom, he has returned once again, and
Beau Lascelles means to have some fun at his expense. The
nobleman is coming closer now, his arms opening as if to
enfold Will in an embrace, but at the last moment he pulls
back with an exaggerated look of distaste.

'A bathtub, Cope,' he exclaims, waving a hand before his
nose, to the further mirth of the company. 'For the love of
Christ, have someone bring Mr Turner a bathtub.'

*

The portrait is an odd one. That Will must admit. It took
him a minute to find, the canvas having been skyed, in the
parlance of Somerset House, as best Harewood can manage:
hung above a door in a shadowy corner of the gallery, almost
as if its owners wished it out of the way. The commission had
been reported around London, as further evidence of the
favour the Lascelles were showing Hoppner, but the work
itself was withheld from the Academy Exhibition. Standing
before it, Will can certainly see why.

Mary Ann is shown as *fat*, in short, markedly fatter than
she is now. She is ungainly also, lumped on a seat like a sack
of goods, her pose – left elbow at an angle, propping her

up it seems, right hand lying in her lap – both listless and vaguely discomfited. The soft line of her neck, so admired by Will, is broken meanly by a pronounced double chin. An attempt has been made at modishness. Her hair is powdered and dressed; her cheeks blush with carmine; her gown of yellow-green silk is fashionably cut, with mid-length sleeves, a plunging neck and a bow tied beneath the breast. The voluminous skirts, however, suggest not the graceful weightlessness of antiquity, but a futile effort to disguise the extent of the sitter's bulk. The actual brushwork is expert, the colouring utterly assured. Hoppner could have helped Mary Ann in a dozen different ways; he could surely have transformed her. Yet he has done nothing.

Will steps back, bemused. Why the devil would such a picture be taken? The first law of society portraiture – flatter your subject – has been contravened. The very opposite result attained. Will knows John Hoppner; he's been careful, since he began exhibiting, to keep up a certain sociability between them. Tom Girtin might hold him in disdain, but the fellow is a senior Academician, a pupil of Sir Joshua at the peak of his ability and reputation. Hoppner would depart from his profession's governing principle for one reason only: the specific instructions of his patron. Could Tom's interpretation be correct? Was the portrait a spiteful trick, orchestrated by Beau?

The gallery extends over the whole west end of the house, a long chamber of splendorous emptiness. Will looks down it, ignoring the stucco, gilt and marble, his eyes picking out a second canvas hanging above the southern door. He strides over, through the warm, slanting bars of early evening sunlight that fall across the polished wooden floor. It's a second portrait by Hoppner, another lady, of the same dimensions and even the same heavy golden frame as Mary Ann's. They were plainly commissioned together. This one is more favourably positioned, however, and painted with a lighter palette; and as Will approaches he sees that it is a far more typical example of the portraitists' art. The lady's gown is an iridescent lavender. Its arrangement, the way it flows around her slender limbs, holds a clear echo of the Sistine Chapel. Her face is a perfect oval, the even features regarding the viewer with serene elegance. Will squints at the label, but it is too high up for him to read.

'Mrs Henrietta Lascelles, by Mr Hoppner of London. Principal painter to the Prince of Wales.'

The servant, the corpulent under-butler Will had followed inside when he first arrived at Harewood, is standing in the doorway beneath the painting. Ellis is his name; appointed to dress Will for the ball, he has overseen a bath, the supply of fresh hair powder and a clean stock and shirt, the extensive brushing of the Vandyck-brown suit and the polishing of the evening shoes, which he has also somehow cured of their squeak. His supervision, in general, has been extremely close. Only a last-minute absence to resolve some confusion over wine glasses enabled his charge to slope away.

'Indeed,' Will mutters, a trifle embarrassed to have been thus discovered. 'Most fine.'

'She is the wife of Henry, Lord Harewood's second son. They reside presently at Buckden, sir, in Huntingdonshire, with their two infant boys.'

Ellis's voice has a pained, stilted quality to it. The servant obviously suspects an ulterior motive for Will's presence on the state floor and intends to stress this by pretending the opposite: that it was driven solely by an overpowering curiosity for Harewood and its treasures. Accordingly, he embarks upon a great long list of facts about the gallery's other ornaments and items of decoration, in which Will is obliged to feign interest.

'What, though,' he manages to ask, after the subjects of the hack paintings fitted into the ceiling have been exhaustively detailed, 'of that other portrait down there? Above the other door?'

'That is Miss Mary Ann Lascelles,' comes the flat reply, 'Lord Harewood's youngest daughter.'

Will pauses. 'Yet—'

The under-butler resumes his list, requesting that Will give his attention to the curtain pelmets, which, despite their luxurious appearance, are in fact made from wood, ingeniously carved and painted in the workshops of Mr Chippendale of London. Will obeys, noting the evasion, and is looking up at the ruby-red folds, marvelling at both the illusion and the pure aristocratic strangeness of the idea, when he sees movement through the tall windows behind. Past the flower garden, over the hedges, a procession is starting up from the stable block.

'The carriages,' pronounces Ellis. 'Come, Mr Turner. Mr Lascelles will be expecting you in the hall.'

The chattering mounts as Will is ushered across the dining and music rooms, rising from a distant murmur to a muted roar; then the final door is opened and it engulfs him completely. He halts, quite oblivious to Ellis's efforts to nudge him further forward. His mouth goes suddenly dry; a cool droplet of sweat breaks free of his armpit and races down the side of his ribcage. There are fifty of them at least, heavily scented and powdered, dressed to their best and in a state of high excitement. Beau is somewhere by the main doors, more audible than visible; but Mary Ann is nearby, only five yards to the left, surrounded by the same young ladies who were with her in the flower garden. They stand in a circle before a bronze Bacchante, daintily lifting the hems of their gowns to compare shoe-roses. Will recalls the portrait's flabby, vacant visage; the actual woman is so much livelier, so much *finer*, that his teeth grind at the injustice of it.

A single, tentative step is taken; and the carriages cut fast along the northern façade, drawing up at the main entrance. This sight – the colours of the speeding conveyances, the discipline and co-ordination of the horses, the smart uniforms of the coachmen – prompts an immediate shift towards the doors. Will is steered out into the twilight by the house servants. Casting about for further guidance, he spies a thin ribbon of white smoke, winding around one of the stone sphinxes that are set on either side of the steps.

Tom is leaning against the front of the sphinx's plinth, his pipe in his mouth. Like Will, he has no formal hat and is again wearing his one acceptable suit of evening clothes, brushed clean but still rather too plain for the occasion. London sparrows, Tom and me, thinks Will with some gladness; then he notices the new silk waistcoat beneath Tom's jacket, pristine white and of the highest quality, and the golden watch-chain that loops over it. His shoes seem different too, better made, and his stock as well. The suit, in actual fact, is the only constant component.

'I knew it.' Tom's voice is huskily quiet and his breathing shallow, as if there is barely space for air to be drawn into his body. 'I knew that you'd have to see the thing for yourself.'

Will grunts; he adjusts his cuffs. 'Keeping watch on me now?'

Tom's reply is lost in coughing, which he tries to smother in his sleeve. The evening is balmy – by Yorkshire standards, at least – yet he appears distinctly cold, his long arms crossed tightly.

'Are you well, Tom?'

Tom takes a pull on his pipe; he looks away. 'It'll pass.'

Will turns to the flight of steps and the noisy cascade of revellers that is rolling slowly down them. 'Did you know of this before, at the rocks? This . . . dance?'

Tom is unrepentant. 'Beau wanted you to come. *I* wanted you to come. Is that so very strange?'

'It was a lie, then. As good as.'

150

'Christ in Heaven, Will, it's one evening only. And it's a *dance*. An entertainment.' Tom spits something on the gravel. 'Familiar with the idea, ain't you?'

There is a great hoot of laughter from the steps as a young gentleman, giddy with Harewood champagne, stumbles midway and ends up sprawled upon the drive. Will is about to state that he sees no entertainment here, none at all; but Tom manages to pre-empt him.

'Rich men will be present. Console yourself with that. It's a public ball, and among the guests will be many from outside the Lascelles' acquaintance. People they'd usually have little to do with. Patrons, quite possibly, who might be inclined to offer us better terms for our labour.' He uncrosses his arms; he weighs the watch-chain in his fingers. 'Whose wealth ain't drawn from such a polluted well.'

A public ball.

Instead of supplying reassurance or provoking curiosity, Tom's words serve only to deepen Will's dread of what lies before him. He's made a very determined point of avoiding balls and dances of every description, believing them to be for the moneyed, the idle and the vain, and no place whatsoever for an artist of any seriousness or ambition. He considers flight, hiding away in the flower garden or the stables, or just bolting into the park. Tom has begun to wheeze like a man several times their age, but Will can't help regarding him with a measure of envy. This affliction of his would surely be enough to excuse a fellow for the night, should he wish it. Might they be permitted to retire together, perhaps, with Will playing nurse? He's seen Tom weather similar episodes, after all. He's pondering how best to propose this when Tom overcomes his difficulty and speaks again.

'Would that damn Hoppner have painted her with a beard, I wonder, or tentacles in place of arms, if Beau Lascelles had given him enough gold?'

The portrait. 'It's odd. I grant you that.'

'It ain't odd in the least. It's *despicable*.'

Will sighs. 'Who can say what really occurred. A painter and his patron – and the sitter as well – it's a complicated—'

Tom won't hear this. 'The villain was humiliating her for his sport. That's what damn well *occurred*, Will.' He pulls himself up and knocks out his pipe against the plinth. 'See there. He's doing it right now.'

The party has started to disperse – to locate their carriages and climb aboard. Beau stands by the three large vehicles that belong to Harewood, their panels painted ivy green, which have been brought up for the family and those among their guests who lack conveyances of their own. He looks remarkable: sleek and huge in a coat of rich russet, hat set just so upon his powder-dusted hair, an unmistakable member of England's very first rank. Adopting an air of patriarchal sternness, he sets about extracting Mary Ann from the company of her female friends, ordering her to Frances's side and into the lead carriage. She obeys, walking over with a shuffling, reluctant quick-step, her head bent down in an attempt to hide her infuriation.

This matter dealt with, Beau's gaze alights on his painters. Tom clears his throat and straightens his back, masking all sign of infirmity as he returns their patron's hail. It's hidden from them, Will thinks, as best as he can do it. It's hidden along with everything else.

They are directed, with Beau's compliments, to one of the other Lascelles carriages, further from the house. As they move through the remains of the party, Will overhears its whispers – many of which are so vocal and indiscreet that they scarcely deserve the term.

'Of course, she is under their supervision. Their guardianship, I suppose. They are putting a brave face on it, but the situation is most lamentable. So upsetting for them all.'

'I could provide a name – the author, so to speak, of Miss Lascelles' distress – but I fear dear Beau would not be forgiving . . .'

'Extraordinary, really, that the girl is not confined to the house. Were she *my* responsibility, I'd have her shut up in a tower somewhere, like a maiden of old.'

It occurs to Will that Tom has said nothing about Mary Ann's eventful London season. He decides that he will ask him about it now, and learn how it might fit into his strident account of the young lady's hardships. Tom is some yards ahead, however, his passage through the Lascelles' milling guests proving rather easier than Will's; and the next minute he is against a span of green-gold spokes, looking up at the carriage, introducing himself to the ladies and gentlemen already seated within. Before Will can speak, or reach out to tug at his coat, he has mounted the iron steps and ducked in through the door.

*

Will and Tom are placed on different ends of the same seat. Between them is a garrulous, bovine lady who talks without interruption to those opposite – a well-to-do couple in early middle age and an elderly gentlemen with a clerical bearing – about coiffure and costume, the particulars of dance steps and who else might be present at the ball. Any communication between the painters is impossible. Tom opens his window an inch or two and seems to concentrate on his breathing, while Will does his best to ignore his fellow passengers and savour each moment of the drive, each moment that is *not* the Crown Hotel at Harrogate. He studies the cottages and country churches; the roadside taverns and the shabby gaggles who come out to watch them pass; the fields that dip and rise in the diminishing glory of the dusk. Within a few miles, however, the scattered farmsteads and hamlets start to coalesce. Houses grow higher and group together into terraces of dark stone. Lanterns appear at corners, or suspended over doorways. Next there is a common, a broad blue expanse criss-crossed with paths; then the streets and sloping lanes of a prosperous market town; and finally, across a loose, leafy square, the façade of the Crown Hotel, a queue of carriages coiled before it.

The Lascelles' carriage is waved to the front of the line, Beau emerging to a round of welcomes so effusive it sounds almost like an ovation. Tom's door is nearest to the hotel and he is out the instant they stop. Will sets off in pursuit; he climbs into the street, strides around the rear wheels and makes for the entrance, joining the small crowd that is filing inside after the Lascelles.

The hallway beyond is dim and packed with people. Neither Tom nor any member of the family can be seen. The heat is staggering, rather like being slowly poached within your clothes; a salty human mist clouds the air and the very walls are stippled with moisture, as if they are sweating along with the multitude they contain. This suffocating atmosphere positively throbs with flattery and forced laughter. The Lascelles are much discussed. Will hears a great deal of admiration for Beau, the bachelor heir – for his person, his aristocratic mien, his tailoring – and at least three breathless accounts of his association with the Prince of Wales, who he resembles so closely (it is asserted) that even George's intimates struggle to tell them apart. The scandalous Mary Ann proves an equally irresistible topic. It is noted how her brother and sister appear to be warding away introductions, more or less, ensuring that the girl's invitations to dance will be non-existent. An ignominious night for *her*, certainly, but who'd want to risk offending Lord Harewood's son?

Distracted by all of this, Will's search wanders off course. He becomes wedged in a corner – stuck in a still pool at the margins of a wide, wallowing river. At his back is a sooty painting of a prize pig; while enclosing him to the front and side are infantry officers from some local regiment, resplendent in the sashes and baubles of their dress uniform. Blatantly bidding for female attention, they are engaged in a shouted exchange about the state of the war with France – the deplorable stalemate, the cowardice of Austria, their longing for action. Will addresses them, requesting his release. The officers respond with supercilious glares, as if an awful liberty has been attempted. Like many others in the hotel that evening, they seem to take him for a trades-man or clerk, presumptuously using a public ball to move among his betters, and will afford him no courtesy.

Will considers the pig, a piebald creature so bloated that its head is receding into its body; and he pictures Tom some-where beyond, simpering at Mary Ann in such a clumsy, doting fashion that he's given away in a trice and they are both tipped forever into ruin. This vision is enough to propel him forcibly between the soldiers' scarlet-coated elbows. There are exclamations – egad, bounder, et cetera – and a hand fastens on his collar. He shrugs it off easily, some-what violently, and without looking around; and by God does this improve his mood. His clarity of purpose, mislaid at Plumpton, is abruptly recovered. He must find Tom. He must make him face their situation; obtain a vow that he will break from the Lascelles' household; and plan their depar-ture, their *imminent* departure, for their rightful quarter.

The lope and trill of dancing music draws Will down a cor-ridor and into the ballroom. Two lines of dancers are arrayed along it, the gentlemen to the left and the ladies to the right, performing a sequence of precise, interlacing steps, to the stentorian instructions of a dance-master. Onlookers border them, four or five deep; commentary is being given, various persons identified and gossip shared. A dozen musicians are up on a stand at the far end, delivering a workmanlike rendition of a tune Will doesn't recognise. The Harewood party arrived late, it appears, no doubt intentionally; this ball has plainly been underway for some time.

The dance ends to applause, the lines dissolving. A murmur goes up as Beau Lascelles takes to the floor, somewhere towards the ballroom's centre. Bows and curtseys are made, and the music resumes with a flourish. Will secures a vantage point of sorts, craning and peering between the shoulders of those in front, but he cannot see the baron's eldest son, or his mastery of the Scotch Reel – which is being reported throughout the company as a matter of urgent interest.

Tom stalks by, then circles back sharply to Will's side. It seems, at first, a rare piece of luck. Will opens his mouth to propose that they head outside, to discuss their situation. But Tom's expression stops him from speaking. With the slightest of nods, the other painter directs his attention to the opposite wall.

It's a perfect little scene, in its way – an incidental group worthy of Hogarth. Mary Ann is positioned by the ballroom's yawning, unlit fireplace with a single companion, the bovine lady from their carriage, who talks on at the same indefatigable rate. Just behind them is none other than Mr Cope, standing bolt upright and impassive against the cream-and-blue wallpaper, deterring all who might approach – ensuring that there is a boundary around her, several feet in radius, which none will cross. A young lady who would normally expect to dance for much of the evening is being made to stand idle. Boredom, anger and acute embarrassment all boil within her, barely contained beneath a thin shell of gentility. She looks up fixedly at the chandeliers, her fan flickering in her grasp like a snared bird.

'I'll do it,' says Tom. 'Why shouldn't I? I'll ask her.'

Will's shoulders fall. 'Tom—'

'But why the devil *shouldn't* I, Will? What right have they got to shame her like that?'

Will nearly laughs. How exactly, after everything he has experienced, does Tom manage to remain so innocent? 'You do *know*, don't you? What happened in London in the spring?'

Tom doesn't reply. He's following the patterns of the dance – the bobbing of heads, the arcing of arms, the little jumps and hops. It leaves him undaunted. 'This ain't so hard. If this collection of blockheads can keep up with it, then so can I.'

'There's rules here, Tom. Rules we ain't privy to.' This earns Will a look of absolute derision. He moves nearer; he grows desperate. 'We've got to stay *quiet*. For *God's sake*. Plan for our departure. Not draw unnecessary notice.'

Tom raises a hand. 'Enough, Will. Honestly. If I need an address on decorum, on probity and suchlike, I'll find myself a damn vicar.'

He steps back and is gone. Will loses sight of him almost at once, becoming trapped behind a range of velvet and satin, topped by heaps of over-powdered hair. He's rooting about for another gap when the moment arrives. A quiver of alertness travels through the company. Everyone who is not presently dancing looks towards the fireplace. All conversation dies away. Even over the music and the noises of the dance, Will hears the question and the confidence with which it is asked; and he hears Mary Ann's immediate, affirmative reply.

Tom returns. He walks with his chin up, proud of himself, unmindful of the speculation that hums around him, both scandalised and delighted, concerning his identity, his intentions and so forth. The disposition of the ballroom has been reversed. Whereas few paid him notice before – and then only to admire him in passing, as a well-made young man of no obvious consequence – now few do not. There is a cautiousness to this fascination, however, as towards someone diseased or condemned to die. No one wants to be standing too close when the Lascelles' hammer falls. A small circle quickly clears around the two painters, much like that which isolates Mary Ann.

'It's done,' says Tom, rather unnecessarily. 'To hell with them all.'

Will cannot speak; he cannot move, even, or make a sound beyond a low, tortured growl.

'What other path was open? Tell me that, Will. What man of honour could watch as—'

'Honour! *Honour!*'

Tom smiles. 'You don't understand. I knew you wouldn't.'

Will imagines himself gripping hold of the fellow's lapels, wrestling him to the ground and banging his head repeatedly against the floor. 'Tom,' he hisses, 'you are rutting with the *baron's daughter*. While you are a *guest in his house*. I believe the position on *that*, as regards to this honour of yours, is pretty much universally agreed upon.'

Tom merely smiles again; and before Will can make another appeal for prudence, for sanity, for simple self-preservation, the Scotch Reel prances to its finish. Amidst the clapping, under the eyes of the entire ballroom, Tom pulls his fine white waistcoat straight and walks out onto the floor. Mary Ann comes forward to join him. The lovers take a mischievous, almost childlike pleasure in the other's proximity, and reveal not a single hint of discomfort or regret. He bows, she curtseys, both exaggerating the action very slightly; then they join hands and wheel around to find their place.

A Country Dance is announced, with the Right Honourable Mr and Mrs John Douglas leading, to a piece entitled 'Summer's Bounty'. As the music strikes up, Will sees Beau and Mr Cope, over by the fireplace, close to where Mary Ann was situated. Beau glistens with heat, mopping at his brow and grinning, working hard to appear as if nothing unusual or improper is going on; but the way Mr Cope holds his arm, a thumb hooked into the elbow, and whispers rapidly in his ear, speaks of considerable alarm. He gives a near-invisible signal of assent and the valet is away, heading for the orchestra stand.

Will moves towards the dance and the empty circle moves along with him, providing an uninterrupted view of the proceedings. The couples are arranged in two facing lines, performing simple, reciprocal steps and taking turns to sweep down the middle. Frances and Douglas, the leaders, go first. They are magnificent to behold, veterans of a thousand balls far more grand than this one; graceful yet rigorous, stately yet really quite fast, whirling from one end of the dance to the other at a racehorse pace. It is a display plainly intended to remind the room of the aristocratic plane upon which they dwell – which they never leave, regardless of their surroundings – and which will protect them, ultimately, against the evening's petty controversies.

Tom and Mary Ann come eighth or ninth. Their progress has a rather different effect. He plays the rank neophyte, wearing an expression of humorous vexation as he attempts this alien discipline; while she is his tutor, patiently guiding him through the movements and smiling at his frequent missteps. They edge along the central channel at a fraction of the normal speed. At one point he stumbles, in an effort not to tread on her gown, bringing them into an accidental half-embrace. Hands linger upon arms as they right themselves; their spectators practically convulse with mock-indignation.

When every couple has made their run – a duration of perhaps ten minutes – the dance ends. It feels premature, even to one as unversed as Will; a first act, as it were, cut off from the remainder of the drama. The Lascelles begin to withdraw from the ballroom, taking Tom Girtin along with them. This is noticed, of course, and prompts a rush of conjecture; but fresh information is also beginning to circulate.

'A painter, up from London,' says a gentleman, somewhere to Will's left. 'He's staying at Harewood. I'm told that he asked Miss Lascelles to dance at her brother's particular request.'

'But why in heaven,' a lady enquires, 'would a noble gentleman such as Mr Lascelles desire a *painter* to dance with his sister?'

Across the room, in an adjoining vestibule, Beau is laughing, clapping Tom on the shoulder as he directs him down an unseen corridor. Here it is, thinks Will. Our end has arrived. He's tempted to flee, to hurry from the hotel, through the kitchens maybe, locate a coaching inn and start for some remote region of Wales or Scotland. He pictures a cabin beside a lake, several miles from any road; a spread of mountains in the background, with forested slopes and snowy peaks; a lifetime's work, just beyond his door. No one would find him.

Yet he does not move. Should he run now, London would be closed to him. His rise, barely begun, would be halted categorically. The two sketchbooks back at the house, the precious seeds they contain, would yield nothing. Father would just have to get on as best he could, denied his dearest ally and his greatest chance for the future. And Tom, brainless hot-head that he is, would no doubt secure his own fate with some mutinous pronouncement – dig a nice deep grave into which Beau Lascelles had only to push him. No, the sole remaining option is an appeal: an abject and heartfelt appeal to Beau's Christian mercy, coupled with a sincere apology for the stupidity, the bestial impulsiveness, the very *existence* of Tom Girtin. Will makes for the vestibule at a panicked trot. He tries to convince himself that Beau's professed love of art, of *their* art, may trump all other concerns. This idea is so nakedly improbable, however, that it brings him despair rather than hope. Destruction, right then, seems assured, the situation irresolvable.

The Lascelles are already gone from the vestibule, and Tom along with them. At random, Will selects the leftmost of three doorways and discovers a large dining room, with places set for two hundred or more. After the humid, over-crowded chaos of the ballroom, the order of its long tables has an almost mesmeric quality; the dense pattern of the cutlery, all those blades and prongs and spoon-heads shining against the white cloth, slows his step.

At the other end of the room, a waiter is folding napkins. 'Might I be of assistance?'

Will stops between a table end and a tall window. He looks back at this man – the uniform, the scrubbed complexion, the officious, faintly distrustful manner – and is preparing to answer when he hears another voice, far quieter, somewhere outside.

'Do you imagine that will help us, Frances? Ending the dance, dragging me out here?'

It is Mary Ann, and she is livid. The waiter's face is unchanged; the young noblewoman is beyond his earshot. Will makes a reply, saying he is well, his every need met. He turns to the window as nonchalantly as he can manage. It is open at the bottom, the lower pane propped two inches above the frame. Peering into the glass, attempting to catch sight of her, he sees only himself and the room behind, reflected in a liquid blackness.

Frances answers, her voice muffled by distance. Will can't distinguish the words, but her tone is one of gentle admonition – rather gentler than might have been expected. The waiter states that guests are to remain in the ballroom until supper is called, that this is a strict rule of the house. Will nods absently, mumbling something, and bends a little closer to the window.

'No one will think any such thing,' Mary Ann retorts. 'Why would they? You are being perfectly ridiculous. And what is a *dance*, by God, beside everything else you've had me do – that I have done without the smallest complaint?'

Will frowns down at the floorboards, his eyes straining on the whorls of the grain. Before he can wring any sense from what he has heard, the waiter loses patience and starts towards him. The man has perhaps four inches' and two stones' advantage – and a plain appetite for confrontation, despite his well-groomed exterior. Thinking that he has caught an interloper, he drops his civility and demands to see a ticket. This secures Will's full attention. He straightens up, explaining that no ticket was ever given to him – that he is a painter staying at Harewood House, and a member of Mr Lascelles' party. The waiter is not persuaded. He advances further, in the manner of one ready to seize hold of a fellow's collar and then box his ears *en route* to a swift ejection.

'I can vouch for this young man.' Mr Cope stands five yards to the rear, having materialised, once more, from empty air. 'What he says is true. Return to your napkins.'

It is unclear whether the waiter recognises the valet or is merely responding to his chilly authority; but he bows and retreats, leaving the room entirely. Will glances at the window, praying that the baron's daughters have concluded their disputation. Mr Cope stays very still, a firm black stroke atop the smooth sepia washes and soft highlights of the dining room. Will was dreading such an encounter. It would be Cope, he'd assumed, who'd come to claim him – to lead him out into a back alley to face the baron's vengeance. Now, though, he sees that there had been a basic error in his understanding. This tableau is too simple by far.

Everything else you've had me do. That I have done without the smallest complaint.

'Mr Lascelles has a request.'

By which, of course, he means an order. Instead of fear, Will feels a prickling, insolent anger. What is Mr Cope actually doing there at the Crown Hotel? Is it *usual* for gentlemen to take their valets out dancing with them? These bold questions go unuttered; he shifts about warily, stepping away from the window.

'What is it, then?'

A very slight depression appears at the edge of Mr Cope's mouth. 'Supper will soon begin,' he says. 'When it is concluded, and the music resumes, he would have you ask Miss Lascelles for the first dance.'

*

Will ventures onto the floor with all the ease and confidence of a man atop an icy pond, who suspects that it might not support his weight. His right hand is joined with Mary Ann's left, at a shade below shoulder height. He looks to her and she turns away immediately; if this really was ice they trod upon, the baron's daughter would gladly see him fall through it.

The dance is called, a French name that sounds to Will like *boo-launcher* – he can no more speak French than he can dance – but those around him are smiling in recognition and making knowledgeable comments. They form into large circles, five in total, along the length of the floor. Will and Mary Ann are accepted into the central circle. There are none of the scandalised stares and grave shakes of the head that greeted her previous dance. Everyone is aware that Will is a second Harewood painter, in the employ of the Lascelles. This is generally considered impressive, an aristocratic attribute akin to their vast mansion or fleet of carriages: a rich man may have one artist draw his house, but this noble family has *two*, brought up from London especially. Nevertheless, a number greet their pairing with amusement, the half-hidden smirks and titters to which Will is almost becoming accustomed: 'The princess and the tar,' he hears someone say, to stifled giggles.

A change in the music announces that the dance is about to begin. The fact of this ordeal dawns on Will anew. He ate copiously at supper, unthinkingly, spurred on by nervousness; his stomach, as a result, is painfully full, an aching ball strapped to his midriff. The taste of the soup – an odd, creamy concoction, redolent of almonds and lemon – still seems to coat his mouth. Furthermore, he is quite abominably hot. His clothes, the clothes of all at the Crown Hotel, are growing dark with perspiration, the folds and flaps of fabric wilting like dying flowers. Perfumes, although applied in prodigious quantities, are beginning to give out, allowing more animal smells to prevail. Even the light seems to be muddying, melting somehow, colours and their shadows mixing together into a grubby, brownish mid-tone.

Will looks again at Mary Ann. Her curtsey is perfunctory, to say the least. His request was met with a combination of contempt and resignation; she'd been prepared for it and instructed to accept, however reluctant she might be. It is a countermeasure, this *boo-launcher*, intended to show the loose-lipped company that if Miss Lascelles would dance with one painter, she would happily dance with the other as well, it being no particular sign of favour.

Tom Girtin is at the fringes now, standing between Beau and John Douglas, recounting some tale or other with every appearance of levity. Another part of the display, Will thinks. They are stressing the blamelessness of Tom's dance – that it was done at their instigation and caused not even the slightest offence. The two painters were seated near to each another at supper, in amongst the rest of the Harewood party – who sought to shield the Lascelles from any further mutterings by conversing as vociferously as they could on any topic that came to mind. Once again, therefore, it was impossible for them to talk. Will caught Tom's eye several times and tried a range of significant looks on him. None elicited anything but puzzlement.

The dance advances into its opening figures. Those in Will's circle adopt various peculiar poses, which he does his best to imitate; and then they are off, rotating in a clockwise direction. Will falls in, half a step behind, only to be caught out when they suddenly reverse course, colliding with the gentleman to his right. This happens twice more, before arms are raised and everyone spins about, bobbing up and down. Will is lost, hopelessly hesitant, like a country visitor trying to pick his way across a busy London street. Mary Ann grips his elbow, quite savagely, to halt him in the middle of a superfluous turn. She drags him forward, taking his slippery hands in hers, and they stand there motionless while the dance skips on around them. Her features remain composed, more or less, but her cheeks, neck and breast are all roaring red; strands of powdered hair are sticking to her face and her grey eyes are staring at him as if he'd just dropped his breeches and bared himself to the room.

'My apologies, miss,' says Will. 'I ain't no dancer.'

'That much is obvious.'

'This weren't my idea.'

'Nor mine.'

Provoked by this lack of fellow feeling, Will decides to speak plainly. He's still too angry, in truth, for any consideration of delicacy or tact, and there's enough commotion on the dance floor to confine his words to his partner alone. 'Yet you do it anyway,' he says. 'You do what's asked of you.'

Her stare intensifies. 'Explain yourself.'

'I heard you. In the garden, with your sister.'

Now Mary Ann looks ready to bite out his throat. 'You heard nothing whatsoever.'

'About Tom, was it? What I saw in the castle yesterday?'

'You are babbling, Mr Turner. Drunk, I shouldn't wonder.'

'Did they tell you to do it?' Will pauses. 'Why in heaven would they *tell* you to do it?'

At this Mary Ann lets out a revolted gasp, casting Will's hands away from her; then, unexpectedly, she comes right up close, her embroidered hem swishing over his evening shoes as her feet interlock with his. Confused by her nearness, by the sharpness of her sweat, he realises too late that she means to trip him. A discreet, well-placed shove and he's falling free, his left arm flailing, the gleaming brass bulb of a ballroom chandelier listing across his vision.

All of Will, his entire person, seems to connect with the floor at the same instant. A hard light flashes through everything, then fades quickly through a succession of humming colours. His breath is gone, his bones and organs horribly jarred; his supper, that cloying white soup, threatens to make a dramatic reappearance. As he struggles to recover he sees her towering over him, a hand on her hip, contriving a loud remonstration.

'Honestly, is this how the painters of Covent Garden choose to deport themselves? By taking so much wine with their supper that they cannot even remain *upright* afterwards?'

Will rolls over, wanting to protest, but he has neither the words nor the air to utter them. The dance has stopped, and the music too, he thinks; and there, off in the corners, the laughter is beginning.

'It is an impertinence, a blessed impertinence! If you are capable of shame, you . . . you *oaf*, I believe you should feel it now!'

The baron's daughter turns, her skirts whipping against Will's cheek, and marches from the ballroom. Flopping onto his back, panting raggedly, he finds that he is indisposed to move any further. It isn't so unpleasant down there; rather cooler, in fact. Overhead, the chandelier holds a reflection of his prone self and the curious dozens who encircle him. Compacted and tinted in the polished brass, the scene has a distinct feeling of remoteness, as if the splayed form at its heart belongs to somebody else altogether. It looks like a death, Will decides – like a dancer has keeled over mid-step and lies waiting upon the floorboards for the undertaker. This thought brings him a strange satisfaction.

*

Mr Purkiss's voice blares out over the Yorkshire fields. Liquor elongates his vowels, clips off his consonants and at times frustrates his meaning; it's made very plain, however, that this worthy gentleman's evening at the Crown Hotel, although less eventful than Will's, has been no more gratifying. He reviles the people and the clothes they wore, the wretched food, the dismal music; not a single aspect of the occasion seems to have met his exacting metropolitan standards. Below them, one of the carriage windows is shut with a force that makes the lanterns swing on their hinges. Purkiss doesn't notice. Well settled in his diatribe, and indifferent as to who hears it, he moves on to their host.

'And of course, the whole business transforms old Beau into the most miserable bore. I've said this to him, to his face. Poor devil don't even realise when it's happening. Those long years among the outliers, awaiting the inheritance – they take their toll. I know it. Dear God, I know it.'

Purkiss falls silent. Half a minute passes. Will wonders if he's gone to sleep. He chances a sidelong look – and the man next to him abruptly reanimates.

'But he's up among the gilded now, is Beau Lascelles, among the *elect*, and he wishes to revel in it. Play lord of the town. Have these simple-minded provincials plant kiss after smacking kiss upon his puckered arsehole. I understand the temptation, but by Jove it is *dull*.'

Purkiss lifts a buttock and squeezes out a voluptuous fart. Its repulsive heat coats the upper part of Will's thigh, the thick, meaty odour reaching his nostrils a few moments later. He inches queasily to the left, across the leather upholstery – towards Mr Cope, who sits gazing off into the night, appearing to ignore them both.

'Duller even, I daresay, than a discourse on his damned china. You've seen something of this, Mr Turnbull, I take it?' Purkiss snorts in scornful amazement. 'The money he has spent already in that quarter, and in that quarter alone . . . why, it would be enough, *comfortably* enough, to rescue the fortunes of a dozen who – a dozen lesser – men to whom—'

Will glances over. The gentleman is lolling somewhat, mouthing words he's clearly thought better of uttering aloud, even in his present condition. Then he sucks in a great sniff, rubs at his pock-marked chin and resumes.

'One specimen, I've heard tell, is worth three hundred guineas. A damned *table centrepiece*. Christ alive. Once we threw such things from windows, Beau and I, right through the damned glass.'

Purkiss mimes the action with his arm, making a smashing noise that flecks the air before him with spittle. The sleeve of his lemon-curd coat, the same one he wore on the evening of Will's arrival, is faintly luminous in the moonlight. The front now bears a large stain, left by a splash of wine or sauce; his wardrobe is not nearly so bottomless as that of his noble friend.

Recollection of their past, of their happily destructive youth, causes Purkiss to turn on Mr Cope, suddenly and viciously, lurching through a litany of grievances. The foremost involves a London gaming club called the Four-in-Hand, where Beau and Purkiss meet on the fifth of each month, a long-standing appointment which the latter regards as sacrosanct – but which the former, of late, has begun to skip. There's no doubt in Purkiss's mind as to the reason for this.

'What tricks do you perform, you black-leg rogue? What is it that you whisper about – about his *blood*, and his *money*, and his damned *name* – that makes him dodge me in this wretchedly shabby fashion? What *wires* have you strung him with? What foul passageways do you draw him down, eh? With what manner of *beast*, precisely, d'you have him frolic?'

The valet does not react, knowing that he has only to weather this tirade for a certain period; and indeed, Purkiss is soon winding down like a clockwork automaton, retreating into muttering, then embittered silence, then sleep. He starts to lean outwards, head tilting to the side, a glittering pendulum of drool swinging from his lower lip. Spotting this, Mr Cope reaches over Will to adjust the insensible gentleman's pose and ensure that he's in no danger of toppling off. Will shrinks down upon the bench, trying to avoid any contact. After the many stinks of the evening – that of Purkiss's expulsion still lurks around them – Mr Cope's odour is slight, fresh, something like clean linen. He has none of Purkiss's dishevelled mass; his weight, his presence, seems to be only that of his clothes, which remain in inexplicably perfect order. They pass the pale cottages of a small farm; several dogs bark behind a wall. Beau Lascelles' man sits back – a single, disciplined movement. The fingers of his right hand, the one beside Will, drum upon his knee.

It was Mr Cope, of course, who salvaged Will from the dance floor and brought him out to the square before the hotel, instructing him to remain there until the Lascelles' departure. Will disobeyed at once, re-entering barely six yards behind the valet. Stares and sniping remarks followed after him, the cockney boor who shamed himself with poor Miss Lascelles, as he skirted the main hall and slipped into a corridor. He didn't heed any of it. His sole concern was locating Tom. This latest intelligence would be shared and a new plan formulated. Will couldn't quite imagine what it might be, not right at that moment, but he knew that something drastic was required.

Tom eluded him completely. The Crown Hotel was not so very large, yet an entire hour ran past without result. He was searching the uppermost floor when Mr Cope claimed him again. There was no recrimination, but the young painter was led directly to his place on the roof of this carriage – a last-minute hire from the look of it, found somewhere in the town and already filled with the Lascelles' other guests. The Harewood party was taking its leave, the family itself having gone twenty minutes earlier. Will heard

Mr Cope telling someone inside that Mrs Douglas had fallen ill after supper; although why this unfortunate occurrence had called for all three of their carriages wasn't explained. Of Tom Girtin he could still find no sign.

'A marvellous night.'

At first Will doesn't understand – surely the night had been a disaster? – then he sees that Mr Cope is referring to the view, to the nocturnal world around them, rather than the ball at the Crown Hotel.

'It must hold you rapt, Mr Turner. It must have an effect on you that those who lack your training, your artistic sensibility, can scarce comprehend.'

Will loosens his stock. In truth, what with Mr Purkiss on one side of him (who might vomit, or mess himself, or grow violent, all of which seemed equally probable), and Mr Cope on the other (who could well have learned about his dance-floor exchange with Mary Ann and been ordered to take steps), he hasn't given his usual attention to his surroundings. He looks now, and by God it is achingly fine. A full moon lies against the sky like a new shilling. Around it, in every direction, the clouds are in retreat – dark, trailing strands, wispily thin, banished by the great brightness behind. The landscape below, the rocks and winding hedgerows and patches of woodland, is coloured through a scale of silver-white to blackish blue; but he observes a note of gold as well, where the moon's influence is strongest, a faint corona that projects earthwards, lending a warm contour to a range of distant hilltops.

'Pretty,' Will manages to say, wanting very much to curse; there's light enough to work up here on the carriage roof, but he neglected to place any sketching materials in his formal clothes, assuming that propriety and circumstance would forbid their use. Squinting skywards, he begins to fix the view in his mind, intending to carry it within him until he can sit before a page and set it down. He's well practised at this.

Mr Cope, meanwhile, is talking again, about a painting Will showed at the Academy the previous year – his first in oil and the product of much toil, trial and anguish. A night scene based on sketches taken on the Isle of Wight, it features a moon not unlike the one above them now, illuminating a pair of fishing boats as they sailed out onto an unruly sea.

'Mr Lascelles and I stood before the canvas for some considerable time,' the valet says, his fingers still drumming away. 'He admired it enormously, and could hardly believe that it was the work of a man but twenty-one years old. It already rivalled Mr De Loutherbourg, he said, in terms of mystery and power. Much of the composition, as well, struck him as very true, the form and colour of the waves in particular. He spoke of this at length.'

Like most young artists, Will has a ravenous hunger for praise – for that instant of reassurance, of validation, that dwindles so quickly to nothing; that feels, on reflection, like such inadequate recompense for your efforts, yet is craved again so soon. This offering, though, is oddly deficient – not false exactly, but hollow, contrived, a means to another end.

His concentration broken, Will sits forward awkwardly, rubbing one damp hand with the other.

'I still have it,' he says, 'if he's inclined to buy.'

This amuses Mr Cope. He might be wearing that spectral smile of his; Will can't be certain without turning to study him at close range, which he has no intention of doing. The valet, he realises, is *pleased*. His calamitous dance with Mary Ann fulfilled its purpose, exceeded it even, supplanting her earlier performance with Tom as the talking point of the evening and creating sympathy for her only at the expense of an unknown painter up from London. It is impossible to tell how much Mr Cope knows about what happened out there on the dance floor, but Will reckons that the fellow isn't planning any imminent reprisal.

'You've sailed, I take it, upon the open ocean? Surely you must have done, to have acquired such a deep understanding of its nature.'

Will shakes his head. 'Boating at Margate as a boy. Ferry on the Solent. The war—'

'The war will end,' Mr Cope interrupts, 'before too long. The ports will reopen. You'll be able to cross the sea – and should you wish it, carry on into the European mainland. Mr Lascelles holds this to be the necessary course for all artists of ambition.' The fingers stop their drumming. 'You'd describe yourself as an artist of ambition, wouldn't you, Mr Turner?'

Here we are, Will thinks. Here's the nub of it. He stares down at his evening shoes, the black leather nearly invisible in the darkness. He doesn't answer.

'The Louvre. The Alps. And beyond them, Italy. Celestial Rome. My master frequently asserts that experience of these marvels separates the good from the truly great. You'd have yourself placed among the great, I assume?'

Still Will says nothing. The carriage rocks upon the road; Purkiss's bulging, loose-limbed bulk presses against his arm, then sways away.

'It's Mr Lascelles' belief that true ambition, in any sphere, must recognise the importance of *pace*. Of advancement by degrees. Of retaining your patrons' custom, and their good opinion also. Of avoiding their displeasure, or becoming a test to their patience.'

Now Will turns to Mr Cope. The lines of his tapering face are further whetted by the moonlight; his eyes, half-hidden in shadow beneath his narrow-brimmed hat, seem weirdly flat, lifeless, as if painted on. 'I ain't—'

'My meaning,' the valet continues, 'is merely that it would be wise for you to affix your thoughts to your commission. To keep to your proper pursuits.'

Will looks back to his boots. This is precisely the sort of warning you'd expect from Mr Cope's type – the threat well disguised, wrapped in the velvet glove of implication. It might also be argued that it is sound advice. Father, Will knows, would certainly argue this. *There is no affair.* There is no assault on this grand family's honour. Will's complicity, as he conceived it, now counts for naught. The Lascelles know. They *desire* it, for pity's sake. He could make that sketch in the morning, the replacement for the one lost at Plumpton, and be on his way, finishing off the northern tour before returning to Maiden Lane. This quandary of his is an illusion. If he provides the drawings, if he honours his terms, then Beau Lascelles surely will as well.

Sixty guineas.

But no. It can't be done. These people have treated him like the lowest species of idiot – worked him into place like a knobbly foot into a stiff new boot. Even as he threatens, Mr Cope is plainly unconcerned by what Will might actually have learned of his master's orchestrations. He expects silence. Complete capitulation to the interests of the Lascelles, regardless of what this might spell for Tom Girtin. The cowed, unquestioning obedience of a servant. Will smiles grimly. He will not give it.

'The commission's my only concern, Mr Cope. Always has been.'

Mr Cope is still for a moment, as if assessing the truth of this avowal; then he nods and points towards a vein of lights, twinkling weakly through the trees ahead.

'Harewood village, Mr Turner. We are home.'

Sunday

The returning guests are directed through to the saloon. They are being received with an extra trim of courtesy and concern; Harewood is recognising their right to grievance after they were abandoned in Harrogate and is seeking to make amends. Will gets in front of Mr Cope — who is caught up with the revival and unloading of Mr Purkiss, and the payment of the coachman — and skirts the meandering crocodile of ladies and gentlemen. The saloon doors open; he glimpses Beau Lascelles beyond, out in the middle of the carpet, giving a demonstration of one of his acclaimed dance steps. Frances is in a window, apparently recovered, with her husband at her side. Mary Ann is there as well, and a handful of others — and Tom, standing rather closer to his lover than might have been expected. His shoulder slopes slightly and his face is blank; he is uncharacteristically opaque amidst the laughter and champagne.

Will swerves, descending from the hall's cool vault into

the close warren of the service floor. The casket chamber is just as he left it. He shrugs off his jacket and removes his shoes. By the light of one of Mrs Lamb's contraband candles, he sits himself on the edge of the bed with the larger sketchbook laid across his knees and a stiff leaf of Whatman positioned atop its cover.

'Colour.'

The word hiccups from Will's lips, almost catching him by surprise. It seems wholly correct, the prompting of a pure artistic instinct. He leans down to retrieve his kit. There isn't much time for this, really there isn't; five minutes' diligence, though, while the scene is so present in his mind, could conjure the beginnings of a picture – of an oil that would set Somerset House ablaze. Before leaving Covent Garden he bought a dozen fresh paint blocks from Mr Reeves's shop, every pigment he might have need of, from Roman Ochre to Burnt Sienna – a black hour indeed for his pocket book, but worth it. The little cubes, glued into the kit in an uneven row, rattle together like dice as Will rolls it out. He runs his eye along them, all other thoughts held in check, and settles upon the last: Mars Orange. This particular block has not yet been used and still has its crisp, newly pressed shape; Reeves's emblem, a seated greyhound, remains clearly stamped on its upward face. It has a rich, mineral brightness, like something precious dug up from the soil.

Will stares at the block. A touch of this in the correct place, the subtlest glaze, would supply that singular golden quality he observed from the carriage roof, hazing the night sky. It would be there, on his page; he would *have it*. His wash bowl contains an inch of water, clouded by dirt and soap. Good enough. Reaching out with his foot, he draws the bowl across the floor towards him, readies his palette and selects a red-handled pencil of medium thickness – a current favourite of his, due to the tidy narrowing of its bristles.

Marriage.

Will stops; he sits upright. Could this be it? Could it be that Beau, in an attempt to wipe away his younger sister's humiliation, is seeking to have her wed as quickly as possible – and, seeing no obvious candidates, has opted to create one of his own? Is his aim to take this impecunious young painter from St Martin's Le Grand and remake him as a gentleman? Will thinks hard. More improbable schemes have been enacted within the fashionable world; and besides, the fathomless wealth of the Lascelles can bring almost anything about. Tom Girtin is known in some select circles, but he is hardly famous. Should he vanish, and a handsome fiancé of means and manners appear on Mary Ann Lascelles' arm that autumn, next to no one would perceive the connection.

Hurriedly, Will dips the red-handled pencil in his wash bowl and transfers three or four brush-loads to his palette, until a small puddle wobbles in its centre. Switching his attention to the dried paint block, he dabs the wet bristles on the greyhound's back, rotating them until Reeves's stamp is effaced and the Mars Orange revived. Just the moon, he promises, and the light around it, and perhaps a suggestion of the terrain upon which the strongest beams fall. Just the heart of it. Then he'll steal up to the top floor, find Tom's room and lie in wait; and when he returns, they'll talk. Everything will be explained and a new strategy devised. Will mixes the wash, charges the pencil and sets to work.

The great question, of course, if such a mighty fraud has really been initiated, is whether Tom is a willing participant. It seems very unlikely, given his stated hatred of the family and the version of the affair he spun at Plumpton. How the devil, in that case, are the Lascelles planning to ensure his co-operation? And why would they parade him around as they've done, loudly identifying him as a painter up from London? And invite Will to Harewood in the same week? And draw so much damn attention to themselves, with their assemblies and dinners and balls?

These queries are preoccupying and quite spoil the moon. Will scowls at it – botched, ugly, all power missing, a poached egg drenched in cayenne sauce. He scratches around a bit, orange pigment banking beneath the scraping nail, but to no advantage. Dropping the pencil in the wash bowl, he takes up the porte-crayone and scribbles some notes beside the sketch, upbraiding his own labours, informing his future self how to address its deficiencies; he forgets his spellings, though, and the form of his letters, and struggles to read back what he has written. Too much time has passed. The moment, that exhilarating view from the carriage roof, is gone. He lays his materials on the bed, blows out the candle and hastens into the corridor.

Two minutes later, Will reaches the summit of the service staircase. He looks across the wide landing, at the panelled walls and the many doors they contain, and realises that he hasn't the first idea where Tom's room actually is. All he knows is that it is modest – the kind allotted to a ladies' maid or a valet, Tom said. This is of little use.

'Blast it,' he mutters. 'Damnation and buggery.'

No candles burn up here. There is a soft, greyish atmosphere, derived from the moonlight outside; and the occasional luminous line, shining from beneath the doors of occupied rooms. These, at least, can be discounted. Will is certain that Tom remains on the state floor, with the party in the saloon. A tactic proposes itself. He will try all the other doors in turn, opening them very gently and then poking the smallest possible portion of his head within. If someone is there, if he is seen, he'll duck back, offering an apology in the manner of a mistaken servant. It's a nerve-wracking prospect. His fingers tingle as he closes them around the first moulded doorknob; his stomach, still fragile after the ball supper, flutters and coos like a startled pigeon.

Not a single soul is encountered, awake or asleep, in the entire eastern half of the floor. The doors reveal only empty bedchambers and dressing rooms, varying in size but all luxuriously appointed and scrupulously neat. No trace is found of Tom – no travelling clothes, no artistic equipment. Will heads down a corridor to a second, even broader landing, the dark well of Harewood's main staircase falling away on its far side. He pads over the carpet, towards the nearest door. As he prepares to open it, the landing grows suddenly lighter, its tones warmer; a candle is being carried up the staircase, the shadows of the balusters wheeling around the walls like the hands of clocks, followed by the murmur of refined voices. He is through the door without a thought, closing it behind him as swiftly and as quietly as he can.

The rocking horse, skilfully carved and slick with varnish, stands in the middle of the floor. It seems positively monstrous, a polka-dotted harbinger of doom; for it indicates with dismaying certainty that Will has taken refuge in a nursery. Sure enough, the two beds beyond this dreadful horse each have a pair of little bodies tucked into them, and the paraphernalia of privileged childhood – toys and toy chests, half-sized wardrobes – is arrayed all about. He doesn't know whose children these might be; he has no precise recollection, even, of having noticed any children at Harewood. There can be no doubt, however, that this would be the worst, absolutely the *worst* place in the entire house for him to be discovered. His end would be assured.

No use will come from panic. Will takes a breath, and another; then he crouches at the door, bringing his eye to the keyhole. It affords only a partial view of the landing, but he can discern a group of ladies and gentlemen, perhaps half the total staying at Harewood, bidding each other good night. They move apart, one of the ladies making straight for the nursery. It is Frances Douglas, her purpose plain. Will jerks backwards. He tries to swallow; his tongue is coarse and dry and strangely thick, like a length of old dock rope running down his throat. Should he move? Should he hide somewhere? Might this only worsen matters – lead to him being found yet closer to the children? The chocolate silk of Mrs Douglas's gown fills the keyhole; the doorknob by Will's ear rattles in its housing as she takes hold of the opposite side.

It is over.

'For goodness' sake, Frances.' Douglas has arrived next to his wife; he speaks in a loving, vaguely exasperated whisper. 'Now is not the time. They are well. Nurse has seen to them.'

There is a pause a hundred years long; then the doorknob clinks faintly, shifting as Frances lets it go.

'I can't help but think of Henry.' Her voice is fearful and sad but quick as well, as if something she has been holding in among their guests is finally being released. 'Of the baby. I wish ... I wish Edward would not talk of it so *easily*. He cannot understand. How can he understand?'

Douglas's manner suggests that he has talked this through a number of times before. 'I know, my love, but Edward—'

'The coffin. The little coffin, carried to church. How did Henry bear it? How did he not go *mad*? And Henrietta, dear Lord, the poor creature must—' Frances stops. 'I try to imagine, John, I try ...'

'Do not try. *Do not*. The other boy survived. And they have their first, Frances. They have their Edward.'

Frances turns; candlelight ripples across the silk. 'Would you be able to take such consolation, I wonder, if one of our children were to die? If it were George, or Harriet?'

'That will not happen. The child was newborn. Ours are grown, almost. They are *grown*. There is no danger. Do you hear me?'

Another pause. 'I merely wish—'

'Dearest, they would not benefit from the disturbance. Harriet especially.' Douglas steps between his wife and the nursery; a stretch of snuff-coloured satin replaces the chocolate silk. 'And besides, as I said, now is really not the time. We should be in our room.'

Frances accepts this – and at once, without resistance or complaint. The couple move away, restoring Will's view of the empty landing; he hears another door, the one to their bedchamber he assumes, being opened and closed again. Whatever it is that has been binding him in place, strung tautly across his shoulders and along his spine, now lets him fall. He slumps from a crouch to a kneel; his sweat-sheened forehead presses against the nursery door, squeaking a couple of inches down the polished mahogany.

Minutes pass. Will does not move; he barely breathes. He listens keenly to the silence that has settled upon the landing. All seems clear.

Then comes the cough.

Immediately, he is at the keyhole again. The candles are gone, but he can see the tall figure leaning on the banister, watching the stairs below, the toe of one shoe kicking idly at the other's heel. Tom could be standing at the bar of the Key, or on the balcony at Adelphi Terrace, composing another of his five-page drawings. Will twists the doorknob, thinking to scurry over. As he opens the door, however, he hears a rustle from the stairwell – the sound of an expensive hem being raised, to ease a lady's ascent. Tom coughs again, straightening up and running a hand through his hair. Will perceives that his carefree attitude is a disguise of sorts, assumed rather than genuine; that this is a *rendezvous*, and for all his self-assurance and charm Tom Girtin is itching with nervous anticipation.

Mary Ann arrives on the dark landing. They exchange a couple of inaudible words before disappearing into the shadows of the south-western corner. It has the appearance of a clandestine meeting, urged by a forbidden love, in the spirit of Shakespeare or some medieval verse play; and it's just as *fake*, just as staged and scripted. This is what John Douglas was referring to – *now is really not the time* – the reminder that won his wife's compliance. They knew what had been arranged and removed themselves to prevent its interruption. Tom imagines that he is defying this great family, outfoxing them, yet they are directing his every step, shepherding him into Mary Ann's bed.

It will end now. Will's temper flares with a searing bright-ness. He will give chase and he will have it out, regardless of the intimacies he might disrupt. He will demand that she supply a full account of the Lascelles' plan. Tom will be shown that they mean to draw him in and consume him entire; to obliterate him, in effect, and divorce him forever from his art; to consign him to their corrupted, frivolous world, which he holds in such disdain. Righteous intention seems to flame out from Will's brow. His heart breaks into a hard canter. He's going to confront them, this very minute, and to hell with the consequences.

There is another rustle, this one closer and crisper – not silk or satin but starched cotton. Bed sheets. Will turns. A child is stirring, rubbing at its eyes, mumbling a question. Had he, in his great anger, been speaking aloud? Or moving clumsily, forgetting the need for stealth? It hardly matters now. He steps towards the bed, extending his hands as if to capture a fugitive songbird.

'No, no,' he murmurs, desperately kind, 'do not be afraid, I merely—'

The sound is absolute, pure and shrill, a drill-bit inserted into the ear and whirred around at phenomenal speed. It lasts for longer than one would have thought possible – fifteen seconds? twenty? – followed by shrieks for Nurse, for Mama, for Papa. The girl, for it is a girl, springs out of bed. She is perhaps four feet tall and clad in a white nightgown; she points at the intruder with a fearlessness rather at odds with her frantic squealing.

Abandoning placation, Will scrambles from the nursery and into the corridor that leads back to the eastern landing. The screams continue behind him, with other children joining in. Doors start to open; candlelight rushes over ceiling and walls; bare feet thud on carpets. He all but throws himself down the service staircase, hopping around its tight spiral two or three steps at a time, only to be halted abruptly by the mutter of Yorkshire voices below. Three footmen are gathered at the base of the stairs, on the service floor. Two bear trays, upon which is a cold collation of meats and cheeses; the third is shaking his head, claiming that there has been an error, that Mr Lascelles asked for cakes and sweet-meats instead. Will flattens himself against the wall, waiting for them to finish their dispute and go about their duties.

They do not. The moments squeeze by with excruciating slowness. Noises gather above, and the lambent aura of candles; and it seems certain that he'll be caught there on the stairs, the obvious culprit, his motives for anyone to guess at. Thief? Kidnapper? Or something worse?

One chance remains. Near to the casket chamber is another narrow staircase, connecting the levels of Harewood's east wing. Will has never troubled to investigate it, but there must be an opening among the state bedrooms – which, in Lord Harewood's absence, are left standing empty. If he could reach them and locate this staircase, he'd be able to return to his berth unobserved.

Will steps onto the state floor and enters the grand room that holds the portrait of Lady Worsley. Although not in use, it's hardly safe: immediately to the right is the saloon, glowing like a bawdy house behind its door. A committed band of revellers is still within, with Beau at its head. Will hears Purkiss bellow and spit, that fine gentleman having evidently been raised, Lazarus-like, for the purpose of further intoxication. As he weaves between the furniture he notices that they are in fact discussing *him* – enacting his mishap on the dance floor of the Crown with thumps, crashes and much raucous laughter. Will bites his tongue – literally bites it, his teeth sinking into the muscle to the point where they seem almost ready to meet. He carries on his way.

The left door opens onto virtual darkness. Clouds have obscured the moon, reducing everything to a two-tone scale: black, and that shade of grey that is closest to black. Outlines are rendered slightly imprecise, rough-edged, lent the burr of a dry point engraving. One object, however, can clearly be distinguished: a four-poster bed of massive proportions, protruding majestically from a broad alcove in the inside wall like the prow of a royal barge. Will has only to cross the front of the room, he reckons, to reach the next eastward doorway – the next in a line of facing doorways that will run the length of the southern façade. He goes in.

Past the bed, something moves; a form rises, drawing itself upright.

'Mr Turner,' says Mrs Lamb. 'Why sir, you caught me quite unawares.'

*

The witch will give me away again, Will thinks; she'll stride around that bed, go through to the Worsley room and create a racket that will see me captured, beaten bloody and probably worse. She's a shape only, both her features and her stance impossible to determine. Her voice is good-humoured, amiable even, but this could easily be deception.

When Mrs Lamb moves, however, it is in the direction Will himself has decided upon. She opens the east door and beckons for him to come over. She's been eavesdropping, he assumes, and seems, with this gesture, to be making common cause with him. He doesn't trust it, not one inch; this is the woman who delivered him to Mr Cope and brought his situation at Harewood to a new level of complexity. But her knowledge of this place wholly surpasses his. Playing along might aid his return to the service floor. Will approaches, his eyes growing accustomed to the gloom; and he sees that she's grinning, a little breathless, as if upon a wild lark.

Beyond the door is an ante-chamber. A corridor runs off it, cutting across the house; at its far end, a figure with a candle waits by a window in the northern façade. Mrs Lamb takes him sideways, into the corner bedroom. She shuts the door behind them, setting it soundlessly in its frame. The room is of similar dimensions to the last, arranged around another looming four-poster, with its second door set in the north-facing wall. He turns, waiting for her to lead them on to the eastern staircase – and sees that she is in fact advancing towards him, readying to act, her silhouette giant against the surrounding greyness. Will makes fists, bracing himself for defence. He has been terribly naive. A damn *simpleton*. That murderous look, shot across the saloon the previous night. The slam of the door an instant afterwards. She means him violence.

The softness of her touch, when it comes, is scarcely less alarming. Disarmed, somewhat perplexed, Will is guided to the lordly bed, sat between the curtains and laid out upon the satiny counterpane. Her fingers close not around his neck but the top of his breeches, whipping them down to the knee-buckles, underthings and all; and then they are *on him*, waking him, working him in a manner both tender and brisk. He stares helplessly into the bed's black canopy. All control of his thoughts and person is removed. Every sensation but one is shut from his brain.

Suddenly it stops. Will tries to lift his head. The still-room maid is rummaging beneath her skirts, making adjustments and hoisting them up, climbing nakedly atop him – and *joining them*, easing their bodies together just like that. He stays perfectly, rigidly still, legs straight and arms outstretched. Her smell rolls between them, sharp and warm and utterly confounding. She plants a hand on the mattress; the palm sinks in and his head slides after it, off to the side, coming to rest by the ball of her wrist. He can see almost nothing but has a vivid sense of her – of her weight and the arrangement of her limbs. The bottom of her thighs rest on the top of his, engulfing them, the flesh smooth and slightly sticky. Her apron, stiff with sugar, crackles against his chest. Her breath has a gooseberry bitterness; it gusts over his forehead, stirring his powder-caked hair. She begins to move.

It doesn't last long. Will tenses hard, reeled in very tight; then emits a small, strangled bark as he is released. Mrs Lamb slows, coming to a halt in the space of five strokes. He pants awhile, suffused with a sweet, numbing calm, tiny sparks worming about at the margins of his sight. She looks down at him for a few seconds. He wonders if she can see any more of his face than he can of hers.

'No shoes, Mr Turner,' she says, as if nothing unusual has occurred. 'No jacket neither. Honestly, sir, to what odd tribe do you belong?'

Is she disappointed? Will thinks she must be. He knows very well from tavern talk, from innumerable arguments overheard in the environs of Maiden Lane, that stamina is what's prized in lovers – and that brevity most assuredly is not. Before any more can be determined, though, she's off him, reassembling her garments, leaving him lying there, cold and damply exposed. When she touches him next it is to pull him from the grand bed, much as she pulled the breeches down his legs, and bundle him underneath it. He fits easily, sliding on the varnished floorboards. She squeezes in behind with rather more trouble, her head pushed close to his, a heavy breast nuzzling his forearm. Greasy, cinnamon-scented curls pile around his cheek.

'Madam,' says Will, fumbling with his disordered breeches, 'what in the name of *God*—'

'Someone in the corridor,' whispers Mrs Lamb. 'Heard your noise, I should think.'

Will freezes, leaving himself undone, too fearful to be embarrassed. Candlelight licks along the edge of the western door.

'No cause for them to enter,' she adds. 'This is the baron's own bedchamber, and he in't at home.'

The light fades away; and the fact of what they've done, of where they are, snaps at Will like a dog bite to the buttocks. He starts, thinking to flee, knocking his pate on the bed's underside. 'But he's *coming back*,' he yelps. 'The baron's *coming back*!'

This isn't news to Mrs Lamb. She presses him to her bosom, pinning them together for a second time, but for the purposes of restraint rather than desire. 'Monday,' she tells him. 'Monday at the earliest. We're safe enough, Mr Turner.'

Will struggles, but it's no use. Her words do not reassure; he hasn't the least idea when Monday might be. The past few days, in all their madness and muddle, have made him lose track completely. He finds, furthermore, that he's annoyed by this woman, who runs so damnably hot and cold – baiting him with mysteries, pricking him with adversity – and now, apropos of nothing, smothering him in the most intimate friendship. She seems to be upending him merely for the fun of it.

'Why the devil should I listen to you?' he gasps. 'Why are you so concerned for my wellbeing all of a damn sudden?'

The still-room maid watches the door. She speaks intently, seriously, her mouth an inch from his ear; he can feel her voice as well as hear it, reverberating in her breastbone. 'You're thinking of the night just passed, in the saloon. I was cross, Mr Turner, I admit it. I thought we understood each other, you and me. I thought there was sympathy. Then I hear that you're going. Then staying. Then going once more. And then you're sneaking through the house like a spy. To be frank, sir, I decided to draw you out. To see what you truly are.' Her manner hardens. 'And I wanted you to *battle them*. I wanted to show you the falseness of this gathering of theirs, this summer season they've crafted up here. Mr Lascelles has made you a part of it, after all. You should know its real nature.'

'Its real nature,' repeats Will flatly, from within her décolletage. This speech has only deepened his unease. There's an expectation here that he's done little to encourage; an assumption of allegiance, of comradeship, which he doesn't recall having granted.

Mrs Lamb's humour creeps back in; she loosens her hold, from a confining clasp to something like an embrace. 'And the scales are falling, sir, in't they? There's much talk of you downstairs. You've had quite the day.'

'Madam, I—'

'Word is that Mr Ellis, that slippery slug, had to fetch you from the gallery earlier. Was it the portraits, perchance, that commanded your notice? The one of Miss Lascelles in particular?'

Will stays quiet.

'It must be difficult for you,' Mrs Lamb continues, 'as an artistic gentleman, to understand why the baron's own daughter was taken so unsparingly. With such brutal attention.'

'Distortion,' Will mumbles, his lower lip dragging very slightly against her skin. 'Of a cruel sort.'

'No, sir,' she corrects him, 'it was truth, no more and no less. The cruelty lay in making her sit, and having that fellow paint her so much as she was, so soon after the birth.'

The birth. Imparted casually, this is intended to stun: a choice morsel from the still-room maid's store of Lascelles secrets. Once again, everything begins to shift, to pivot and realign, like the parts of a celestial model.

'You're saying . . . you're honestly saying that Miss Lascelles is a mother.'

Mrs Lamb goes on to explain, in her steady, under-the-bed whisper, how the unlucky girl had returned from London early in the summer of 1796, with three trunk-loads of fashionable gowns, a case of new jewels and some gallant's seed growing in her belly. He'd already exited the stage, an eminently unsuitable fellow whom Mr Cope (she believed) had been obliged to dissuade. As fortune would have it, her sister-in-law Henrietta was then at Harewood also, and with child as well – for the first time, before the twins. They entered their confinement together, up on the top floor of the house. Two expectant ladies climbed the stairs, yet only one baby was brought back down: a healthy boy who was accepted by Lord Harewood, by the world, as Edward Lascelles the third, his grandson and eventual heir. Of the other child there was no trace.

'My guess would be a still birth,' says Mrs Lamb, 'and a switch. A solution to satisfy all parties. Anyhow, the portrait painter was on his way up from London before the babe was even baptised. To take the new mother, they said – meaning the son's wife. And the gentleman certainly earned his money there. Every effort was made to mask Mrs Lascelles' recent ordeals and picture the lady to her best advantage.'

She sighs; Will's head moves with her chest. 'It was her elder brother's idea that he take one of Mary Ann too. As a punishment for her carelessness – for what she might have put them through, had those around her not managed things as they did. How she might have tarnished this new title of theirs. And it stays at Harewood as a badge of her shame. A warning, if you like, against further misbehaviour.'

Will is unconvinced. 'Ain't that an awful risk? Might someone not—'

The still-room maid pulls back, breaking their clinch. 'Is it, though, Mr Turner? Who'd think to tie an unkind likeness of Mary Ann to her brother's infant child? Did *you*, sir? Her condition was concealed. Nobody suspects, save a few Yorkshire servants. They hang the canvas poorly, as you saw – move it between the very worst spots in the house. And if it did ever receive any proper notice, who'd dare to make anything of it? Who among the fops and toadies that they invite out here would take the chance of insulting Lord Harewood?'

This interpretation feels rather determined to Will, like forcing a hat down upon a head that it doesn't quite fit. He says nothing.

Mrs Lamb senses his scepticism; she seems to smile. 'They're right harsh with her, Mr Turner. Always have been. The youngest daughter, the late addition, and with a temper that does her no favours. A burden of worry to her parents and nowt but a nuisance to the rest of them. ' She peers out again, into the dark chamber. 'Until this spring, that is.'

'Beg pardon?'

Instead of supplying an explanation, Mrs Lamb releases Will completely and rolls onto her stomach. Light is gathering beneath the northern door. There are footsteps; two male voices, one sounding disturbingly like that of Mr Cope, engage in a brief discussion. The still-room maid crawls from beneath the bed. She listens hard and hisses an oath.

'Appears I was mistaken. They're searching for someone. Come, we should get downstairs.'

Will emerges, floundering in his haste, buttoning the slap of his breeches. 'What ... what happened in the spring, madam? What changed?'

Mrs Lamb doesn't answer. Six strides take her back to the western door; she inches it open, alert for any sign of life in the corridor outside. The light is strong now. Will can see the impression on the counterpane, where they lay not five minutes before; and a curious crowding of objects across the bedroom's buffets and side tables. It is china, he realises, Beau Lascelles' haul of fine French porcelain, most probably being stored in here for safekeeping while the baron is absent. No individual pieces can be made out, just the odd spout or handle; and a tiny, naked arm, extended with graceful languor, which can only belong to the Endymion centrepiece.

The still-room maid isn't going to wait. Will stumbles after her, fastening the last of his buttons. 'Mary Ann's much the same, ain't she?' He thinks of the castle, of the lovers squirming in the hearth. 'Their punishment failed. She was just as careless this season as the last.'

Mrs Lamb almost laughs. 'Oh no, Mr Turner. This time the whole thing was quite reversed.' She steps into the doorway. 'This time the poor sow was *looking* for pregnancy.'

*

A hunt is in progress. Footmen are combing the state floor to ensure that no interloper is at large; that the upset up in the nursery was an accident, the mortified perpetrator now hiding in their quarters, too embarrassed to come forward; that no vagabond or burglar or professional child stealer lurks among the Chippendale, waiting for their opportunity.

Mrs Lamb leads Will across the corridor, heading diagonally down it, neatly evading a patrol. They arrive at a far smaller room, about the size of one of the four-posters, intended for a personal servant. It holds a mean bed and a modest wardrobe, and has a single window facing onto the eastern court, through which a weak, soapy light filters up from the service floor. She closes the door behind them with the same silent speed and tells him that this room will be checked last, as nothing of value is housed within – that they should be safe for a short while. He nods, glad of her assurance. It strikes him how very good she is at this.

They remain upright, ready for a prompt exit. Mrs Lamb comes near, taking Will's hands in hers. A new awareness of what has just happened on the baron's bed sounds through him, sudden and staggeringly loud, making everything reverberate at a strange new pitch. Her latest claim is forgotten. All intention, opinion and judgement are gone. He tries to catch his breath, but misses it slightly; he stands there like an imbecile, mute and idiotic, quite unable to meet her eye.

Mrs Lamb speaks fast and low, her lip twisting, taking her usual pleasure in the spinning out of privileged, provocative information. She starts with a question.

'What do you know, Mr Turner, of Prince Ernest Augustus?'

Like most London artists, Will maintains a certain familiarity with royalty: their habits and preferences, their residences and haunts, and especially rumours of any need for paintings. This particular Prince is the fifth son of the King – raised, it is said, in deliberate counterpoint to the libertine Prince of Wales. Accordingly, Ernest Augustus is an officer of the cavalry, and a veteran of many battles against the French on the European mainland. He is described as being solemn and private by nature, and a determined philistine – of no use to artists whatsoever. Will has seen him but once, riding through St James's. Tall and solidly built, the Prince was no more than five-and-twenty, with a plain, Hanoverian cast to his features – enlivened by a fearsome scar carved across his cheek, reportedly the work of a French sabre, and the unsettling deadness of a blind left eye.

'Not overmuch.'

This wins him a sly look. 'Our baron,' Mrs Lamb confides, 'considers him a dear friend. They sit together in the Lords, you see, high Tories both, and concur on many matters. I hear that they saw a great deal of each other over the season just past. Lord Harewood bent the whole of his London household to the diversion of the Prince, including his unmarried children. The son, that Beau, was a failure, all cards and theatres and tours of the auction houses. Too different from Ernest in character and inclination. Too like his degenerate elder brother.' She comes nearer still. 'The daughter, though, was more successful. At least at first.'

'This Prince was the lover,' says Will, who'd guessed half-way through. 'The one who jilted her.'

Mrs Lamb's black eyes grow narrow. 'Imagine their pride,' she murmurs, 'as people talked of it. Prince Ernest in't known for his amours. Don't form attachments with the frequency of his brothers. I'll bet their hopes were high indeed. They'll have been urging Mary Ann to make herself amenable, to do exactly that which had brought so much trouble the previous year. And then to have it come to nowt; to end only in embarrassment and bitter rejection. Imagine their distress.'

The two things are mixed – blended to a glaring tone. Will pulls his hands free. 'Tom,' he says. 'They don't want *him*, they ...' Disbelief hampers his speech. 'He's to – he's to provide a ... give her a ... a child.'

This pleases Mrs Lamb; she clearly knows the full extent of Tom's activities at Harewood. 'The Prince is a lofty one, like our Mr Girtin. His nose ... well, it in't *small*, if the newspaper sketch artists are to be believed. There's a resemblance. Queen Charlotte is a moral sort, so they say; and her husband too, when his mind is in order. Prince Ernest heeds his parents. This in't some actress or painted lady. Our Miss Lascelles is the unmarried daughter of a loyal nobleman. If she's revealed to be carrying a royal baby, the expectation must be that matrimony will follow.'

Everything else you've had me do. That I have done without the smallest complaint.

Will looks out into the court, at the dark windows piled up in the opposite wall. 'So the dinners and balls,' he says, 'parading before all these people . . .'

'A balance has been sought, Mr Turner. The brother and sister wish to present Mary Ann as a young girl bruised by circumstance – who's under their protection, and restricted in her acquaintance – but who, at root, is a guiltless victim, pining for her lost love. She's on display. Being talked about. The affair is kept fresh. And then, if Mr Girtin's efforts bear fruit – if the timings work as they should – the Prince's cut can be refashioned as a minor quarrel. A *misunderstanding*, from which she fled in confusion. Reunion, betrothal, would be the natural consequence.' Mrs Lamb settles on her back foot, crossing her arms; she angles her head towards the saloon. 'Course, having all these extra bodies about the place, drinking and shouting and so forth, only makes it easier for your friend to get up to her and do his duty.'

The timings. Will thinks. Mary Ann can't have seen this Prince for a fortnight at least. 'They don't have long.'

'That they don't. A week at most, sir, if there's to be any chance.' Mrs Lamb shrugs. 'It's a desperate plan.'

Someone passes outside, stopping at the corridor's end. 'Lord Harewood's bed's seen use. Counterpane's all creased.'

'The doors are locked, yes?' Mr Cope – for definite this time. 'Go through the blue room again. The fireplaces. These wretches will hide up chimneys if they have to.'

Mrs Lamb lets a minute go by, and then they are out – with perhaps thirty feet between capture, utter destruction, and blameless safety. They are on the staircase; they are around a corner, and along a passage; they are at the casket chamber. No one has seen them. Will scampers up to the door, into shadow. Mrs Lamb has rescued him. Glancing back at her, he both hopes and fears that she'll come in, to join him in his tiny pallet; and is both relieved and disappointed when she steps away, as if to continue into the service floor.

'What about me then, madam?' he asks. 'Why am I here?'

The still-room maid adopts an air of mock surprise; of mock mystification. 'You, sir? The great Mr Turner, up from London? One of the pair of prodigies who Mr Lascelles has employed to wander the grounds, to sketch the house – to be seen by all these visitors who stream through Harewood's gates? Not to mention the worthy crowd that filled the Crown Hotel, where you was such an uproarious success?'

Will sees it; he feels acutely stupid for not seeing it sooner. He is cover. Part of the distraction staged to conceal the scheme. To have had two young painters residing at Harewood – and old associates to boot, in whom Beau Lascelles has an established patronal interest – is surely less likely to attract suspicion than if Tom had been here alone, should the events of this crucial week ever be scrutinised. Will can almost hear Beau's explanation. *It was an artistical partnership of my designing. They were together for all of every day, out in the park, each inspiring the other. Raffaelo and Michelangelo. Claude and Poussin. Murillo and Velazquez.* He thinks of the ball, of how he was ordered onto the floor after Mary Ann's foolhardy decision to dance with her latest lover. The transgression was diluted, forgotten; the company's attention redirected. This is it, in essence. This is the task he'd been summoned to Harewood House to perform.

Mrs Lamb is smiling at him from the edge of the door frame – a broad, wry smile, bearing friendship and fondness and a plain trace of pity. She takes his hand again and kisses it, quite enveloping the knuckle, her mouth cool and oddly dry. This leaves Will yet more awkward. He wants to retreat into his room, he wants it with an aching intensity; then she bids him good night, telling him they'll talk more in the morning, and is gone; and he's sunk in darkness, somewhat at a loss.

Will sits on his bed. His earlier theory, hatched in this room not half an hour before, now seems contemptibly dim-witted. The Lascelles' aim is rather higher than a husband. The entire drama is rewritten, with new roles for all. Beau and Frances are schemers of the lowest order, prepared to pimp their own sister for advancement. Mary Ann is a wanton harlot, wholly without compunction, who will apparently fuck any man placed in her vicinity. Bold, brave, rebellious Tom Girtin – who cannot know anything of what is truly going on – is but a dumb beast, a stud bull led by the ring Beau Lascelles has punched through his nose.

And Will Turner is a dupe. A hopeless ass, kept on hand to provide diversion. A jester gambolling in the background. His art, his ability – his *genius*, as many in London were calling it – is irrelevant to these newly minted aristocrats. They merely required a biddable being who they could warp to their purpose. His house portraits, keenly desired by patrons up and down the country, are here but an excuse.

It is wounding, this realisation, but the raw sting of anger that might have propelled him Tom-wards once again lay all this bare, to prise the lid off it, to tear it damn well is missing. In its place is simple exhaustion, setting in fast now that danger has departed. Besides, Tom will be accessible no longer. The west landing will be on alert for the remainder of the night; a guard would be posted, most probably, to ward against further disturbance.

Gnawing at him also, however, more insistently than his fatigue, is a need to absorb fully what happened in the baron's chamber. At the forefront of his thoughts is a buckish triumph: *copulation*, and on Lord Harewood's own bed! He can smell it still, beneath his clothes. The memory is almost too potent, too astounding to explore. Very little, of course, was actually visible on that dark four-poster. As he begins to summon a scene, to provide for the absences of memory, his mind reaches not for the monumental nudes of Italy, but those of a more carnal order; for the plump, disporting bodies of Mr Rowlandson, arched and splayed — of which he has a small, clandestine collection in the bottom of his print box, hidden beneath the Dutch seascapes. He fetches a light, using tallow for safety's sake, pulls out a loose leaf and readies the porte-crayone. This one he will capture.

Mrs Lamb's right thigh is dashed in, and her substantial, rounded hip, with the skirts hitched atop it; then the expanse of flank leading up to the daunting vastness of her bosom. Words come too, his own words, for the first time in weeks. He tries them as he works.

'Drunk on the dark we lay ourselves, the moon's pearl—' He halts, frowning; he begins anew. 'The moon, pleasure's bubble, rises in dark wine . . .'

Her arm, the one she used to prop herself above him, is done in three lines only, and he's back to the upper leg, the groin, the points of their connection; to the wide, rough-skinned knee he felt rubbing against his ribs; the stockinged calf flexing along his shin; the ankle that locked around his own.

She can't have been eavesdropping.

The thought arrives unheralded and it quite spoils Will's concentration, causing the sole of Mrs Lamb's slipper to rove off on an unnatural course. He lifts the porte-crayone from the paper. They met in a state bedroom, in the east wing, perhaps the one area of the great house that was empty of people. The one place an eavesdropper *wouldn't* be. It hadn't seemed as if she was on her way elsewhere. She was by the bed when he entered, out of sight; and immediately swept him up, carried him along with her, through to their unlikely union on the baron's counterpane. The still-room maid was supplying some distraction of her own. The design was to throw him completely; to sink him into his present, damp-palmed fervour; to prevent him from asking, from even considering, that most obvious of questions.

What was she doing in there?

*

Routine, observed unthinkingly, takes Will from the house and off into the park. He has slept, contrary to his expectation, four or five hours of dead slumber; washed himself and dressed in his standard outdoor garb; broken his fast at the kitchen counter. There's a dullness about him, though, that he can't shake, as if the tension of all this, endured for many hours now, has stretched him slack. The facts are too familiar; they are losing their bite, wearing smooth, no longer catching in his mind. He goes north-east, veering over the front lawn towards the woods. The spot where he made that first sketch is easily found. Sitting cross-legged upon the grass, he selects a sheet of Whatman and starts its replacement.

The result is cursory, finished in a half-hour, Will begrudging Beau Lascelles any effort – any application of the skill he so undervalues. He watches the sun melt a hole in a floe of gauzy cloud, and the shadows sharpen and darken across the house's blank, black-windowed façade; and he feels a longing for work, for *real* work, of the sort he'd last known out at the castle.

The bells begin, the flat clangs cascading through the trees at Will's back. Like all Londoners, he's well used to this sound, at proximity and in volume. It is expected, also; he's managed to ascertain that this morning belongs to Sunday, with its attendant observances. Worshippers assemble on the steps of the house. They are dressed smartly yet soberly, their conversation reserved, their gestures discreet; the occasional discharge of tobacco smoke is the only sign that this is the same band who crowed and cackled there the evening before, as they boarded their coaches for Harrogate.

Their numbers grow to two dozen or thereabouts; and are then more than doubled by the arrival of servants from both the house and garden, who join quietly at the rear, under the direction of Mr Noakes. They all proceed along the drive to the church path, which leads through the woods behind Will. The green parade, he's heard it called, when Saturday's revellers are summoned from their beds and pressed into Sunday's reverence – marched forth to bend their aching heads in prayer. He has no intention of joining it. His plan is to use the ensuing emptiness of the house to get up to Tom, whether he be in his own chamber or Mary Ann's. That radical quotation returns to him – *my own mind is my church* – and he's murmuring it aloud when he spies the other painter, the man who had once bellowed it so daringly, close to the front of the procession. Freshly shaved and tidily attired, Tom is barely distinguishable from the gentlefolk who surround him. It's a disturbing sight: Tom

Girtin, committed and vocal atheist, going meekly to his pew – trailing, of course, behind the young woman he has unwittingly been enlisted to inseminate.

Will is up, the porte-crayone back in his pocket and the sketchbooks under his arm. His nerve is firm; he won't permit it to falter. This isn't what he prepared for, but the stakes are raised. They couldn't reasonably be raised much higher. What fate lies in store for Tom once his task is complete? When a baby, ready to be presented to the world as the issue of the King's son, is implanted within the younger daughter? His evidence could bring a swift end to the Lascelles' ambitions, replacing promotion and advantage with derision and disgrace. It would be a great risk simply to let him go. Too great a risk.

No: the only hope for Tom, for them both, is *exposure*. This is what Will intends to suggest – what he has to propose right this minute as a matter of urgency. They have to hurry back to London and tell *everyone*. They have to state their case, as publicly as they are able. This will protect them. The Lascelles would be prevented from doing any harm as their guilt would be guessed at once. The support of all decent people would be won. They would be recognised – Tom's amorous incontinence notwithstanding – as the innocent victims they are. It's a hazardous route, and will bring on all manner of unwelcome changes, but no others remain. They cannot stand docile and acquiescent in the face of this misuse, awaiting a conclusion of the Lascelles' choosing. They cannot do nothing.

The parade is approached at speed, Will thinking to slip straight through to Tom and ask him for a word. He's knocked off track, however, by sight of the Douglas family: mother, father and an indeterminate number of offspring. Frances is talking to a girl in white lace, something to do with ducklings; and so tenderly, so plainly fascinated by what she is being told, that it makes the frosty imperiousness of her dinner-table conversation seem the behaviour of a different person altogether. Will is fairly sure, also, that this is the child who screamed at him in the darkened nursery. He slows down, changes course, but too late.

'By Jove, Mr Turner! You impress me, young sir!' John Douglas addresses Will directly for the first time. His tone is that of the gaming table, the gentleman's club, with a brusque edge added. 'I honestly wasn't expecting to see you up and about so early. You were the *victor*, my friend, the clear victor in a rather crowded field. The drunkest of our drunk.' He turns towards the staff; caps and bonnets lower to avoid his gaze. 'Left a mess in the hall, too, I understand, for these poor souls to attend to. Remarkable, really. Your spirit. Your great appetite for life.'

Will can't help protesting here. 'Excuse me, but I weren't – I was not—'

Douglas isn't listening. Leaning down to match Will's height, he points westward, across the front lawn. 'Here's a thing. Why don't you take yourself off and sketch that tree over there? The big one, see it? Looks like a mushroom?' A little push is administered by his grey-gloved hand. 'Very brave, you coming out here like this. Very pious. But you need fresh air, I believe, more than you need a sermon.'

Will considers resistance, a retort, but his anger is tempered by doubt. Douglas is a party to the Lascelles' scheme, obviously he is; this neat repulsion earns him an approving glance from his wife. How much have they deduced? Has Will revealed himself somehow? He stops on the gravel, letting the procession flow on around him. The churchgoers head up the path, disappearing among the trees. For a minute or two, he studies the sky again; the cloud lies now in high, diffuse lines, like chalk skimmed across coarse paper. Then he follows.

The church itself is uninteresting, a plain structure built from the same warm stone as the house, with clear glass in the pointed arches of its windows. It's old, though, the porch robed in ivy, the gravestones blackened and lilting, and has been well placed in a fine grove of trees. The picturesque, in short, is present, and Will regrets momentarily that he didn't discover it earlier, in place of the castle. He'd be far away from here, a serviceable sketch in the smaller book, ignorant of Tom's situation and perfectly content.

But he cannot begin a new scene now. He *will not*. Instead, he strides from one end of the building to the other, and back again; then he starts a loose circuit, widening it gradually until he is out among the trees. The drone of an ecclesiastic can be heard within, leading the congregation into a hymn he doesn't recognise. Churchgoing has never seemed to him like anything but time squandered. He's heard other artists assert – usually after wine – that whatever they know of God is felt beneath the open sky; in a range of hills, with a storm coming on; above a rocky cove, looking out to sea. This all sounds about right to him. He has no wish to see churches burned or broken up, as some do – too much money to be made in painting them – but he doesn't ever plan to waste his Sunday mornings on their cant and hot air.

The eventual opening of the doors catches Will unawares, roaming in a stand of pines. Tom is the first to emerge, hurrying off between the gravestones. He removes his borrowed hat, a shiny black number, and coughs into it six or seven times with ferocious, purgative energy. When he stops to spit, to wheeze in some air, Will nearly winces to see the tiredness on his face; to hear the labour in his breaths, clearly audible from twenty yards' distance.

Beau is out the next moment, pursuing Tom perhaps, batting aside a strand of ivy and yawning hugely. He has his own burden of lassitude – a certain shadowing around the eye, a deeper note to his ruddy cheeks – but is bearing it with determined good humour. Approaching Tom, the heir to Harewood lays a hand between the painter's shoulder blades, murmuring words of light-hearted enquiry. Tom rallies, as is his habit, drawing himself up and grinning, wiping his eyes with a handkerchief; offering some effortless reply that has Beau chortling into his burgundy stock.

Others are appearing, the rest of the family – Frances talking to the vicar, her children skipping on the gravel, Mary Ann peering here and there, seeking out Tom – and then their guests. Beau turns to propose a picnic by the boating lake, with angling for whoever would care for it. This meets with a favourable response. The party wanders down the path, the gentlemen laying bets about the giant fish they will bag. Tom hangs back, though, an arm wrapped around his chest; he's far from recovered, despite the show he put on for Beau. Mary Ann starts to come over, but seems to change her mind, going after her brother and sister instead. Servants are leaving the church in a string of sullen knots, already being hectored by Mr Noakes about the duties awaiting them at the house and the multiple failings of the evening before. Tom pokes the pipe into his mouth and unfolds the charcloth along the top of a gravestone.

Will strides from the pines, out into the open. Mr Noakes pauses his recitation. Every eye is directed Will's way, an inexplicable and rather unnerving level of scrutiny. He doesn't slow or hesitate but lowers his head, obscuring his face with the brim of his sun hat.

At first Tom is pleased to see him, beginning to joke about the *prime view* there must be from down on the floor of the Crown Hotel; then he recognises Will's manner and his amiability vanishes. 'No,' he says shortly, 'not again. I ain't going back to London with you. Wasn't I plain enough at Plumpton?' His expression becomes resentful. 'You've a real taste for this, Will Turner. For upset. For dramatics.'

This accusation, coming from the man who not twelve hours previously danced with his aristocratic lover before an entire public ball, makes Will's intended tone of urgent comradeship impossible to assume. He struggles, in fact, to locate any speech at all; and as his silence lengthens, he feels their last chance for escape begin to dwindle away.

'She's in on it,' is the best he can manage. 'Every man-jack of 'em's in on—'

Mr Cope scythes the two painters apart. He collars Will with surprising strength, damn near lifting him off the ground. 'This way, Mr Turner,' he says, his voice straining very slightly, 'if you please.'

*

Mr Cope's technique is well practised: he shoves, lets Will stagger, grabs him, drags him a distance, then shoves again. The valet works through this cycle efficiently, without malice — without emotional display of any kind. They leave the woods, starting across the wide spread of lawn in front of the house. No one sees them; the servants are still on the church path and the Lascelles' party has drifted off to the east, making for the boating lake. Kept in a state of constant motion, fighting to remain upright, Will cannot collect himself sufficiently to protest, to demand an explanation. Halfway over, he slips on the sun-warmed grass and the smaller sketchbook falls. To his dismay, Mr Cope claims it; and when he objects, with the *oi!* so commonly heard around Maiden Lane, the valet calmly plucks away the other one. Arms free, Will thinks that he can now offer some resistance. He stops and squares his shoulders — only to be clouted about the ear, felled nearly, the sun hat wheeling off

215

in a long curve. Before he can fetch it he is pushed onwards, around the western end of the house.

They arrive at the stables, passing through a high, rounded archway into a colonnaded courtyard paved with grey brick. It is bright with morning sunlight, and quiet; the grooms, Will guesses, are among the churchgoers. One of the ivy green carriages is parked to the side, waiting to be checked and cleaned after its trip to Harrogate. A stable boy is sweeping up spilled straw; he looks over as they enter.

'Out,' says Mr Cope.

It has happened. The very worst has happened, and he is to discover for himself how this family deal with those who oppose them. He remembers the argument at the rocks – Tom's dismissal of his talk of Neville. *Claptrap*, he'd said. Perhaps he was right. Perhaps there's no danger here. No real danger. But Will can't believe it. He looks around him, a palm against his throbbing ear; he senses the weight of finality in the stable's shady arcades. One way or another, he is to be ended.

But by God it's unfair. He has such soaring plans. Those two sketchbooks, right there under that valet's arm, hold the foundations for paintings the likes of which England has never seen. Nature in her most astonishing, most soul-stirring forms: the Sublime, fully and properly expressed, equal to Mr Burke's description. Mountains swathed in thunder clouds. Dusky crags and lonely ruins, and valleys cloaked in radiant mist. The coast, with waves savage against the rocks; and the *sea*, dear Christ, the glorious terror of the sea, the great subject he has barely touched. Would they come to pass, even? Would the Academy ever be shown what he's capable of? Will's chin dips. He imagines all these unpainted pictures, a huge long line of them, gold-framed oils every one; they flicker before his sight like the contents of a print-seller's album. A lone tear squeezes out, a droplet of pure frustration, splashing to a black star on the brick below.

One of the gates, shut by the departing stable boy, opens to admit Beau Lascelles. Leaving it ajar, he strolls over to his valet in a sore-headed approximation of his usual fashion.

'Why, Jim,' he says, 'you're bleeding.'

There is a small, deep cut on the back of Mr Cope's right thumb. Will looks at his hands and sees that the scraping nail has been snapped to a point. It must have stabbed at the valet during the walk over from the church. The two men before him, the gimlet-sharp beanpole and the overstuffed rake, stand close together. Beau is studying the wound, cradling Mr Cope's hand in his, dabbing away blood with a lace handkerchief. His manner is unmistakeable: he is tending to his darling. That this is done so openly increases Will's disquiet. Does it no longer matter what he sees?

'Nipped, you've been, by our little cockney rat.' Beau releases Mr Cope and returns the handkerchief to his pocket. 'You see how easily all this painter business is forgotten and the true London character comes out.'

Will rubs his stinging eyes on his sleeve. He decides upon defiance. 'Liar,' he says. 'You're a damn liar.'

Beau sighs, blandly bored. *'Omnis homo mendax*, Mr Turner,

as David tells us in the Psalms.' He bends a little to meet Will's stare. 'I presume that you are as familiar with scripture, young sir, as you are with the Greeks?'

'You claim to be a friend to art, yet you use artists like beasts. You rate us no more than the man who brings your dinner.'

This charge wins Will an enquiring half-smile, inviting him to continue.

'Tom and me—' *Do not weep*. 'Tom and me, we sought only to make our living. We sought only—'

Now Beau Lascelles laughs, flinching straight after as if the volume of his own mirth has caused him pain. 'Heavens above, Mr Turner, you speak as if I mean you both harm – as if you are afraid of me! You're a peculiar sort, God knows, but I would no sooner see you hurt, for whatever reason, than I would take a chisel to Raffaelo's *Stanze*. And as for Mr Girtin, well, he is almost a member of my family. Loved by us all. Loved dearly.'

Will's ire is confused by relief and a dizzying, directionless gratitude. Those paintings may yet come to be. Then he realises what has occurred. He has given himself away – shown them exactly what he has learned. This was their purpose in bringing him here.

And sure enough, Beau has a question. 'But it is most interesting to discover that you see so much menace at Harewood. And that you harbour such animosity towards *me*, who has offered you nothing but friendship and patronage.' He casts an amused glance back at Mr Cope. 'What could possibly justify these poisonous sentiments, I wonder – these bizarre accusations of abuse?'

Will bites at the remains of the scraping nail – peels it back to the quick in one go. The jagged triangle sits on his tongue like the scale of a fish. He resolves to say no more.

Beau shakes his head, assuming a reproving, regretful air. 'I sought to make you a place here, Mr Turner, just as I have made a place for Mr Girtin. Yet you have rejected it. You have tossed it back at me with contempt, as if the hospitality of one of England's great houses was repulsive to you – quite beneath your acceptance. You have shown yourself to be truculent and slovenly – and dashed ungracious, to be perfectly frank. So you will leave Harewood at once. Immediately. You will not be admitted beneath our roof again.'

Expulsion. It's an end to all this, at least. Will spits the scraping nail onto the grey bricks. 'My things,' he says. 'My clothes.'

Another shake of the head. 'You will not be admitted.'

Will holds out his hand. 'My books, then.'

Beau turns to Mr Cope, who passes him the sketchbooks. He starts to look through the larger one, taking his time; after a minute, feeling foolish, Will lowers his hand. Again, he gets an unwelcome sense of the direction of events. Beau remains impassive as he surveys the results of the northern tour – the sketches and studies that were to fuel Will's next great run at the Academy. When every page has been examined, he moves on to the loose sheets at the back, the images of the Harewood commission. One makes him pause. He holds the place with his finger and looks up.

'These,' he says, 'I think I will keep also.'

Will's scowl clamps across his face, squeezing it purple. He considers barging forward, seizing the books and sprinting into the park. There is Mr Cope, though; there are the servants returning from church, grooms and groundsmen among them, no more than a shout away. He'd be caught and beaten stupid. They'd probably burn the books in front of him. Father's voice sounds somewhere close, urging restraint, acceptance – that he place a limit on the damage done. He'd get out, wouldn't he, with his limbs and his faculties intact? Why not cut his losses, return to London and resume his work?

No. Impossible. He cannot allow himself to be defeated so absolutely. He advances on the precipice. He fills his lungs, wavering for a single second. Then he steps off.

'I'll tell. Damn you, I'll tell every detail of this scheme of yours. Everything I've seen.'

Beau has rotated the sketchbooks, as if to inspect the binding. 'And what might that be?'

'How you're using Tom Girtin as your – as your stud. How you plan to pass the child off as that Prince's. How you brought us here to—'

The nobleman is frowning in an affectation of offence, his hooded eyes dark with amusement. 'Mr Turner, please! Good Lord, man! This is slander of the very blackest variety – sufficient, I daresay, for my family to have you summoned to a court of law. What basis can there be for such claims, beyond your own fervid conjecture?'

Not the reaction Will expected. The word *stud*, he thought, would land among them like a cannonball, changing the landscape completely, but instead he feels things turn yet more cruelly against him. He blinks, wiping his palms on the blue coat. Off to the side, out of sight, a horse snorts in its stall.

'I am aware of how it can be for men of your background,' Beau continues, 'welcomed into houses of the aristocracy and exposed to a degree of female refinement and beauty for which your lives have left you wholly unprepared. That your desire, the tormenting hopelessness of it, can overcome your good sense and lead to all sorts of confabulation and fantasy. But to *insult us*, to malign our young ladies in this dreadful way, casts you in an unfavourable light indeed It cannot be excused.'

Will recovers himself. 'I saw them. Tom and your sister. Off in—'

'What you forget, Mr Turner,' Beau interrupts, 'is that I *know you*. Your reputation, at any rate. Such temper, such imagination, such fire! A sure formula for self-deceit.' His pleasure becomes open, a smirk stretching those mottled jowls. 'Consider yourself for a moment, as the rest of the world might. Really, sir, do it. The only living issue of a back-alley wig-maker and a violent lunatic, grown into a bona-fide oddity. Abrasive company at the best of times. Distinctly curious in both appearance and behaviour. Prone to falling in lakes; to falling over in the midst of dances. A common *thief*, furthermore, who has taken beeswax candles from the butler's pantry and who knows what else. Madame de Pompadour's chocolate cup, perhaps?'

Again Will is caught unprepared. He sees ruin, a miserable cell, the gallows at Newgate; or more likely in some bleak square in York or Leeds, before a baying northern crowd. Desperation hones a memory, perceives a connection, and the words blurt out of him.

'Mr Purkiss. There's your thief. He – he damn near spoke of it last night, up on the carriage. Of the money that china would fetch. Ask your man there. He heard it too.'

Beau glances once more at Mr Cope, seeming to weigh this; it is obvious, however, that the actual question of guilt is of no interest to him. 'Poor Purkiss. Such a sad descent. He has spent his last night at Harewood too, I think. But the fact remains that a penniless cockney painter, staying in the house for a few days only, is a rather better fit for the crime. If an accusation were made, most would believe it, our local magistrates included. It would be the word of one against that of many. That of people of rank.' He hesitates. 'And there is the other thing, of course. The matter of the pamphlet.'

Behind him, the valet produces a sheet of thin, folded paper: the scene from the *Zong*. Will's toes bunch hard inside his boots. He'd tucked the print in his bundle, between a spare pair of outdoor breeches and the rolled stockings; and then he'd gone forth to Harewood Castle, discovered Tom and Mary Ann and forgotten it completely.

'*Abolitionist literature*,' Beau proclaims. 'The ingratitude of it. The shameless discourtesy. Were you thinking to infect our staff, I wonder, with your hare-brained London ideas? Foster radicalism on the service floor? Is this how you sought to reward my disinterested patronage – my benevolence and encouragement?' His satisfaction mounting, the nobleman opens the larger sketchbook, at the place marked by his finger. 'Is this why, despite all the learned, the genteel, the eminently respectable souls that have gathered at Harewood over this past week – including a fellow artist, an old friend of yours no less – I am informed that your closest association has been with a troublesome servant? A woman known for impudence and brawling, and disdain for her betters?' A loose leaf of Whatman is drawn out in a single movement, flashing in the sun like a white flag. 'You'll forgive me, Mr Turner, but this has the look of a very close association indeed.'

Slowly, the glare fades and the sketch is revealed. There's more to it than Will remembers – the broad thigh and the heavy breast, the black locks, the maid's skirts gathered around her waist – easily enough, at any rate, to identify both the subject and the undertaking. Turning away, he stares up at the stable's plain entablature; then down at the iron grate in the centre of the courtyard. He is broiling hot and hollowed out by humiliation. What can he say or do now? They have him. He's been floored, roped like an animal ready for slaughter, and can only await the *coup-de-grace*.

Beau does not delay it. 'You understand, therefore, that

should you decide to *talk*, to circulate these foul stories of yours, they will be met in kind, and with evidence. The injury for you would be far more severe than anything you could hope to inflict upon us. It would mean your end.' He leans in, adopting a quizzical expression. '*Do* you under-stand? Some manner of signal would be appreciated.'

Will nods.

The nobleman straightens up, apparently content; then, suddenly, he seems to tire of the interview – to remem-ber his enervated condition, the party by the boating lake, the lure of seltzer-water and repose. The sketchbooks are handed back to Mr Cope. Will looks over, for a final sight of those volumes, the repository of so much labour and hope; but it is the valet himself that captures his attention. There is the smallest interruption to the line of the coat, and the straight back within; a slight angle between the shining shoes; an adjustment, barely present, to the colouring of the greyhound face. Mr Cope is discomforted. Dutiful as ever, he fastens the clasps on the sketchbooks and stows them under his arm. He acts as if unaware of Will's gaze.

Beau steps to the side and extends a hand towards the stable doors: a curt instruction to depart. 'Your terms are cancelled, Mr Turner. Away with you.'

*

Hidden behind an oak, Will remains unseen until Mrs Lamb is at the garden door. He approaches with a finger to his lips, though she has said nothing; makes a placatory gesture, though she shows no indication of alarm. Her wicker basket is over her arm, full it looks like, and covered with cheese-cloth. She lets him come near, emerging from the woods where he's been stewing now for three anxious, angry hours. Then she opens the door, checks quickly for garden-ers and pulls him through.

They hasten past the vineyard and into the nearest green-house – the same one she was standing outside two days earlier, trimming pineapples. The ripe, still air closes around them. Leaves pack the long building like feathers in a pillow, almost obscuring the brick path laid down its middle and filtering the afternoon sunlight to create a yellowy, under-water ambience. She leads him to a small room at the rear, built against the wall. He watches her legs as she walks – the shape of her haunches, rolling within her charcoal dress. *This is it*, the body that was joined with his not a day ago; and despite everything that's happened since, the hope blooms within him that they might shortly be joined again.

It soon dies. Mrs Lamb swings Will past her, into a corner. The room is crowded with terracotta pots; shelves hold planting tools, bundled canes and balls of twine. There is a mean table the size of a supper tray and a single three-legged stool. She advances, spreading like a blot; soon the only light is that which can fit around the margins of her form. He tries to take her in, to study her properly, but he cannot. They call it having knowledge, do the gallants of his acquaintance, back in Covent Garden – *I've had knowledge of that one*, and so forth. In this instance, however, the act has brought about

225

no new insight or familiarity whatsoever. If anything, he feels more removed from her than before. Alongside this is a deep regard; and desire, still; and fear, quite a strong fear, for it's plain now that she's profoundly annoyed with him.

'What d'ye say to them?'

It's out. Of course it is. Will's ejection would be the talk of the service floor. 'Only what we know. What you told me.'

This is the answer Mrs Lamb was anticipating, but it displeases her nonetheless. She rails on for a while about how the Lascelles are certain to seek out the origins of the story; how she, with her enemies on the staff, will be the prime suspect; how there's already a suggestion, derived from God knows where, that she was involved somehow in the young painter's exit from Harewood.

'It'll see me discharged,' she concludes. 'They've been looking for a reason for longer than I can remember. It'll be the first thing that new housekeeper does – before she even hangs up her hat, I shouldn't wonder.' She broods for a minute longer, following the weave of her basket handle with her fingers; then she shoots him a fierce look. 'Why d'ye come out here, Mr Turner? Shouldn't you be on your way back to London?'

'They took my books,' Will tells her. 'All my work from this summer.'

The still-room maid is unsympathetic. 'And what d'ye expect me to do about that?'

Will's idea, elevated to certainty while he hid in the woods outside, is that the books would be stowed in a cupboard somewhere, or a pantry, that Mrs Lamb could be persuaded to raid. He sees now that this is pure delusion. They'd be upstairs, in Beau's rooms most probably, well beyond the reach of a still-room maid. His heart sinks, his spine bowing; it's as if the bottom has dropped out of him and he is spilled on the ground, spoiled for good. He mumbles something.

'So that's why you told,' says Mrs Lamb. 'You were trying to get back at them. To strike a little fear into our masters.' Her tut has a glass-cracking sharpness. 'Didn't do you no good, though, did it? They know very well that nobody'll heed a strange little puppy like you. There in't any actual *proof* of their connivings. Just your word, a low-born artist hardly clear of boyhood, against that of a millionaire noble-man. A lord of the King's party. Gossip, they'll call it. Preposterous rumour from an unknown source. Lands on them like rain on a roof.'

All true. Will stares dazedly at the dirt floor. Beau Lascelles was right. In real terms, in terms of a case that could be made to the world, he has nothing. The books are gone.

The faintest touch of compassion passes over Mrs Lamb's features. 'I might've heard summat,' she admits. 'In the servants' hall.'

Will can't quite credit it, initially; then he wants to kneel, to clutch at her hands, to worship her like a saint in an old Italian altarpiece, brought before the Holy Virgin. 'But what – where are – how can we—'

She stops him. 'A deal, Mr Turner. I propose that we make a deal.'

The basket is set on the table, the cheesecloth folded back and an object carefully lifted out; she moves to one side to allow the light to reach it. Will sees a covered porcelain cup trimmed with gold. The decoration is oriental and rather dense: pagodas, butterflies, twisted trees and luscious flowers, wandering Chinese folk clad in robes of pink and blue, all arrayed across a dark ground. The saucer is thin as a lettuce leaf, and shaped like one too. The lid is crowned with a tiny gilded rose.

Madame de Pompadour's chocolate cup.

Mrs Lamb seems to grow, the cup rising towards the greenhouse's narrow beams; Will realises that he is flat against the wall – sliding down it to the floor. She is *proud*, openly so; she places the cup and its saucer on the table and sits upon the stool.

'You're the thief,' he says.

She laughs. 'Why sir, had you really not put that one together? What in heaven did you think I was doing up on the state floor, creeping around in the dark?'

Will doesn't answer. Within the basket, he can see part of a small jug, teeming with painted parakeets; and what appears to be a sauceboat, its gold and blue handle curling like that of an antique lamp.

'How much is there?'

'Less than there should be.' Mrs Lamb laughs again, more harshly. 'A lot less than there should be.'

There's a new quality to her, a righteousness not unlike that of Tom Girtin over in the saloon, when he talked of smashing Beau's china with a hammer. Is this thieves' logic, Will wonders – some convenient notion about the immorality of wealth, and the obligation of ordinary people to spread it about if they spot the chance?

'You speak as if it was owed you.'

Mrs Lamb leans forward, linking her hands. She looks off into the greenhouse, at the tropical leaves swimming in sunlight; she grows both more calm and more incensed. 'That's because it *is* owed me. Me and many others.' The stool creaks beneath her as she turns back – not to Will but the chocolate cup on the table, so absurdly ornate against the bare, bleached wood. 'Where does it come from, d'ye reckon, this fortune of theirs? What is it that grants them this wondrous life, so far beyond the imaginings of the vast bulk of humanity? This in't some ancient noble line, with country estates and tenant famers and suchlike. No, Mr Turner, the Lascelles harvest their gold from a different field altogether.'

Sitting motionless on the dirt floor, Will recalls Tom's talk at Plumpton, of floggings and shackles; the terrible diagram of the *Brookes* and that scene from the deck of the *Zong*. He gazes at the still-room maid's enlaced fingers – at the slightest tint of ochre that warms her skin, which he in his ignorance took for a sign of gypsy blood.

'I'm a slave,' Mrs Lamb says simply. The disclosure has a strange effect on her, a deadening effect, causing her fury to decline rapidly to weariness. 'There it is, sir. I was born a slave. The legal property of the Lascelles family. And I'm their slave still, I suppose, in the eyes of the law.'

Will rubs his nose. His mind has acquired an almost animal emptiness, wholly beyond thought. Sweat wells above his brow and runs down the side of his cheek. He says nothing.

'None of them knows,' she adds. 'It wouldn't even enter their damn heads. Irish is what they're content to think.' She shrugs. 'It is but an eighth share. Mestee, the plantation masters call us.'

The story is told matter-of-factly, without self-pity. Born on the Nightingale Grove estate in Jamaica, she was the issue of a clerk and a coloured domestic, put to work in the kitchens of the manor house. At the age of fourteen she witnessed a plantation visit by Daniel Lascelles, the first baron's brother. For a week afterwards the estate hummed with talk of the family's riches – and particularly the palace they had just built themselves back in England.

'It fired summat in me, Mr Turner, and I ran away the first chance I got. A damn *palace*. I barely understood what I was doing, or what I was letting myself in for, but I knew where I was bound. I was coming to Yorkshire. I was coming to see this palace. I made it the business of my life.'

There was a punishing trek through the jungle; a month on the streets of Kingston, dodging the Lascelles' slave-catchers; a stowaway's voyage to Bristol; and then she was in England, seeking employment in guesthouses and hotels – in kitchens not so very different from the one she'd fled in Nightingale Grove. But she was free. When she moved on, nobody attempted to hunt her down. And this girl, light-skinned enough not to draw any special notice, had her skills.

'I know sugar,' says Mrs Lamb. She recoups her energy, and her pride along with it. Her chin lifts; she smoothes that stained apron. 'I know it damn well. It won't surprise you to learn that in Nightingale Grove there was a boundless supply. My mother taught me to make puddings and cakes. Flans and tarts and ices. And I was good at them all. The still room, though – that was where I shone. The more places I stayed, the clearer it became to me how I'd get inside their palace. I worked my way northwards, Mr Turner, from household to household. I climbed this country like it was a ladder.'

Will looks over at the chocolate cup. He tries to concentrate on something simple. 'Why do all that?' he asks. 'Stage is sixpence. Why wait all this time?'

'And break in, you mean? Force a window, grab what I can and run off?' Mrs Lamb grimaces at her lap. 'No, sir. I wanted to know what I was doing. What I was taking. I wanted to leave with as much of their wealth as I could damn well carry. Not so I could have it, you understand – but just so *they* could not.' She pauses. 'Then I saw my first *Brookes.*'

Of course. 'You met with the Abolitionists.'

Mrs Lamb did more than this. She attended addresses by the movement's great figures – and in Yorkshire, on the very doorstep of her target. Mr Clarkson giving a lecture in a Leeds tavern. Mr Wilberforce speaking before a huge public meeting in Harrogate. She saw the campaigners toiling in the streets and squares, and at the gates of the factories, quickly filling their petition sheets with the marks of ordinary working men. And she learned how their efforts were opposed by lords, princes and dukes, by King George himself; and how the war with France was being used as an excuse to let the notion founder, to silence its proponents and permit the evil to continue – to expand, even. What was needed, her Abolitionist friends told her, besides political will, was *funds*: ready cash so that literature could be printed and posted, notices placed in newspapers and speakers dispatched about the country. The matter had to be kept before the British people.

'I knew then what I was to do. I'd use my skill with their slave sugar to gain entrance to their palace. And then I'd use my position to help halt that sugar's flow.' She smiles tightly. 'A pleasing shape to it, wouldn't you say?'

From here to Harewood, by Mrs Lamb's account, was a series of straightforward steps. She took a cook's post with a solicitor in Harrogate. Discovering the shops frequented by Mrs Linley, the housekeeper from Harewood, and the days on which she called at them, didn't prove too difficult. An acquaintance was engineered, and presents made of Mrs Lamb's most splendid preserves and chutneys. And when the still room fell empty – the maid having experienced a powerful, unexplained urge to return to her family in North Wales – Mrs Lamb was the obvious replacement.

'It's been nearly three years now. I've a bale of silver forks, hidden over in the village. Various jewels and gimcracks. A ring or two.' She picks up the chocolate cup and its saucer and puts them back in the basket. 'It's almost too easy at times, especially since this current lot came into the house. They spend without thinking, and they barely damn well notice when it goes.'

Will catches a glimmer of intent. 'You're going to take more.'

'Mr Turner,' replies Mrs Lamb, 'I'm going to take every last thing that I can. You know what them bits of china sell for to the idiot gentlemen of London. And I'll put the money to good use. It'll go to aid those who seek to end this wickedness of theirs forever.' She reaches for him now; her hand is on his thigh for perhaps three seconds before fastening around his forearm, just above the wrist. Her eyes, quite black, are open wide. 'This is my chance, sir. They'll be ridding themselves of me tomorrow. I must act.'

Her meaning is plain: she's going thieving again, over in the grand house, and Will Turner is coming along to help. This is the deal she wants from him, and it's not a choice. He's being pressed into service like a man grabbed from the docks.

'Madam—'

'The house will be quiet. Early bed for everyone after the fuss last night – upstairs and down. We'll move about like ghosts, Mr Turner. Spectres made from mist.'

Will thinks of the *Zong* – of the sketch he made of the woman now attached to his arm. 'They found—' He swallows. 'They found one of them pamphlets. The ones you wrapped around my candles.'

'What of it?'

'They knew it'd come from you. Seemed to, anyhow. That we two are – that there'd been – that we'd—' Will frowns; his cheeks and brow are bristling with violent heat. He abandons the sentence. 'If one of us is caught, they'll go after the other directly.'

Mrs Lamb is unimpressed. 'Neither of us will be caught. I know this damn house better than anyone else alive. All I need is a second pair of arms. You'll walk behind me. You'll carry what I give you. That's the whole of it.'

'Madam,' Will insists, 'I ain't no robber.'

Now she is impatient. 'This is the only way you're ever getting those books back, Mr Turner.' Her grip grows firmer; her face is brought nearer. 'And you feel the rightness of it. I *know* you do. I saw you with that print, with the *Brookes*, back in my still room. You're of our party. I shouldn't have to plead with you like this.'

Will's heels dig into the floor, as if bracing for a tug-o-war; he twists his arm a fraction within Mrs Lamb's grasp. Could this be true? The horror of those images is still imprinted upon him, that he can't deny, but where an actual opinion should be – the granite conviction that must govern people of principle and impel them to act – there is only blankness. He's a *landscape painter*, schooled by the Royal Academy. A man of dawn and dusk, of clouds and atmospheric effects; of the Sublime and the Picturesque Object. He has his path and it demands every last thing he's got. What, really, does he know of all this? What does he *want* to know of it?

Mrs Lamb turns, leaving him facing the top of her mob-cap, the curls packed beneath the white cotton, always attempting to escape. She shuts her eyes and sighs, dispelling her irritation, collecting herself for a final amendment of manner; then she releases him, her fingers playing along his arm as they withdraw.

'D'ye not think that we make a fine partnership, sir?' she asks. 'Why, last night we got past Mr Cope and the others without the least bit of trouble. We sported about them bedrooms like we owned the place.' Her left boot inches forward, nestling against his right, underscoring her meaning. 'It could surely be done again.'

Will colours anew, more savagely than ever. Squirming in the loose dirt, he steals a longing glance at her knees, and the open inch between them; at the way her buttocks softly overhang the stool.

A sly line appears at the side of Mrs Lamb's mouth. 'And there's summat else you might care to know. It's Mr Girtin who's got your books.'

It's a double blow, expertly timed; Will is left gaping, radish-faced, his objections obsolete. 'Beg – beg pardon?'

'A regular scene, there was, when Mr Lascelles arrived at the lake. Your friend Tom was sorely put out by your dismissal. Requested in the strongest terms that the books be placed in his care. Mr Lascelles weren't best pleased, but he permitted it for the sake of harmony. To keep Mr Girtin applied to the task at hand, I suppose.'

Will sits up. Tom Girtin has the sketchbooks. He'll be at leisure to look through them; to survey what Will has gathered; to examine the points of contact with his own northern tour the previous year, and the significant points of departure. And there's the drawing of Tom's, the infuriatingly brilliant drawing Will salvaged at Plumpton. Tom can't discover that he has it. He just *can't*. And that accursed sketch of Mrs Lamb, which Beau Lascelles waved at him with such glee. Why the *devil* did he make it? What in *damnation* was he thinking? Tom would consider it hilarious, and lay it open to the inspection of all artistic London. Academicians might hear of it. Conclusions might be reached about William Turner's character – his ability to conduct himself in a manner befitting one of the king's painters. The door to membership, the door to his future, might well become obstructed.

Dear God.

Will scrabbles against the greenhouse wall, clambering to his feet, accidentally kicking over a stack of plant pots. 'Mrs Lamb,' he begins – stopping to right his waistcoat, which has ridden a distance up his stomach. 'Madam—'

Crossing her legs, the still-room maid places her elbow on her thigh and her chin on her palm, a pose of incongruous elegance. Her eyebrows rise in expectation.

'What do we do?'

Monday

This woman is a saviour. Will is certain of it. Mrs Lamb will deliver him from the fix he's in and set him back on his rightful course. Following her up through the park, he feels immensely grateful and slightly awestruck; and protected, shielded from harm, like Tobias on his journey with the Angel. Both of them are wearing black cloaks, which she brought with her when returning to the greenhouse. Will's is at least three inches too long and reeks of horse, but out in the moonless night, pulling it on provided a distinct and exciting sensation of invisibility. The house is ahead, so dark and silent that it appears uninhabited. Exactly as she assured him it would be. The route to his books seems direct, secure and safe. He'll be rescued from his present difficulty and freed from this place for good.

They enter at the kitchen corridor on the western side. Embers still smoulder in the range, dry-brushing door-frames and floor tiles a deep, tarnished red; but otherwise this end of the service floor is unlit and its passages empty. She takes them right, towards the still room. The lingering odour of dinner, of roast chicken and suet, gives way to the thick, sweet smells – fruity, spicy, waxy – that cling always to her clothes and hair. Reaching the threshold, she comes to a halt, her purpose suddenly suspended. Ten seconds go by. Will nearly nudges her, to prompt continuation, but thinks better of it.

This woman is a victim. It cannot be forgotten. The victim of something unspeakable. Will peers into the room, at the copper pans piled dully in the darkness, at the jars and bottles and trays – the instruments both of her enslavement and her revenge. Waiting in the greenhouse, watching the afternoon's tones shift and dim, he wondered at some length about her experiences. Had she felt the slavers' whips cut into her skin, or endured their abuses in closets and thickets? Had she seen others, relatives and friends, suffer the lurid horrors detailed by the Abolitionists – hung on hooks like butchered meat, dragged behind traps, lashed until dead? And the voyage to England, Christ alive; had it been on a slave ship, like the abominable *Brookes*? There's much he would have her describe. He thinks these questions at her broad back, thinks them very hard, as if she might feel it somehow and turn to reply.

She doesn't, of course. Will realises that this is a farewell. She stands in place for a half-minute more, contemplating it all; then she leans inside, scoops up two small sacks and quietly closes the door.

'They've been moved to the gallery,' she says, as they mount the western service staircase, 'on account of Lord Harewood's return.'

She's talking about the china. Will stops climbing. 'Are we to get all that first? Won't it be heavy?'

Mrs Lamb looks back, her face in shadow. 'Porcelain,' she tells him, taking off her shoes and tucking them in her belt, 'then books. Remove your boots, Mr Turner.'

With its sumptuous decorations muted by the night, the long reach of the gallery, could be that of an exhibition hall or large shop. Mrs Lamb passes Will one of the sacks and is off across the cool, smooth floor. Beau's pieces are arranged in front of the west-facing windows, on a row of small tables. She moves through them like an authority, unhampered by the lack of light, making her selections and transferring them to her sack. Any caution regarding what she takes has obviously been dispensed with. She's departing Harewood, never to return, and is grabbing the best loot she can.

This woman is a criminal, calculating and ruthless. She's spied her opportunity and is using it to rob a nobleman of more money than country-house drawings would yield in a decade. And Will Turner is her accomplice. Staring about in panic, he sees his silhouette in the blue pane of an enormous looking glass: a runtish figure in an oversized highwayman's cloak, boots in one hand and swag sack in the other, breaking into a grand house like the lowest blackguard of St Giles. He must have lost his mind entirely. Father would reel at the sight, that's for sure. Mrs Lamb's tale of distant sufferings, of girlhood ordeals, would mean precisely nothing to him. His response would be one of absolute incomprehension.

There's causes, boy, he'd say, *all sorts of very laudable causes, for which it's worth doing all sorts of things. And then there is the law.*

'D'ye hear summat?'

Mrs Lamb has reached the far end of the gallery, her sack almost full. She's staring back at Will. He realises that he's standing quite rigid, glued in place, as a man might if he'd caught the sound of approaching footsteps. He shakes his head and hurries over to her, intending to ask how much more there is; how much longer they must remain so exposed. Before he can speak, however, she heaves up an object from the nearest table and turns about to present it to him.

The Endymion centrepiece. Its separate forms – the shepherd and the goddess, and the slab of rock upon which they so gracefully recline – are jumbled together in the gallery's gloom, a tangle of glistening, rippling whiteness. The statuette looks large indeed in her arms, much larger than Will remembers. He doesn't take it from her.

'This they'll miss,' he says, 'and soon.'

Mrs Lamb angles her head an inch to the left – a plain warning against nonsense. 'I can sell it,' she states, 'for two hundred guineas. Put it in the sack.'

Will doesn't move.

'Put it in the sack,' she repeats, more clearly and rather more coldly, 'and we'll go for your books. Mr Girtin's room is straight above us. At the western corner.' She adjusts her hold on the centrepiece. 'No one will connect the two things, Mr Turner. They'll come looking for *me*, and me alone. And they won't have a single hope of success. You think I in't prepared?'

Still Will does nothing, so Mrs Lamb pushes the statuette over in a way that forces him either to accept it or let it fall. It is weighty, even more than he expected, and a damn awkward shape; as he works it into the sack, trying to keep hold of his boots as he does so, the pointed parts of miniaturised anatomy press uncomfortably into his belly. His fright is impeding him now, dimming his awareness, gumming up his mouth with the foulest taste. He barely registers their exit from the gallery, passing beneath the empty gaze of John Hoppner's Mary Ann; the scurry along the border of the dining room, back to the dingy confines of the western service staircase; the action of his legs as he climbs to the upper floor. Mrs Lamb sees it as they reach the landing and she's on him at once, all tartness gone, drawing him under her cloak – reclaiming him as a lover might, her right breast flattening against his face.

'Come, sir,' she whispers, guiding him around a corner, 'nearly there.'

Will moves the bulging sack from his midriff to his shoulder and attempts to peer out. 'Which door is it?'

'You're doing so very well, Mr Turner. You're proving a true friend.'

'Which door?'

Mrs Lamb stops; she lifts her nose, as if sampling the air. 'I'll go. Won't take a moment.'

Will has a different vision. He pictures himself striding across the bedchamber, wresting the books from Tom's grasp and then conveying a few dark truths about the Lascelles before he leaves. He wriggles, testing her grip, and lets out a dissenting grunt.

'Me and Tom need words.'

'He'll be over with her. Every hour's important to them.'

'Let me see.'

Her embrace hardens. 'There in't time. We can't risk you two squabbling. Him deciding to alert the family.'

Will's fear of this situation, of what he's done and is doing still, switches to stubborn anger. He arches his back, pushing away from her, wobbling slightly as he breaks out onto the landing. She's brought them before a pair of doors, set close together. He points.

'This one?'

Mrs Lamb lowers her sack to the carpet, her face strong and serene in the low blue light. She's not going to oppose him, but neither will she help; so Will advances on the door, reaching for the handle.

'If I hear trouble,' she says, 'I'm damn well coming in.'

*

The room isn't large. That it's lit – a single beeswax candle over on the mantelpiece, close to guttered – gives Will pause, but he sees no one. A moderately sized four-poster is set against the opposite wall, its crimson curtains drawn; two tall windows look out into the empty night. It's Tom's, though. That cheap suit lies carelessly on a chair and those are his shoes on the rug, four feet apart, arranged as if kicked off. And there, under one of the windows, laid in the middle of a small desk, are the sketchbooks.

Will goes over to them. The clasps are fastened – the loose leaves present. It looks as if they haven't even been opened. He's frowning at this, mildly perplexed, when he notices the album beneath: dark blue board with a spine bound in black canvas, laced shut with a length of black ribbon. Tom prefers these to sketchbooks, liking to shuffle his sheets about, pass them around, lend them to people. Will deliberates for a second, then gently sets the Endymion centrepiece between his feet. He picks this album up, unties the ribbon and eases open the cover.

It holds a number of watercolour drawings, each at least twenty inches by twelve, and all of London – forming a continuous view, like the five-page sketches Tom would make from Adelphi Terrace. Although it's clear that these were also taken in the open air, before their subject, they're far more considered in effect. The vantage point is different as well: somewhere on the southern bank of the river, a roof-top close to Blackfriars Bridge, looking north. Several are unfinished. Will can tell that they are preparatory, the basis for another work – a great metropolitan vista, no doubt to be executed in oil on a significant scale. He selects a drawing that is more or less complete, representing the stretch from the spire of St Mary Le Strand to the borders of Westminster, and conducts a swift evaluation.

It's a fine effort. This can't be denied. The faithfulness to the atmosphere and arrangements of life is amazing, in fact, beyond anything Will himself has attempted. Tom has captured precisely the low chiaroscuro of a squally London afternoon, with its translucent greys, settled blues and browns, and fleeting smudges of sunlight. As always, the technique is rough in places – jogs and blots, and the occasional bleeding of pigment caused by hasty washes – but Will notes that correct local colour has been painstakingly applied to every building, along with specific shadow tones. It has a breadth to it, also; that indefinable feeling that tightens your chest and quickens your heart. Elevation, he supposes. Tom is serious. He's coming at this with his very best blood.

Among the edifices that line the Thames's northern bank is the vast silvery block of Somerset House, dwarfing everything around it. This is where Tom's monumental city piece is surely headed. If he can transport the effect of this drawing, of all the drawings in this album, into a single epic canvas, the Academy Exhibition will rest in the palm of his hand. The laurels will be set upon his brow, by general demand; the Royal Academicians will usher him into their ranks at the first opportunity, perhaps even forgoing the vote. Will tries to take a calming breath and finds he cannot. His muscles and sinews have contracted to an insupportable degree; it feels as if, were he to be caught by a draught, he'd topple to the floor locked in his current pose.

'Will Turner.'

Beside him, not three feet away, a forefinger has drawn

back a portion of crimson bed-curtain. Candlelight falls through the long triangle it creates, revealing an eye, Tom Girtin's eye; and past it, the contours and furrows of a landscape of naked flesh. This sight releases Will from his seizure. Gasping, he shuts the album and returns it to the desk, swapping it for his sketchbooks. The rest of Tom's head appears, his short hair sticking up; he's grinning, unperturbed by Will's appearance in his bedchamber in the dead of night.

'You've come for the books. Course you have. Can you smell them, perhaps?'

Will wipes his face on his sleeve. 'I ain't—'

'And dear Lord, look at that *cloak*. Will Turner the burglar. Rather a drastic shift in occupation.'

Will is looking into the bed, at the other person who lies there. He wonders if he should run.

Tom takes this silence as a sign of umbrage. His grin falls and he apologises for his behaviour at the church – for not giving chase when Mr Cope towed Will off to the stables. 'My chest,' he says, by way of explanation. 'I couldn't breathe, really.' He moves atop his disordered sheets; the curtain opens further. 'It was harsh, what Beau did. Throwing you out like that, just for taking a couple of candles. Far too harsh. Word'll get about, back in London. A boycott, Will, of this damn place. It'll happen.'

Behind him, Mary Ann Lascelles sits up. Will glimpses the loose, powder-grey tresses falling about her shoulders; the pillowy roll of her stomach as she drops a shift over herself.

245

'Tom,' she says wearily, 'don't talk rot.'

'Rot, my dove?' Tom replies, glancing at Will. 'How so?'

This was not anticipated. Will assumed either that Tom would be alone, or the chamber would be empty. The lovers didn't need to fear discovery, he reasoned, so they'd meet in her room, surely the more spacious and comfortable of the two. He sees now, however, that they are in here for Tom's sake, so he doesn't guess that this affair is taking place with the sanction – with the active encouragement and assistance – of the very relatives he imagines he's defying.

Nonetheless, Will is disconcerted by how indifferent Mary Ann is to his presence; and by the casual, faintly sardonic familiarity between them, as if their connection, their fornication beneath her noble father's roof, is of no particular significance. He can hardly reveal what he knows now. Tom would be staggered, incredulous and then hugely wrathful. Who wouldn't be, upon such a discovery? He'd turn on her, shouting his questions. And Mary Ann is no timid maiden. She'd respond in kind. A dreadful row would ensue. Someone would come running, most probably Mr Cope. Will would be caught red-handed with the Endymion centrepiece, and destroyed. The black cloak is becoming unbearably hot. He stays quiet, watching the couple in the four-poster very closely.

'You are poor,' enlarges Mary Ann from the shadows of the bed. 'Whereas my father and my brother are rich. It doesn't honestly matter what they do, does it? Your kind will always be scratching at their door.'

'My *kind*, Mary Ann?'

'Painters and furniture makers. Silversmiths and jewellers.' She shrugs. 'Professional men.'

Tom manages to remain cool. He turns towards her. 'Your father and brother will learn that change is upon us,' he says, 'very nearly. Proper, effective, *improving* change. The true artists, those like Will and me, will soon be freed from their control.'

Mary Ann sighs, not without affection. 'But they have the gold. They are the source of it. We all must heed them, all of us, no matter how it might sicken us to do so.' Will sees her fingertips skim idly along Tom's hip. 'What will it be, precisely, this freedom of yours? The freedom to starve, and wander raggedly through the streets?'

'If that's what we choose.'

'Oh Tom,' she says, lying back, 'you will not *choose*.'

Will has heard enough. It'll do him no good to tarry here. He's got his books; he's got a sizeable burden to carry, in fact, what with his boots and this damn sack at his feet. The plan is that they'll leave the house as they entered it and march up the drive to the village, where Mrs Lamb says she has a gig waiting to take them off to Leeds. He lifts up the sack, working it onto his shoulder.

Spotting Will's intention, Tom breaks from his debate and hops naked from the four-poster to intercept him. Will swerves, stops, trying to avert his eyes from the lean limbs, the long, bony torso, the flapping genitals. Tom doesn't want to bar his path, he sees, but to assist him – to collude in this illicit escape from Harewood and demonstrate to his aristo-cratic lover exactly who and what he is. Mary Ann, vaguely irritated, tells Tom to come back to bed. He ignores her, snatching up his shirt and riding trousers. Will steps around him and slips through the bedroom door, thinking to hurry off before he's dressed.

Mrs Lamb is gone.

Will curses; he peers hard into every shadowy nook. She's gone for certain, swag-sack and all. Voices sound in a corri-dor, somewhere to the east; candlelight rises against a wall, carried up from below. The thefts have been discovered. What else can it be? His one hope is to bolt as well. Get outside as fast as he can. Make for the village. But urgency numbs his mind, leaving him quite unable to orientate himself. The only route he can summon is a plunge down the main stair-case, perhaps a dozen yards from where he now stands. It seems empty, for the moment at least. Light-headed with terror, he scuttles towards the banister.

Tom catches up with him at the landing, just as he's start-ing onto the second flight. 'Why's it so damn *difficult,*' he whispers, hooking a hand around Will's shoulder, 'for you to accept an honest offer of help? What is—'

Will twists about, glowering in readiness – and finds that astonishment has dashed every other emotion from Tom's face. The head of the moon goddess, tiny and perfect and brilliantly white, is poking out of the sack, framed by a neat escarpment. Light lances through the darkness above – through a spread of glass cases mounted high on the wall, in which a menagerie of stuffed birds are forever unfurling their wings, about to take flight. Will attempts to rush onwards, but he treads on a fold of that wretched black cloak and is tripped; Tom grabs for him and together they begin a tottering descent, revolving clumsily, shedding boots and sketchbooks as both fight to keep the sack aloft. After a half-dozen steps Will is thrown aside, dropped on his rear, and for an instant his legs are windmilling through the air; then his left knee slams against the staircase, a stone corner driving between the parts of the joint. The pain is startling, spearing up his thigh and on into his trunk – straining, even, in the tendons of his neck. He bites hard on his cuff, to stem an untimely squeal, and rolls down helplessly onto the fine carpet of the state floor.

Before this first shock has faded, Tom's arms are under his, dragging him up, urging him to continue. More people are gathering on the upper floor. Candles seems to be converging on the staircase from several directions. Will draws in a shuddering breath. He manages to stand on his sound leg and experiments gingerly with the other one. The results are not heartening: barbed daggers, searing pins, the clear sensation of damage. Tom is busy nearby; he has the sack and is retrieving the sketchbooks. He passes them to Will with an enquiring look.

'Knee,' Will mutters. 'Buggered.'

Tom moves to Will's side, bending to offer support before steering them towards the hall; only to reverse abruptly at the sight of a footman, already posted at the front entrance. There's another door, thankfully, just past the staircase. It opens into a drawing room, the yellow silk of its walls hushed to a soft brown-gold. Tom bears left, without deliberation. He's taking them somewhere.

'Hold,' says Will. 'What—'

'The saloon,' Tom tells him, as if stating the obvious. 'The portico.'

The doors are unlocked and swing back on well-greased hinges. The painters go out into the night. The Lascelles' artificial valley is laid before them, between smooth columns; stars glint through a tear in the cloud, adding a pure white highlight to the lake. It's a false release. They are enclosed by a balustrade. And beyond it is a fifteen-foot drop.

'What in God's name is this? Are we to glide off into the trees, Tom, like a pair of merry pigeons?'

'It's an easy jump. Fairly easy. You saw me do it on the night I got here.'

Will leans against the balustrade. He tries his left leg again, but it will take no weight at all; the least bit of pressure is like a hot tack hammered into the kneecap. His gut stirs uneasily. He ate a quantity of fruit in the greenhouse – peaches and figs, and something purple he couldn't identify – and he tastes it again now, mixed with the shivering sourness of bile.

'I can't walk,' he states, gesturing at his knee, at his stockinged foot – realising as he does so that his boots are gone, left behind on the stairs. 'This is – I don't know – this is broken, I reckon. Hurts like damnation. How exactly am I to *jump*?'

Tom gives up. He crosses his arms. 'You're the one who's turned thief, Will. You're the one who's stealing Beau's china. Why the devil don't *you* decide what we're to do?'

'The service stairs,' Will says. 'There's a flight just through there, that door on the right. We can—'

Mr Cope enters the saloon from the hall, candle in hand, once more hunting out the source of the disturbance. The two artists go still, though God knows why – he'll have seen them the moment he came in. They are caught. What will he do? Fling open the doors and overpower them, as he did Will at the church? Call for others and have them beaten down?

Neither of these. Mr Cope hesitates for perhaps five seconds; then he sets his candle on a table or sideboard and simply stands there, in that sentry-like way of his, his hands by his sides. Will meets the valet's level stare. Later on, he'll try to convince himself that he detected the chink – the minuscule shift of the brow, the bend of the mouth, the almost indiscernible dip of that narrow chin – but in actuality there is nothing. Mr Cope could be a lofty, rather hollow-cheeked plaster-cast, painted to resemble life and dressed up in a modest version of gentlemen's clothes.

'He's waiting,' murmurs Tom.

'For our surrender?'

'No, Will.' Tom moves to the side of the portico and swings his leg over the balustrade. 'For us to go.'

*

The cough echoes about the ice house. It's a hard sound to hear, both grinding and rending – and as suggestive of distress, of raw plight, as any cry for aid. Will looks in; he can make out a crude domed ceiling and a curve of brick-work below, but Tom himself is lost to sight, down among the straw-bales. Abruptly, there is respite; the scraping of a chisel. Then something is inhaled, or some inflamed part chafes against another, and the cough begins again.

Will is seated in the passage, just by the door, which has been propped open to admit the light that slowly gathers outside. The left leg is extended; the black cloak rolled into a ball and wedged underneath it. They've been in here for minutes only, but a thin slime, halfway between moss and mud, has already found its way onto everything – Will's blue coat, so far from new now that it might as well be used for a scarecrow; his breeches and stockings; and the goddess of the moon, broken off from the rest of the centrepiece, who he cradles in his arms.

It should have been predicted. It should have been *avoided*. Tom took the lead, and without accident – dangling at arms' length before dropping to the lawn, as he'd done the previous week when hurrying over to greet Will. The sketchbooks were next, small after large; but as Will prepared to lower Mrs Lamb's sack, the candlelight from the saloon became stronger and a voice addressed Mr Cope; so Will simply jumped, the sack against his chest, the black cloak flowing out behind him like a spout.

After an instant of improbable grace, he came thumping

down upon Tom, confounding efforts to be caught, flooring them both. There was a brittle snap from the sack; and as they struggled to rise, Will felt a new motion inside it. One route – the safe return of the centrepiece, as part of a bargain for his life – was viable no longer. The injured knee, jarred during the fall, prevented him from standing. Light moved over them as candles were brought to the windows behind the portico. Tom collected the sketchbooks and stepped back, and for a moment Will feared that he was to be abandoned for the second time that night. Instead, he found himself lifted clean off the ground, onto Tom's shoulders; no mean feat as Will, although short, is a solid specimen. Thus arranged – Will's face angled towards the lawn, the blood surging thickly to his head – the painters lurched off at a diagonal, away down the slope.

Tom returns from the chamber. He drops a packet in Will's lap and sits across the passage. 'Artemis,' he says, pointing at the detached goddess. 'See, I've read my legends too.'

'Or Selene. There's different stories.'

The packet consists of a Whatman leaf folded around a piece of ice the size and shape of a prayer-book. Will sets the broken figure aside and presses the ice to his knee. The relief is immediate.

'Now,' says Tom, 'what in the name of *high heaven* is going on?'

He's trying to sound amused, detached even, but Will recognises the excitement in him. A grand piece of disobedience has been enacted, a play made directly against the Lascelles, and he wants to hear everything.

'Why'd he just stand there? Why didn't he stop us?'

Tom allows this; it's not as if Will is about to leave, after all. 'What d'you know of them? Of Beau and his Mr Cope?'

Will thinks of that glimpse in the near-darkness of the state floor, during his first failed attempt to reach Tom's room, and the way they embraced; of the cut hand in the stables and the lover's concern with which Beau made his examination. 'I've seen them. Together. Each holding the other like they was—' He stops. 'As if they was—'

'As if they're on *closer terms*,' Tom supplies, 'than is generally assumed.'

He rubs his nose on his forearm and coughs as gently as he can. Will realises that he's trembling, chilled to the marrow by the time he spent chipping at the ice. His shirt is damp, clinging to his skin in places; on its front is a fresh bloodstain, its source unclear. The hour since the leap from the portico has been demanding indeed, a stumbling, panting progress between a string of hiding places. They went first to an arbour in a corner of the flower garden; then to a stone hut swathed in ivy, close to the stables; and then, alarmed by the approach of gardeners with lanterns, they ventured deeper into the grounds, until they arrived at this curious burrow by the lake. Will's guess is that these are trysting sites. He tries to picture Tom and the baron's daughter coupling against the rough walls, or down on the grimy wooden floorboards; and he considers the other painter now, hugging his knees tightly, the breath grating in his throat. Had he not entered that bedchamber, Tom would still be behind the curtains of his four-poster, well warmed by Mary Ann Lascelles. Will takes the balled cloak from beneath his leg and lobs it over.

Tom nods in appreciation and wraps himself from shoulder to calf. 'They conceal it,' he continues, 'in plain sight. That they're master and valet prevents the questions. Permits the nearness. The private hours they pass together. The adjoining bedchambers. My sense is that it was his idea for Beau to become a patron of art. That he's directed his master's taste almost from the beginning.' He chuckles hoarsely. 'For all Beau's talk of Michelangelo and whatnot, I'll wager that it was Cope's notion to have us both come up here.'

'So why—'

'Something's gone awry. You could see it at the lake. Cope didn't much like the way you was handled. He didn't like it that Beau kept your books. And this put Beau on the back foot. He ain't used to them disagreeing.' Tom looks at the sketchbooks, laid atop the sack at Will's side. 'There was a chance, Will, and I took it. I got him to give them up. I was going to post them to Maiden Lane later this morning.'

This is all plausible enough. Things were threatening to become untidy. Mr Cope thought it sufficient that Will be made to feel his place and scared away; it wasn't necessary, in his view, for the young painter to be given cause for grievance as well. This plot may or may not have been hatched collaboratively, but the valet is certainly its stage manager. He arranges the cues and the settings; he ensures the actors are in their positions. And Beau, caught up in his show of lordly swagger, has strayed from the script. Letting Will escape with the books was an easy correction.

'Is this why you're stealing from them? Is it vengeance? Did you want to take something of Beau's – something precious, to punish him?' Tom shakes his head. 'I salute your courage, old friend, truly I do, but you've just created a brand-new difficulty for yourself here.' He nudges the dirty goddess with his shoe. 'Specially now.'

This seems like a reprimand – like a charge of pettiness. Rather tersely, Will says that revenge or punishment were absent from his thoughts, and that he came by the centrepiece for another reason altogether. Tom asks what that was, as well he might; and Will sees an explanation of some kind is unavoidable. His earlier zeal for this task has disappeared. He is so encumbered by tiredness, in fact, that he can scarcely arrange his words. But Tom deserves it. He deserves to be relieved of his ignorance.

'It's all been for you. Everything that's happened this past week. Us both coming here. The family – their arguments, at dinner and suchlike. Even that ball the other night. They've been working you into position.' He shifts his leg. 'It's a scheme.'

Tom's face has darkened. 'Christ, Will,' he says, 'not more of this. How the devil d'you keep it up? These visions of persecution. These dreams of plotting and death. It'll end with me being broken on a cartwheel, will it? Drowned in the boating lake?'

'No,' says Will. 'No, Tom. This is real. Miss Lascelles — what you two have been doing. It ain't what you think.'

'What I *think*?' Tom sits forward suddenly, his knees pushing from inside the cloak. 'What do I think, Will? Pray tell me.'

So it's to be a confrontation. Of course it is. Will gathers his breath. 'There's things about that lady you ain't a party to. Things, Tom, plenty of things, that she ain't revealed to you.'

'The child, you mean,' Tom says, disdainful now, slumping back against the wall. 'The child born last year. D'you honestly think I didn't know? I was damn well *here*. She was still recovering when I arrived from London. That portrait had just been put up in one of the drawing rooms. Beau led me to it afore the dust had been brushed from my coat. That the babe was dead, that his sister was mourning it, didn't sour the joke any, as far as he was concerned.' He covers his eyes. 'The girl was beleaguered. Beset on every side. So I did what little I could to show my friendship — my *humanity*, I suppose, in a circumstance where it was in damn short supply.'

'It lived,' Will states. 'Her child lived. There was a swap, with the brother's wife. A live boy for a dead one.'

Tom's hand lowers. 'How in heaven can you—'

'They're trying to use her a second time. That's what I'm telling you, Tom. They're trying to pull another damn trick.'

Again, Tom attempts to reject what he's being told, as a further figment of Will Turner's garish imagination; but it's plain that his own mind is beginning to reach out, to grope around the possibilities, and not liking at all what it encounters.

'A lie has been spun,' Will says, 'a mighty lie, with you smack in its middle. The Lascelles need your girl in the family way so they can marry her into royalty. To the scarred Prince – Ernest Augustus, her lover from the spring. And they need it double quick.'

Will envisions anger. He braces for yells, for curses, for snarled denunciations; he readies himself to lunge at a trouser leg as it whips past and impede a rash charge back to the house. None of this comes. The other painter merely grimaces; coughs into the folds of the black cloak; knits his brow in thought. When he speaks, his voice is calm, relieved almost, as if he's voicing doubts that have been troubling him for a while.

'It's reckless,' he admits. 'You were right. What you said at Plumpton. *She's* reckless. I ain't unpractised at this, not in the least, but I've never known the like. Today she had me take her in a boat, for God's sake, in amongst the reeds, with her sister and nieces sat barely thirty feet away. Habit of her class, I've been telling myself. Just the way they live.' He pauses. 'And the loathing that family has for each other. It's more poisonous, even, than last year. And worn so openly. There's been no end to it.'

'They're doing it for you,' says Will. 'They know you,

Tom, and they know what'll get at you. Villainy. Suffering. All that.'

This comes out a touch too eagerly. Tom glares in his direction – studies him with distinct annoyance. 'What've you heard then, Will?' he asks. 'Come on. What's your proof?'

Proof. Mrs Lamb used this word, Will remembers, back in the greenhouse, when telling him there was none. He reveals what happened at the ball, in the empty dining room – the fragment of the Lascelles sisters' dispute that had drifted in through the window. Tom dismisses it. Too vague, he says. Mary Ann and Frances frequently differ. Their exchange could have referred to any number of things. So, rather more self-consciously, Will names Mrs Lamb.

'The still-room maid? How the devil would she know of a . . . a *secret plot* among the family?'

'She watches them. She's been watching them since the beginning. She's pieced it together.'

Tom is shaking his head again, more firmly. 'That woman has her hooks in you. I saw it, in the garden. I warned you, Will. I told you to keep well back.'

'You don't know about her,' Will says. 'Not the truth. None here do.' He meets Tom's baffled stare. 'She's from their sugar plantations. In Jamaica. She's a runaway. A slave.'

This revelation, Will thought, would at the very least earn him some understanding. Had Tom not spoken bitterly of the origin of the Lascelles' wealth at Plumpton? Had he not railed against slavery in innumerable taverns and coffee houses, demanding its cessation, heedless of whom he might offend or estrange? But no. Tom is not shocked, nor contrite. He is disappointed. Dismayed by his companion's gullibility. Their course changes – as if a sail has been caught in a brisk wind, the boom sweeping unexpectedly across the deck. Will ducks an inch, into his coat collar.

'That's what she told you, is it? That she's just like them poor souls in the pamphlets?' Tom's tone grows scathing. 'Then how come there's people employed on this estate – good people, with no reason whatever to lie – who'll tell of her family in Leeds, her *Irish* family, that she ain't quite managed to hide from view? Who'll talk of her deceptions and her intrigues? Of how nobody with any brains in their head goes within ten damn yards of her?'

'Stories only. Servants' malice.' Will frowns; he must make a case. 'She's a decent woman, at her heart. D'you hear me, Tom? She's giving the money from this to the anti-slavers. The Abolitionists. To aid those still enslaved.'

'The money?' Tom is puzzled; then he looks down at the broken goddess and joins the parts. He starts to laugh. 'Dear God, Will, has she got you stealing for her? Is that what's really happening tonight?'

'Just once,' Will replies, rather weakly, feeling what remained of his advantage fall away. 'I agreed to help her. So she'd help me get the books. I ain't—'

'She fucked you, didn't she?'

Will's hesitation is his answer. 'We shared—'

'She *fucked you*, Will Turner,' Tom proclaims, 'and she

conquered you completely. The woman's a sharper, and she spotted a juicy mark – a young guest a good distance from his natural place, well supplied with imagination, and pride, and self-regard, but lacking, *wholly* lacking, in worldly knowledge. A fellow she could prime to do her bidding. All it took was the conjuring of some tall tale and a timely lifting of the skirts, and you was risking your neck so she could haul in the plunder – then jump from this house afore she was pushed.'

Will bridles at this account, but can't think of anything to pitch back. 'That ain't how it was,' he mutters. 'Not a bit of it.'

Tom smiles grimly from within the cloak. 'Where is she then, I wonder, your Mrs Lamb? Why ain't she at your side, telling you what to do next? Weren't there a plan for your escape?'

This is more mockery, a ribbing rebuke. Tom has guessed what happened outside his chamber door. The ice packet is melting, the fine paper soaked; a cold drip runs into the underside of Will's wounded knee. He alters his grip, flexing the numbed fingers. One thing, he sees, is certain here. He has done that which he swore early on in life never to do. He has *ventured out*. He has established a connection – a slight one, God knows, but a connection nonetheless – and he has been compromised by it. Made ridiculous.

Tom lets him off. He rises with a groan and moves to the entrance. For a minute he stands looking at the sky, making a landscapist's assessment of the hour; then he runs through the various coaches that stop in the village, identifying Will's options.

'You've missed the post, I reckon,' he says, 'but there's a telegraph at six.'

Will nods, testing his leg – the pain, he thinks, is marginally reduced – then realises what he's heard. 'Ain't you coming?'

'I can't. Not yet.'

'But they might think you knew. About the china. That you was in on it.'

Tom isn't worried. 'There's a clear culprit. They won't be looking for anyone but your friend from the still room. If I'm seen on my way back in, I'll just say I was out studying the dawn for a drawing. I've done such things before. Nobody'll question it.'

'Mr Cope might tell yet. Tell on us both.'

'He won't. Most he'll ever say is that we was getting back your books. None of them would ever honestly think we wanted the china, Will.'

'What if Mr Lascelles asks for the books?'

This question leaves Tom amazed. 'That won't happen. Not in a hundred years. Ain't you been paying attention at all?'

Will's jaw clenches; he drops the sodden remains of the ice packet onto the ground. 'An answer for everything,' he says. 'How about *you* then, Tom Girtin? What I told you is the truth. You talk of tall tales, but you see it. I know you do. They're using you like a – like a *beast*. Don't that trouble you none? Your girl does what she does only because her brother and sister would have her do it. Are you just going to keep playing along?'

'Mary Ann—' Tom lowers his head. 'If there's something to what you say – if there really is trickery here, this scheme for marriage – it won't be of her devising. I can't believe that. She obeys them, Will, because she ain't got a choice. They care nothing for her happiness or her wellbeing.' He gazes sadly at the lake. 'I won't leave her to them. Not like this.'

Will pictures the young noblewoman lounging in Tom's bed; he hears the sarcastic drawl of her voice. 'Touching,' he growls. 'Such loyalty. Such disinterested friendship. Your Miss Lascelles ain't about to extend the same to me, though, is she? She got a proper look at me up in your room, and at the sack too. She could give me over to them whenever the fancy takes her.'

Tom returns to the passage, his patience finally failing, opening the cloak to free his arms. Will thinks that he's to be pummelled and dragged off to the nearest coach stand; but Tom leans across him, reaching for the goddess instead.

'I ain't so foolish as to expect gratitude from you,' he says, 'or respect, or even good manners, but you might credit me with a scrap of insight. I know Mary Ann. Regardless of what she might feel for me, she truly despises her eldest brother. If she thinks that her silence will bring him discomfort – before the world, before their father, or just before his bedroom mirror – then she'll keep it. She'll keep it gladly.' He hefts the goddess in his hands. 'Besides, everything here is about to change. You must've heard this, during your adventures. Lord Harewood is expected today. The other brother, Henry, will arrive within the week, with his wife and two infant sons. Beau will lose his place at the table's head. He'll most probably decide that these losses of his are best left unmentioned.'

Lord Harewood. Will feels fear's fingers creep onto his collar once again and give his pigtail a slow twist. 'What time exactly,' he asks, 'will the baron be here?'

Tom doesn't reply. He walks from the ice house and winds back his right shoulder, the black cloak swinging around him. A heave and a grunt, and the goddess is gone. Will scrabbles into the doorway and spots a last spark of white before she lands, close to the shadowy rushes that fringe the far bank. The splash is small, the dark water gulping the porcelain under; but its ripples roll out to the lake's furthest corners, catching the colours of the early morning sky.

*

Piggyback, reflects Will bitterly, has to be the very least dignified of all the undignified ways that one man can be carried by another. You must cling to your mount like a babe, with feet dangling apart; you must have your head close to his and your tackle pressed against his spine; you must be slipping, constantly slipping, and being grabbed at anew. Tom suggested it as an easier arrangement for them both, but their progress from the valley is proving a good deal more arduous and meandering than the initial escape from the house. As they near the crest of the ridge, he swerves into the blue gloom beneath an oak. Planting a hand upon a skull-sized knot in the bark, he leans over to cough – to really *cough* – in the manner that he must, dredging thick fluid from his lungs and spitting it into a cluster of wild flowers.

Stretched out on his back, Will can feel every strain and spasm. He struggles up a few inches, firming his hold on the sketchbooks and glances about. Farm workers are crossing an adjacent field, tramping through the purple mud. They don't seem to notice the piggybacking paint-ers, or to hear Tom's coughs. Heaven knows what they'd think if they did.

'Tom,' he says, 'Tom, set me down. I'll walk from here.'

Recovered to a degree, panting slightly, Tom gives his head a determined shake; and they're away again, out from under the oak, weaving beside a hedgerow, sending a pair of starlings careering off into the dew-damp air. There's a gate ahead and a gap in the hedge beside it. Will is coming loose once more, sliding between Tom's shoulder blades, his rear drawn ineluctably earthwards, as if weighted with lead. Tom picks up speed, reaching the hurried, tilting pace of some-one about to fall, or let a heavy load drop to the ground. The gap is a foot too narrow. They crash on through it regardless, pushing past twigs and leaves and tiny snagging thorns, and collapse onto a strip of grass.

Will is dumped on his side. The grass is deep, soft; he's overcome by a need to rest, his eyelids dipping. Then a dewy

blade licks his earlobe and he's scrambling upright, yank-
ing the sketchbooks across his lap, conducting an anxious
check for moisture. But all is well. He exhales, frowning;
and discovers that they are at the edge of a country road,
a shallow, rutted channel that runs along the valley's eastern summit. And laid before them, soaring above them, is
the heart-stopping fullness of the dawn. Sunlight rakes over
a mountainous array of clouds. The giant forms are clear
and crisp, tinted with silvery pinks and bordered with a line
of burnished copper. Beyond is a mighty sweep of colour,
ranging from deep indigo and vermillion through to a celestial yellow-white, the transition impossibly smooth. The
effect is one of inestimable distance, of unfathomable scale:
of *infinity*, so awful and elating. It would fit a scene of the
highest dramatic import. A scene of true Sublime poetry. A
great biblical exodus. A tremendous battle, immortalised by
history. The conclusion of a heroic voyage. Will is studying
it, fixing every element in place, when Tom starts to talk of
Wilson – of how this is a Wilson sky through and through,
in its breadth, its grandeur, et cetera. Will knows Wilson.
He's filled a book with sketches taken from the dead man's
pictures. He knows very well which of their qualities he'll
be adapting for use in his own work. And he knows that he
can, that one day he surely *will*, surpass them completely.
He says none of this to Tom.

The painters sit together in the wet grass – Tom eulogising,
Will wordlessly recording – until a clanging noise makes
them look to the left, along the road. Will spies a roof and

part of a gable; a trail of hearth-smoke wafting over the hedgerows. They are near Harewood village, nearer than he'd realised. This spot was carefully chosen.

Tom stands. 'Just cattle,' he reports. 'Telegraph will be here soon, though. And I'll get you on board so damn quick nobody'll have the chance to wonder at it.'

'Go back,' says Will. 'Don't wait.'

'That knee's sprained, Will, more than likely. You shouldn't walk on it, not for a week at least.'

'It ain't so bad.' This is debatable, but Will now wants quite desperately to be alone, and reliant on others no longer. 'I'll manage.'

Tom isn't persuaded. 'If that's how you wish it,' he says; then he cranes his neck, peering into the village, and maps out Will's route. 'Telegraph to Wetherby. Stage to Stamford. Why, you could be in Maiden Lane by noon tomorrow.'

Will nods. He doesn't intend to return to Covent Garden much before the end of the month. He has his books and his painting kit, and three shillings ninepence in his waist-coat pocket, so he's going to finish off the northern tour. This decision was made in the greenhouse; and the injury, although painful, doesn't warrant a change of plan. There are minsters still to see, and a couple of Lincolnshire market towns; and an invitation from the Earl of Yarborough to draw his mausoleum at Brocklesby. Money wasn't mentioned, of course, but an agreement would be reached. The fact of it is that Will's mind has begun to twitch most aggravatingly – to jog about like a restless limb. His terms are struck out.

No one else would want drawings of Harewood House or its environs. Even the castle is not, in all honesty, a first-rate subject. There's dead time to make up for. He has to gather in everything he can.

'How long will you stay?'

Tom is scanning the horizon. 'A week. Perhaps longer. Beau wants me to meet his father, for some reason.'

Had the intention been to provoke, this offhand reply could scarcely have been better phrased or delivered. We've been familiar for years, me and him, Will thinks; we've spent many hours together. Yet we understand each other not a single damn jot. He wants to ask Tom what he imagines will come of his little alliance with Mary Ann Lascelles — how it might end, exactly, and how soon — but he knows it's pointless. Tom won't have considered any of it.

'Ain't you got work to do?'

'A drawing or two,' Tom answers with a shrug. 'No more than usual.'

Will's irritation increases. 'Why d'you do that?' he snaps. 'Why the devil d'you pretend to be of such confined ambition? I *saw them*, Tom. Back in your room. The drawings of the city. I can see where you're headed.'

Tom steps from the verge into the middle of the road; moving, briefly, before the rising sun. 'Will,' he says. 'Dear Will.'

'London on a fearsome scale. Ain't that it? *The London Sublime*. A single canvas, a six-footer — or a series of them? Am I right?'

Will swallows. His heart, he can tell, is squatting right there on his sleeve, throbbing with all its jealous malignancy. Tom seems amused, though, more than anything; and as Will starts up again, asking about the Academy and how he thinks it'll be received, and what he'll do if they offer him membership, the other painter cuts him short with a single word.

'Panorama.'

To his chagrin, and despite his self-acquired fluency with classical legend, Will can't actually speak any Greek or Latin, beyond a handful of commonplace axioms. There was no room in his draughtsman's education for such rarefied attainments. But neither was there in Tom's. His first thought is that the fellow is trying to bamboozle him.

'Beg pardon?'

'Come now. Don't act like you've forgotten. Henry Barker and his father. The rotunda in Leicester Fields. They're making money hand over fist.'

The memory reappears. Barker was an acquaintance of Will's, back in the Academy schools. His artist father had brought them both down from Scotland to realise an unusual idea: the display of a complete view, taken in three hundred and sixty degrees – every element, every detail of a particular spot on earth, painted and displayed to make you swear that you were really there. Panorama, Will recalls, was the term the Scotsmen coined for these spectacles. He's been to see a couple – views of Edinburgh and of London – and thought them impressive enough as feats; but lifeless, topographical only, devoid of art. The method of presentation, furthermore, was unmistakeable: a huge wooden cylinder, temporary in appearance, festooned with hoardings promising *sheer disbelief — a vista that will truly amaze — an illusion the eye will refuse to credit.*

'But that's an entertainment,' he says. 'That's a show.'

Tom explains. His aim is to join his experiences as a landscape painter, as a painter of weather and atmosphere, with practical knowledge gained on the stage sets of Drury Lane. This panorama of his will have artistic merit, he claims, far in advance of any other that has been put on display. It will be modern, also, indisputably modern: the English capital, rendered *as it is*, summoning both recognition and awe. And most importantly it will be *democratic*, open to all London, in a way that Somerset House simply is not. It's a mighty undertaking, though, far more complicated and demanding than pictures, and subject to a great long list of mundane delays. Credit for materials. A place of sufficient size to work in. The patent on the term, on the format — still held by the Barkers and not set to expire until the beginning of the new century. But Tom is resolute. That much is plain. He sees a future here.

Will is left mystified; rather dazzled by the scope of it; and goaded somehow, as if an oblique challenge has been made. He cannot, at any rate, merely give his approval.

'It's against the Academy,' he says.

'More room for others. More room for you.'

This notion, for some reason, does not appease Will at

all. 'They won't ever let you in, Tom, if you do this. It's a—'
He stops. 'You'll be reduced, in their eyes. A showman. A
hack.'

'Will,' Tom says, 'they won't anyway. I ain't made for that
whole business. The endless politicking. Begging those old
mutts for favour. I ain't got your appetite for it.'

'Wilson wouldn't have done it.'

Tom's equanimity slips. 'Wilson *starved*. Died desti-
tute. And your beloved Academy let it happen.' He kicks
at the rutted road. 'You know how I live. Stuck with John
in Mother's back room. Three shirts to my damn name.
There's got to be a way past this, what we're doing here.
This wretched toadying.'

'We chase them that would buy,' Will says. 'We get ourselves known and then they start to seek us out. That's how
it works.'

Tom's kick has stirred up a cloud of pale dust. He steps
back, coughing into a fold of the cloak, and sits heavily on
the opposite verge. Another fit seems to be beginning, but
he stifles it, holding his breath until his skin reddens. He's
shaking his head.

'It *works*, Tom. Look at these people. How they are with
you.' Will's jealousy returns. 'Why, if you was to go to Beau
Lascelles and tell him of your difficulties, he'd give you
terms to last out your whole life.'

The black cloak drops. Tom pants for a while. He spits on
the road. 'Beau Lascelles,' he states, 'is a damn fool. I believe
I'll find my terms elsewhere.'

The dust cloud drifts towards the village. A silence falls between the painters – the disgruntled silence of men whose differences have been exposed, but who lack the energy or the will for further argument. Tom's colour subsides. After a minute he lets out a long sigh, bored with discord; then he looks at Will's feet and starts to smile. Will glances down himself. His stockings are grass-stained, mud-caked, dew-soaked, their colour and shape quite lost. On the right, a big toe pokes through the cotton like the tip of a grubby turnip.

'Boots got left in the hall,' he says.

Tom is already removing his own. He pinches the pair together and holds them out, over the road. Will tries to refuse, so he rises and lopes forward, setting them on top of the sketchbooks.

'Take them,' he says. 'Don't be a chump, Will.'

These boots are better than anything Will has ever owned – a gift, no doubt, from Beau Lascelles or somebody like him – although the leather is cracked and scratched, and the soles nearly worn through. He eases them on. It's a peculiar, not entirely pleasant feeling: they're much too large, predictably enough, and still clammily warm. But he is shod. He is a traveller once more.

Tom helps Will up. By adopting a shuffling, wincing limp, he manages to advance a few yards along the road. It can be done. He turns; Tom is on the verge, watching with his arms crossed, his bare feet half-buried in the grass. The sun is behind him, breaking over his shoulder, obscuring his face with a painful radiance. Will squints, raising a hand to shield his eyes, but to no avail. Nothing else can be seen.

'Thank you,' he says.

Covent Garden

November 1797

Will is caught on Chandos Street, just by the Swan tavern. He's moving quickly, along a route so familiar it can be followed without thought – crossing between the western end of Maiden Lane and the mouth of Half Moon Street, a narrow alley that will bring him straight to the Strand. The Swan serves as a perch for all manner of predators; it stands on a corner where the thoroughfare grows uncommonly wide, allowing the passing multitudes to be surveyed with ease, and targets selected. Will, furthermore, wears no coat or hat, which makes him conspicuous on a cold November afternoon. He's keeping his head firmly down, reciting Thomson's *Seasons* in a gruff whisper, hoping that the verse will sustain him through this unwanted interlude – an interruption that has arrived at the *worst conceivable moment* – when the success of a picture, of an oil destined for Somerset House, hangs by a single straining thread.

'Till in the western sky, the downward sun looks out effulgent . . .'

The leader has Will's arm – is latching onto it as if to anchor something that might otherwise blow away. It startles him quite witless, and for a few seconds he can only continue with his recital, stammering another line beneath his captor's galloping salutation.

'Serendipity, Mr Turner, blessed serendipity! The fates do so delight in it, don't they? Throwing the like-minded together, I mean – surprising them most pleasantly with the society of a comrade!'

'The – the rapid radiance strikes the illumined mountains – a yellow mist . . .'

'But how are you faring, young sir? You must tell me all, every detail. I insist on it. Much has happened, I gather, since last we two spoke.'

Will's poetic momentum runs out. Adjusting his footing in the greyish mud, he sees a pair of greasy green lapels; a cream stock tied a touch too tight; a spatter of pimples upon a jutting, apple-shaped chin. Jack Harris, he thinks. It's Jack Harris. He damn near faints with relief.

Hirelings were the initial fear – the torment, in fact, of Will's first days back in London. Any man of uncertain occupation who lingered on Maiden Lane, any knock that came at the barber-shop door, was a blade-wielding brute sent to punish his thievery. Soon, though, this was supplanted by a vigilance for tall, well-made females and curly black hair; and gypsies too, and people in the plain attire he associates with Abolition. She'll come, he told himself, a strange excitement mixed with his fright. She'll want that centrepiece. She'll talk of slavery, and evil, and the need for funds – and she'll surely demand some manner of restitution when she discovers what has happened. Amidst the doubt and the unanswered questions, this seemed definite.

Yet Mrs Lamb stayed away. Weeks passed without incident. Summer's high stink diminished, leaving Covent Garden to the milder pongs of autumn. Work took over; Will's watchfulness slowly slackened. Then this hand closed around his arm.

The joy Will felt at the sight of Harris's shrewd, spotty visage is extremely short-lived. He's to be interrupted, it appears, even in the course of his interruption; annoyance is to be piled atop annoyance. The fellow is a frame-maker, among other things, with premises on Gerrard Street – one of the burgeoning number trying to make their living off London's artists and print men. An especially bushy-tailed specimen, he's well known for these expeditions out of his shop, in search of advantageous encounters. Will despises this tactic. He needs to be *prepared*, always; to have established in his own mind what he'll pay, and what he'll have in return. He's never made an agreement in the street, not once, and has taken pains to spread this fact about. It doesn't deter them.

Realising that Will isn't going to begin a discussion of his circumstances, Harris does it for him. 'You've had a good summer, I've heard. A *prime* summer. You've been sporting in the lap of Xerxes, ain't you Mr Turner, and you've had your pockets filled with his gold. Seven drawings, was it? Quite the haul, sir. Quite the haul.'

Will is scowling now, vexed as ever by the transformation of his private business into public knowledge. There are any number of suspects for this leak – foremost of which is his own father, who is presently scouring the piazza with a bloody handkerchief clamped to his ear. He glances back into Maiden Lane. The striped barber's pole can just be discerned; and beneath it, through the dark casement, some of the disorder left by Mother's escape. He wonders how much these men have seen.

'I've someone already, Mr Harris.'

The frame-maker ignores him. 'And taking commissions in oil! Heavens above, Mr Turner, you'll be an Associate in no time. We've been talking it over, my pals and I, and we all agree. Next year's elections. Your hour is nigh.'

Two others wait at Harris's rear, lackeys from the look of them. Both are nodding.

'Aye,' says one.

'Next year,' says the other. 'For sure.'

Beau Lascelles' letter was received on the fifth day of September. Will shook it open with quivering, sweat-sticky fingers, convinced that he was about to read words like *theft* and *proof* and *witness* and *magistrate* – that he might as well just cast himself out the damn window right then and be done with it. A minute later, though, he was frowning with perplexity and fast-gathering delight. In his feathery, careless hand, Beau informed him that – on account of the hour or so he'd spent studying the sketchbooks – he would have his six watercolour drawings, consisting of four views of the house and two of the castle; and that he desired to order an additional drawing, taken from the sketches of Kirkstall Abbey, for which he would pay a further ten guineas. Remuneration would be made upon delivery of the completed works to Hanover Square: all at once, individually, or in any combination Mr Turner pleased. For whatever reason, he was pretending that the ugly scene in the stable block hadn't occurred. Will wasn't about to question it. The terms were improved. His finances were secure, until Christmas at least. The hirelings would be held back.

Better was to come. A second letter arrived a fortnight later, this time from Lord Harewood himself, requesting oils of Plumpton, of which he understood Mr Turner had sketches: two canvases, and pretty large ones at that, to add to the decoration of the saloon. The fee would be thirty-two pounds, with nine shillings allowed for materials. Will showed it to Father, who seized hold of him for a bow-legged jig before the parlour fire.

By God, boy, the barber declared, stopping to catch his breath, *you must've charmed them nobs something proper.*

At first, it seemed a great gift. Will could now afford to forswear the likes of Dr Monro and the Sans Souci and concentrate on his Academy submissions – on works derived from the northern sketchbooks, which he's convinced will be his finest yet. Before long, however, he recognised the Lascelles' largesse for what it was. They were binding him with kindness. He was in their service. Toiling for their coin. His silence could be taken for granted.

Harris has started talking up his frames. 'I've this moulding in from Amsterdam – very grand it is, but complimentary also – a fine fit for Romantic matter. The pins, also, are best steel, and fish-hooked so they withstand the sharpest of knocks, such as might reasonably be sustained during the traversal of our fair city. What's more, the gilt I employ . . .'

Street women drift in, carmine over their bruises, murmuring invitations – 'Walk with me a while, my tup? There's a place, not far . . .' – Will they know, and know he's no good for it, but the usual persistence is shown towards Harris and his companions. Sleeves are stroked and shoulders smoothed; and one of the lackeys orders them away, cocking a fist when they hesitate.

'Mr Harris,' says Will over the curses, trying to pull free, 'I have someone. I ain't got time. I must be off.'

It's right there, in his voice: a dread of being asked why he is in such a desperate hurry, clad only in a shirt and nankeen breeches, with the buckle of his left shoe flapping loose. He looks at Harris. The fellow sees his unease, sees it plainly, and is thinking of how it might be used to his advantage.

'What about drawings, then? I know you're busy, Mr

Turner, but anything you have that may be surplus to your commissions, anything that may be in need of a quick sale, would be gladly received. I have my buyers, sir. Five guineas I got last week, for our mutual friend Mr Girtin. Perhaps he's mentioned this to you.'

Will is halted. He shakes his head. 'No. He ain't.'

They haven't met since Harewood. Will's bundle, left behind in the casket chamber, arrived by post at the end of August, the clothes laundered and neatly folded. Even the sun hat was included. Accompanying it was a note from Tom, expressing the hope that he'd recovered from his fall upon *that slippery riverbank*, and had reached home without further mishap. Will sent a reply to the effect that he had, that the knee was fully healed, and that he looked forward to returning *the articles so kindly loaned* in the near future. Before he could act on this intention, however, Father came across Tom's boots lying in the downstairs corridor and gave them to a beggar.

Harris smiles. 'You're aware of our association, I'm sure. Two years now, I've been selling for him. And interest in his drawings has never been higher. Mr Girtin is *thriving*. It's most satisfying to witness. Your own patrons, the Lascelles, are helping him as well. They've appointed him drawing master at Hanover Square, and every day he gains new pupils from among their fashionable friends. He told me that he's looking to leave his mother's house at last. Lodgings on Drury Lane, apparently.' The frame-maker's tone drops; his fingers refresh their grip on Will's arm. 'I'm concerned, though. A touch. I won't deny it. There's a quality about him, Mr Turner, that I can't quite comprehend. Perhaps you can assist me here. A *shadow*, you might call it. Cast, I'd say, during the summer just gone.'

Will is staring into the gutter. 'What is – How do—' He blinks; he clears his throat. Something is coming. 'Beg pardon?'

The plot, as delineated by Mrs Lamb, has certainly failed. No pregnancy was announced. Prince Ernest Augustus was reported to have left the country, in pursuit of battle against the French. Early in October, the Lascelles family arrived at Hanover Square for the season, but Mary Ann was not among them. Will made some discreet enquiries; her whereabouts were unknown. Word around town puts Tom in his old haunts – back on the same circuit of artists' taverns, theatre scenery and drawing lessons that Will is attempting to avoid. Harris's account makes it clear that he too has been bound to the Lascelles. How he might feel about this, though, and what he might say or do, is less easy to determine.

Harris seems to back down. 'It ain't important. Mostly he's his normal self. Starting trouble. Rallying folk to some great cause or other.' He laughs, relaxing; then abruptly returns to it. 'There was a night, however, in the upstairs room of this very establishment behind us here – an assembly of a little tavern club we run, for men of our profession. We was making our toasts, and it was the usual sort of thing: the immortal Muse, so-and-so's pet pug, Miss Emma at the Key. But when Mr Girtin's turn comes, he proposes "the Lascelles family of Yorkshire" — says something like "the most generous of patrons, who only two months previous showed me the kindest and most disinterested hospitality".'

Will stays very still.

'Such displays of gratitude to a benefactor are hardly unknown, of course, in a club like ours. But a couple of things caught our notice. First was that Mr Girtin had told us he was going west this summer, out into Devon. Second, and more striking, was the way he spoke. He wasn't grateful at all, Mr Turner. He was angry.'

Dear God.

'We drank, at any rate, and we sat back down. Several people asked Mr Girtin to enlarge, but he refused. Not a word more. Looked like regret from where I was placed. Like he'd give much to take back that sour toast of his.' Harris turns to his companions. 'What do you say, gentlemen? Ain't that a fair description?'

'Aye, Mr Harris.'

'Poor devil was ready to black his own eye.'

'And afore the next charging of the bumpers he was gone,' Harris continues. 'Thundered down the stairs. All but ran off up Bedford Street. We talked on it a while, as you'd expect, and it transpired that one of us had recently been in Lord Harewood's employ himself. Giuseppe Forli was his name — a decorative painter from Ravenna, originally, brought into Hanover Square to do up the columns so they'd look like marble. This Signor Forli said he'd overheard a great deal from his scaffold, among the family and their callers, of *your* stay at the Yorkshire house over the summer, of the commission made and the results anticipated, yet none whatsoever of any by Mr Girtin. Mr Turner this, Mr Turner that – but Mr Turner only.' The frame-maker pauses, rather pleased; his challenge has been set. 'Odd, wouldn't you agree? This disparity?'

Will suppresses a shiver. More than frames or picture dealing, gossip is Jack Harris's stock in trade. He knows when he sees a kink in the cloth – a loose stitch to pick at. Will's thoughts, unexpectedly, are of confession. He could air the whole damn story, right this minute. The facts of his experience. The memories that swamp his mind whenever he is trying to work, or sleep, or think. This is surely a chance for release. He peers to the left. The Strand can be seen along the crooked passage of Half Moon Street: the carriages and tall carts, the haze of smoke and steam, the endless crowds through which he has yet to search.

It can't be taken. What revelations, exactly, would he make? Where would he break off? It's all roped together, every deed and misdeed of that fretful, tumultuous week. To tell of Tom and Mary Ann Lascelles is to tell of Mrs Lamb, and Abolition pamphlets, and night-time escapades in the state rooms; of Selene and Endymion, stolen, snapped apart and hurled into the boating lake. Harris is no fool. He'd see that he was being given but half a tale. He'd pose questions that Will would be better off not answering. He'd worry the matter like a dog. It'd start too much. The Lascelles have Will's measure. He can't do it.

'Tom weren't at Harewood, Mr Harris. Just me.'

The frame-maker draws back, his brow lifting. He releases Will's arm. 'Really, Mr Turner? Our friend was quite specific. "Only two months previous," he said, teeth gritted as hard as you like, "they showed me the kindest—"'

'He went to Harewood the *year* previous. It was the liquor, I reckon. Muddled his recollection.'

Harris considers Will for a second; then he grins. 'Possible,' he admits. 'Very possible. Mr Girtin seemed certain – but you was *there*, sir, wasn't you! I hope that you should damn well know!' He slaps Will's shoulder. 'You mustn't be nervous. The night I speak of was several weeks ago now. We've seen him since, for business, and had him lecture us on the wickedness of the government with his usual spirit. And only yesterday Mr Samuel was saying that he's become embroiled with a ... laundress, was it?'

'Dairy maid. Near Regent Street.'

'No *enduring injuries*, then,' the frame-maker concludes, 'on our Mr Girtin. This, I think, can safely be attested.'

The three men laugh and begin to discuss the particular attributes of dairy maids; so Will decides that he'll resume the duty that propelled him from his easel, out into this unwelcoming afternoon. He excuses himself, none too loudly, and carries on down his intended path. The sounds of the Strand – tradesmen's cries, the grinding and creaking of wheels, ten thousand voices talking at once – are funnelled up the sloping alley, enveloping Will like a rush of dirty surf; and Jack Harris, calling after him from Chandos Street, is almost drowned out.

'I'd visit the pillory first, Mr Turner, if I was you. That's where you got her last time, ain't it?'

*

An hour later Will is back in his painting room. The latticed window is open despite the cold, in an effort to wring what light remains from the declining day. His oils are mixed and ready, the muddy little heaps dotted across the flat hump of the palette. Before him is a half-finished view of Buttermere, taken from a colour study in the larger sketch-book, one of the best studies of the tour. A rainstorm arches above the mountainous valley, sinking it into a rich pluvial gloom; but at its centre the sun has found a gap in the cloud, and reaches between the foothills to set a golden cradle in the mid-ground. The intention, of course, is contrast: thunderous shadow and blazing brilliance, placed side by side to Sublime effect. His time away, however, has served to underscore the picture's shortcomings. Timid, he thinks, glowering at it. Hesitant. He has it in mind to add a rainbow, curving over the peaks, leading the eye down to the brightest point, but cannot find it within him. Thomson's *Seasons* was the source of this notion, so he gives the lines another try.

'The grand ethereal bow shoots up immense, and every hue unfolds ...'

It's hopeless. The sensibility is fled. These fine words aren't enough. Image and paint aren't enough. They'll *never* be enough. Will slumps onto his stool. He hears Father scrubbing the small courtyard outside his window, working the coarse brush as hard as he can, and Mother's moans trailing plaintively from the parlour. His own search proved unsuccessful. Even the pillory at Charing Cross – where she has indeed been discovered on several instances, making a vigorous contribution to the punishment of the unlucky souls locked within – yielded nothing. Footsore and irritable, he returned to the shop to find both parents already there. She'd been in the yard of St Paul's, Father told him, looking for their daughter's grave, the location of which she could never be made to learn.

Will sets his palette on the mantelpiece and gazes around balefully at the cramped, cluttered room: at the table piled with papers and books, the muller lolling on its stone plate, both coated in orange dust; the washing line pegged with drying drawings, running diagonally from one cobwebbed corner to another. The problem here, the cause of his restiveness, is obvious. That brief conversation with Jack Harris has brought about an unsettling change. No longer has Will simply been used and then bought off; he has colluded directly. The Lascelles' calculations can be imagined with infuriating ease. They've decided, plainly, that William Turner is *safe* – a neutered, brainless creature, as unlikely to challenge their account, their manipulations and omissions, as the staff up at Harewood. And he has proved them right. He has lied. Obliged himself to lie again.

Beau's drawings hang together at one end of the washing line. The close views of the house are complete, ready to be taken over to Hanover Square. No chances have been taken. Dutch-style details of rustic life, Vernet skies, the lightest gloss of Claude: everything that could be desired. Will wasn't going to give them the slightest reason to deny or reduce his payment. The other four are all at roughly the same stage, being worked up for a simultaneous finish early in the new year. Those of the castle are turning out especially well. He decided on the eastern view, with the ruin in the left foreground and Wharfedale off to the right – the first of the day, sketched with such exhilaration – and one of those from the north, the triangular composition, taken just before the breaking of the storm. Before he sought refuge inside. Before he found them.

Suddenly, Will's discontent points out a course. He pulls down the eastern view, flaps it against a board and identifies a suitable spot: a section of mossy bank, perhaps an inch long and a half-inch wide, just beneath the castle. The scraping nail, grown back to its old dimensions, is brought to bear and the paper cleared of pigment. Then he takes up the smallest of his watercolour pencils, charges it with the very darkest mix of Cologne-earth and makes his addition. Five minutes' labour puts two tiny figures forever in the foreground of Beau Lascelles' drawing. One sits in a sun hat and blue coat, sketching diligently into his book. The other, bareheaded in a suit of burnt umber, is stretched out on the ground beside his companion, watching him work with idle interest.

Will and Tom.

Charing Cross

April 1803

'Stories,' says Morland now, sitting back with the air of an expectant king. 'We must have stories.'

The company shifts about, arranging its recollections; glad, in truth, of this new purpose. Little Louis Francia speaks first, his usual trim precision compromised somewhat by port, telling of the severance of Tom's apprenticeship to Edward Dayes. Jealous of his pupil's ability, this ill-famed master used to delight in assigning him the most tedious labours imaginable. One task eventually proved too much: the colouring of five hundred prints of Coldstream Guards, of five hundred tunics and sashes and tri-cornered hats, each identical to the last. So Tom, at only seventeen years of age and with four years of indentures still remaining, decided that he would add great long beards to the soldiers instead, and devils' tails, and tackle of the most extraordinary proportions; and leave Dayes' house for good, plunging into the city to live off his own brush alone.

'Independence,' Francia concludes. 'Even then, he prized it above all else.'

Bob Porter goes next, standing grandly as if addressing a public meeting, and barks his way through a tale of an artists' outing into Kent. An old mill was discovered beside a stream, at a picturesque degree of ruination. The painters agreed that this was their subject, to be taken in colour, with the results compared at the day's end. An hour later, though, Tom was finished, his drawing so fine that it left the others very much inclined to abandon theirs; and when a pair of dairy maids came over to see what they were about, he made them a gift of the sheet like it was nothing at all.

'They strolled off together, of course, arm in arm.' The company starts to laugh. 'Didn't see the scoundrel again for the better part of a week.'

Third is an affable, diffident fellow called Holcroft – an amateur, it turns out, and a medical student, who went with Tom on his journey to Paris. 'He wanted to see every last inch of the city, and record it also. We were warned that sketching in the open might be dangerous, that we might be taken for spies and possibly harmed, and should really remain in our cabriolet. But he wouldn't have it. The hazard simply did not apply to him. And his energy was remarkable. Greater, certainly, than mine.' Holcroft's smile falters; he looks to his glass. 'Although by then, the cough was . . . it really was very bad.'

No one can follow this. All good humour is dispersed, melancholy building in its place. Morland, plainly experienced in both dissipation and grief, moves to quash it.

'Save us, Turner,' he cries, rapping on the tabletop with his cane. 'Save us, sir, if you please. They tell me that you were his boyhood companion, with all of London as your stamping ground. By God! Days like that must surely never dim.'

Sat in a corner, Will is almost hidden between Georgie Samuel and Paul Sandby Munn. He eyes Morland, the bane of his afternoon: the old coat, the broken veins, the drink-swollen jowls. The exact link between Tom and this sorry figure is unknown – Jack Harris, kept away himself by an attack of rheumatics, remains the best guess. A prodigy in his youth, Morland smothered his talent with a profligacy so reckless it has seen him confined to the King's Bench, cast from his home more times than can easily be counted, and required to throw out pictures at a rate that has made any quality or originality impossible. He's a failure, in short; but today he finds himself in the company of success, and is determined to have his fun. Addressing Will often, he tries to drag him into the foreground and inflict whatever embarrassment or disquiet that he can.

Will shakes his head. 'Damn shame, that's all. Poor Tom.'

Morland pushes no harder, for the moment. He drains his glass and supplies them with his own tale, a florid account of a night spent coasting through the low taverns, including the one they presently occupy – the Rummer, which he claims was Tom's special favourite. There's boozing and singing, wenching and spewing; and then a running battle with the militia – the 'agents of repression' as Morland terms them

– involving hats tipped into gutters and the liberal slinging about of dung. It's an evocation of Tom Girtin that his circle of intimates struggles to recognise. They listen with forced smiles.

Will's attention drifts. He looks out into the tavern, at the ancient black beams and warped floors; at the sallow faces that watch them steadily through the tobacco smoke. This occasion is starting to feel rather pointless, as if he's waiting for something – for someone – whose arrival is less likely with every minute that passes. He wants very much to consult his watch, a handsome piece bought last year after the conclusion of his business with the Earl of Egremont. Another glance at those sallow faces tells him this would be unwise.

Fresh bottles are brought and glasses charged, and the toasts begin again. This is Morland's other method of choice for fending off the gloom: port-induced insensibility. They work through a list, more or less identical to the one trotted out in the Crown and Anchor, and the Three Tuns before that. Liberty, poetry, love; their brother Thomas Girtin, and his wife and son; and his paintings, his magnificent paintings, sure to immortalise him in the annals of art. Will hangs back, feigning participation, barely touching the thick liquid to his lips. He needs to keep a clear head.

Morland is watching him. 'Perhaps, Turner,' he calls, 'if you won't talk of Tom, you'll be so kind as to talk a little of your pictures. What've you got on the stocks this year, eh? What astonishing feats can your public expect?'

Will's frown weighs down his features, tilting his head towards the Rummer's cracked floorboards. The old reprobate has put this to him in the certain knowledge that he wants nothing less than to answer – and that everyone present will be eager to hear whatever he might say. Sure enough, he looks up again to find himself hemmed in by expressions of deep interest and enthusiasm; of reverence, almost, in a couple of cases. They're *leaning in on him*, it feels like. It's extremely discomforting.

'This and that.'

'I understand you were in Switzerland, Mr Turner,' says Holcroft. 'Few have been, especially of late. One can only imagine the effects. The sentiments they inspire.'

'There's Alpine pieces,' Will allows. 'A large marine.'

'With tall ships, I hope,' booms the rosy-cheeked Porter, 'and stormy seas. Good God, that one last year, of the fishing boats – I swear it made the carpet move beneath my feet. Damn thing was quite *nauseating* to behold. And I say that, you know, as the highest possible praise.'

'New one's better.'

Four or five questions come at once, along with more half-heard impertinence from Morland. Will protests, telling them that he can reveal no more – thinking that this really is intolerable, that he might well be justified in getting to his feet and heading straight home. Georgie Samuel intervenes. A degree less drunk than the rest and plainly seeking to rescue Will, he reminds them loudly of the evening's purpose.

'The hall shuts at nine,' he says, 'and we are not, I think, at our fastest.'

Drinks are finished off, chairs scraping back as the company heaves itself upright; and not long afterwards they are walking out from the darker regions of Charing Cross, over the broad thoroughfare and around the end of a neat terrace. Sight of the pillory, empty for once, on its platform beside the statue of King Charles – standing in the lamplight like a barren, battered fingerpost – brings Will a jolt of alertness. His fists clench; he scans the people milling at its base. But she's not there. The realisation comes cold and clear. She'll never be there again.

The shops, kitchens and concert rooms of Spring Garden are lit merrily against the coming night. A chain of coloured lanterns leads away from the main parade to a small park behind, from where Will can hear a fiddle, and the claps and whistles of a dance. Set on a corner, the exhibition hall is a smart, square construction of red brick, and it is busy. This is troubling. Will's understanding was that Tom's venture had foundered. His expectation, when he agreed to this jaunt, was that the place would be deserted.

They approach, weaving and slurring yet also markedly sombre, like a well-oiled funerary procession that has mislaid its coffin. Morland is at their head, swaggering in a wide-brimmed hat; he starts proclaiming about *genius* and *hallowed ground* and asking the people on the steps if they understood, really *understood*, what they have been privileged enough to see. Will lingers at the rear, making discreet efforts to determine who might be within. Academy life, it has turned out, is quite viciously political, and there are several among the senior members who he'd like very much to avoid. But it's futile, the view too partial to be of any use. He looks to the sign pasted up by the doors: six feet high, printed in large, plain script – and bordered, since last November, with black.

EIDOMETROPOLIS is emblazoned across the top; *The Form of the Capital* below, in letters half the size; and beneath this, arranged in a tidy block, the description: *A situation so chosen as to show to the greatest advantage the Thames, Somerset House, the Temple Gardens, all the churches, bridges, principal buildings etc., with the surrounding country to the remotest distance.*

He must enter. Of course he must. To hell with them all. If Northcote or Hoppner are in there – both broadly supportive during his election the previous year, but conspicuously less so since – he will merely tip his hat and continue with his study of the display. Let them see Morland and the rest. Let them form whatever conclusions they pleased. As he's climbing the steps, he notices a builder's cart, drawn up in the street on the other side of the hall. Two others are behind it, and around them a team of labourers smoke their pipes and drink pots of beer. They are set-breakers, he realises, ready to start demolishing Tom's great picture the moment the doors are shut, in preparation for the room's next exhibit.

Payment appears straightforward: a coin box on a table, just beyond the entrance, watched over by an attendant. No sum is given, however, a handwritten notice stating that this is being left to the discretion of patrons, with all proceeds going towards the relief of the deceased artist's family. The company from the Rummer are dropping in shillings, three or four at a time; half crowns too. Even the impecunious Morland manages a stream of pennies that must add up to at least two and six. Then, as one, they are all looking back at Will: at J.M.W. Turner R.A., the most successful and affluent of their number by a considerable distance – widely known, despite his attempts at concealment, to command prices that are double their own, with another nought stuck on the end. *Ambush*, he thinks, fishing out his pocket book. A clean golden guinea nestles in its folds, earmarked to buy a new hat for Father, to smarten the old fellow up a touch and protect his bald pate from the last pinches of spring. That'll have to wait. He drops in the coin with a private wince and trundles through to join them.

A simple wooden structure fills the hall's main chamber, something like a drum on a ten-foot stand, with a flight of stairs leading up inside it to a central viewing platform. The company's excitement suddenly flares, Morland and Bob Porter racing to the summit. The autumn before, in the galleries of the Louvre, Will glutted himself on Napoleon's plunder – poring over the works of Tiziano, standing stunned before the grand canvases of Veronese, remaining until the guards ushered him out. Following the others up, he's reminded of those days; of the jubilation that would build within him as he walked into a certain room and approached a particular painting; of the sure belief that he was about to be made wise, elevated, both improved and renewed. The sensation is not so strong here, not nearly, yet it is undeniably present. He can't help but be irritated by it.

This isn't Will's first visit to Tom's show. He came alone one morning in late October, the day after his return from the continent. A letter seemed an inadequate way to convey his opinion, so he resolved to travel up to the house in Islington that Tom shared with his wife and infant son. There was some Academy business, though, and a few patrons to see, along with a print man in Oxford Street; and then Tom Girtin was dead, killed by the complaint that had hounded him since childhood, and buried before the week was out. Emerging onto the platform now, experiencing the thing again, makes him quite sick with regret.

That it is lit artificially this time, by a huge lantern suspended from the skylights, scarcely diminishes the impact. Many hundreds of buildings are arrayed along the river: foundries, palaces, warehouses, tumbledown tenements and churches by the dozen, steeples of slate and stone sprouting amid the surrounding rooftops. The very best effects enwrap certain sections – the interplay of sunlight and coal smoke, of cloud shadow and morning mist – and thin away to nothing in others, allowing for great clear distances to open up, off towards Lambeth fields and the low hills of the western horizon. The Thames, also, is a marvel, its reflections rendered with unusual detail, and a multitude of complex tones accurately captured; it has a *current*, furthermore, the water seeming to inch mightily around the room. Will knows very well how damn difficult it is to bring this off.

The company's initial awe is giving way swiftly to sorrow. Georgie Samuel and Louis Francia embrace, both weeping openly, the Frenchman burying his face in his friend's lapel. Porter, who claims to know panoramas, holds forth with some vehemence about how this one is the finest ever put to canvas, the very *finest*, the absolute pinnacle of the form; while Morland, wet-cheeked, is gesturing with his cane, insisting that those in his proximity attend to certain passages and incidents that he deems especially excellent. The refrain from all is *Promise Denied*: what else Tom Girtin might have done, had he lived just another ten years. Another five.

It is, on one level, a chastisement. Will believed Tom was lazy. It can't be denied. He thought that indolence lay at the root of the fellow's many casual attitudes towards his profession; of his refusal ever to make a serious run at the Academy; of his tendency to lose himself in implausible, unachievable schemes. Yet here is an emphatic contradiction, a scheme fully and gloriously realised – and one that represents so much labour, so much concentration and effort, that it makes Will faint-headed to consider it. He looks to Blackfriars Bridge, its stone channel jammed with carts and carriages, pedestrians and riders; to the expert perspective of its arches and the gentle rise in its middle, a miracle of exactness; to St Paul's beyond, a looming citadel several times as tall as the next tallest structure, the dome sheened with rainwater as a storm closes over the City from the east; and he feels a hot, shameful relief that this man, this great rival, is gone.

It fades almost at once. Will's eye halts at the border of this storm, snared by a singular effect above the Monument that escaped him during his first visit. The light of an unseen sun infuses one of the uppermost rain clouds, restoring its whiteness – appearing to illuminate it from within like a paper lantern. This brilliant spot lies against a patch of blue on one side and a thunderous darkness on the other. It's familiar, annoyingly so, like something he himself has witnessed but failed to record. A similar passage, he realises, could correct a deficiency in his latest marine. His largest yet – although not seeming, right then, so very large at all – it is a remembrance of his return journey from France; of a hazardous embarkation, a tiptoe along the lip of a hungry sea. It has power in the water, that he knows, in the waves that lick and froth and gape, but the sky isn't as effective as this one here. Not by a good distance. Will glances at the rapt, tear-tracked faces around him. He has a small book in his pocket, and a piece of chalk. Could he make a sketch – a quick, ten-stroke impression? Jot down a note? Or simply make his excuses and rush home for an adjustment?

Hissing disturbs the platform's worshipful hush. Will turns; the artists have huddled at the top of the stairs and are waving him over.

'Edward Lascelles is here,' Georgie Samuel informs him as he comes near. 'Down with the French prints.'

'You've had dealings with him, Will, haven't you?' asks Porter. 'Drawings of the family house, wasn't it?'

Will answers warily. 'A while ago now.'

Several of them talk together. The fellow is fabulously rich, and free with it too. They say that he was in Paris last year buying china – splashed over six hundred guineas. And he loved Tom, really *loved* him. You know how these noblemen can get. Kept a room empty at the country mansion just for his use. Commissioned a veritable stack of drawings. Even fixed up his marriage, some have claimed, to that goldsmith's girl. Tom certainly wouldn't ever have got round to such a step on his own.

Tiring of preamble, Morland strikes his cane against the platform floor. 'Turner,' he says, 'someone needs to buy this thing. The widow can't store it. Poor creature's in dire need of funds – I believe she'd let it go for a hundred pounds and the costs of transportation. That's nothing to a big beast like Lascelles. Nothing whatsoever.'

'It needs to be preserved,' states Francia stoutly. 'It should stand as Tom's memorial.'

'Better it be bought by some blockheaded aristocrat,' Morland continues, 'than left to those wreckers outside. There's no saying what might result if they get their hands on it. Philistinism prevails in England, gentlemen. We all know that. It could end up as decorators' rags. Beggars' blankets. Paupers' shrouds.'

'You must approach him,' urges Porter. 'Make the proposal. For the sake of our friend.'

Beau Lascelles.

For a time, Will was cautious. The pictures, both drawings and oils, were received and paid for without comment.
They're at Harewood, as far as he knows. He spent the
money and forgot them. But there was a sense of something unfinished; a suspicion that despite the reinstatement
of the Lascelles' patronage, an opposition lingered. He
began to hear of Beau consorting with his detractors and
voicing public criticisms of his art. It was even rumoured
at one stage that Lord Harewood's elder son had been plotting with Lady Sutherland to set Tom against him in the
Academy elections. This came to nothing, of course. Will's
preparations were too painstaking. And Tom would hardly
have co-operated.

Now he's beyond Beau Lascelles' reach: a full Academician
at seven-and-twenty, with earls and dukes lining up to purchase his canvases, and true connoisseurs seeking him out
like votaries approaching an oracle. He's safe, he's sure of
it, but he can't rid himself entirely of that old unease. That
intimation of doom attached to the name Lascelles. He still
takes care to leave any room he thinks Beau might be about
to enter. Throughout Tom's funeral, he was watching intently
for an aristocratic mourner who never appeared; and the
month before that, in a Louvre swarming with English visitors, he hid behind a majolica St Francis while the heir to
Harewood's party passed nearby. Right then, flight seems
the best option. There must be other exits, over at the rear
of the hall.

'I don't know,' he says.

This prompts his companions to make their case again, in more forceful, voluble terms – to embarrass him into capitulation, perhaps even drawing the attention of the very man he seeks to avoid. It's an effective ploy. Simply to stop them, Will signals his assent and starts grumpily down the stairs.

*

Beau Lascelles proves difficult to locate. He's alone, for a start, without friends or servants; a lofty, greyhound-faced absence, in particular, seems to hang at his shoulder. His clothes are more reserved, as is now the fashion, even among the highest – linen for satin, cotton for silk, powder all but absent. There's less of him, in every sense. The figure from Will's memory has grotesque, caricature proportions, with its strut, its gesticulations, its irreducible lordliness. This man here, however, makes him wonder at his years of worry. He looks ordinary.

The area below the viewing platform – the crypt, as it were, beneath the chapel – has been given over to another of Tom's projects: a series of picturesque aquatints depicting the environs of Paris, taken from drawings made during his stay. The nobleman is studying one of them in the low light, a valley view done in the broad format Tom had come to favour. He notices Will's approach, but does not break off from his inspection until the painter is at his elbow. Will feels the brush of nerves, as one might before a confrontation, along with a certain detached curiosity as to how this might actually go. Up close, he can see the additional years on Beau, how the architecture of his face is entering the first stage of its collapse — the fault lines appearing, the downward slide beginning. Those hooded eyes, also, are raw. He has been weeping. There is no vulnerability in his manner, though, and his greeting is one of sardonic distaste.

'I'm most honoured, Mr Turner, to be granted your society once more. The man of the hour. The Rembrandt of our age — greater than Rembrandt, so the newspapers would have it.'

He wishes it had been me, Will thinks. He wishes me dead instead of Tom. He mumbles something.

Beau is scrutinising him now. 'You *are* different, I must admit. Urbane, very nearly. Who'd have thought that such a change could be brought about? What can the secret possibly be?'

This riles Will. 'Damn hard work,' he replies curtly — and has a strong desire to add, 'd'you know of it?' But he restrains himself; forces himself to remember the task at hand; and realises that he hasn't the first idea how to begin.

'An old friend of yours is here, you know,' Beau tells him. 'An erstwhile benefactor of yourself and Mr Girtin. The gentleman, in fact, through whom we all came to be associated.' He pauses. 'The esteemed Dr Monro.'

The urge to flee returns. Will absolutely does not want to encounter the mad-doctor in here, alongside Beau Lascelles, with a gaggle of spectators assembled at the summit of the viewing platform stairs. Their artistic connection ended some time ago, but Will has since had cause to call upon Monro's professional influence. Only last Christmas, the doctor arranged a visit to Bethlem Hospital, to the Incurables' Ward, without an entry being put in the book. Will sat in that bare cell for the better part of an hour. Mother didn't move from her straw bed, and gazed over at him with no more recognition or feeling than if his chair were empty. He left in a state of dull distress, resolving not to go again.

Dr Monro, though, isn't anywhere to be seen. Will looks back to Beau. This is not an innocent mistake. The villain is implying knowledge – letting on that he's uncovered that which Will and Father have done their level best to contain, and could tell others if he so wished. He's trying to intimidate.

A riposte, for once, is right there in Will's mind – ready for utterance in the same mock-casual tone used by the nobleman. *You here by yourself then, Mr Lascelles? No other members of your family interested in attending? That younger sister, perhaps?*

The elopement is nearly two years old, but allusion to it would still smart. All tolerance of her situation finally exhausted, Mary Ann deserted her father's London home in the early morning with an armful of clothes, married her paramour in the nearest church and absconded forthwith to Swansea. Tom, thought Will immediately, as Father read him the details from one of his gutter rags, he's gone back for her; but that couldn't be right. He wed his goldsmith's girl the previous October. Their stories had diverged for good.

Mary Ann's choice, at any rate, was almost as inappropriate: the son of a Leeds merchant, some distance beneath her, and a terrible mortification for her family. Rumour held that the Lascelles' chances for advancement, for royal preference, had taken a grave knock — that the much-prized earldom had been shifted years beyond their reach. Hinting at this humiliation would be a blow to match Beau's own. It would show him the true change in William Turner.

But no. Again Will resists. He decides to be direct and dispense with this matter as quickly as he can. 'I'm told a buyer is needed,' he says, 'for the grand piece upstairs. For the ...' What the devil is it called? 'For the Idatropolis. Might you be interested?'

Beau is equally direct — and firmly, decisively negative. 'Mr Turner, I'm afraid that I cannot consider it. Where would it *go*, for heaven's sake? I am an art collector, a connoisseur. What use do I have for a public showpiece? An exhibit of these proportions? Should I put it up in Hanover Square, perhaps, and charge sixpence a peep?'

'Mr Lascelles, if you won't—'

'Could *you* not take it? You're having a private gallery built, so they say, on the side of your new house, to accommodate your legions of admirers. Up behind the fine gates of Harley Street. Quite an enterprise. What reserves of capital you must have at your disposal. Could you yourself not find space?'

More knowledge of Will's affairs. The fellow plainly makes it his business to learn everything that he can. Will frowns, both at this and at the absurd impracticality of his suggestion. 'It don't need to be *displayed*,' he says. 'Preserved only. Safeguarded for the future.'

Beau shakes his head. He is becoming angry. 'I cannot bring myself to look at it. There you are. That's the truth. I have been in here for twenty minutes and I cannot even mount the damned stairs.'

Will blinks; he notes the strain gathering in the nobleman's voice. Something rather different has been broached. He stays quiet.

'It killed him, Mr Turner. Can you honestly deny this? The act of producing it, this inexplicable thing here – it hastened his death. He would never do what was wise. *Never*. I had him leave this damned city as often as I could – to Wales, to the coast. I bought the drawings that resulted. I ordered more, more than my father's houses can reasonably hold. And I had him stay at Harewood – every summer, nearly. The Yorkshire air is a tonic. So very clean. One could see the good it did him, day upon day. Hear it in his breaths.'

Now Will must speak. 'He coughed still,' he says, 'as I recall.'

Beau stares at him. Understanding connects them like a bright bolt. All at once that turbulent, peculiar week is resurrected; the harshness, the abruptness of its conclusion; the family's subsequent omissions, and their calculated munificence; the two tiny figures, the young artists together, drawn on the mossy bank beside the castle. Instead of spitting forth venomous threats, however, or vows of ruin, the nobleman folds straight away into fresh dejection. His talk grows mournful, of the sort Will has been listening to all afternoon: youthful genius so cruelly attenuated, the potential left unfulfilled, the great dearth inflicted upon the world. *Promise Denied*.

Will nods along – increasingly aware, for his own part, of the contrast between their last conversation, his ejection with menaces, and this uncomfortable truce. Between a time when Tom Girtin was alive, away in a rowing boat with Mary Ann Lascelles; and one where he is dead, buried not two hundred yards from where they stand, in the yard of St Paul's. The pain of it surprises him. He saw Tom over the intervening years, of course, on many occasions – at the Academy Exhibition, and in a miscellany of coffee houses and taverns, streets and hallways. Their final meeting was at the Key the previous June, deep within a large and boisterous group. Just back from France, Tom was visibly weary, but as usual he had much to communicate. Learning of Will's own travel plans, he offered his advice on the sights of Paris and the landscape surrounding it; on where to stay, who to seek out, what to eat and drink. Will made a few notes, and gave his thanks – neglecting to mention that his initial goal, and his priority by an enormous distance, was not the Champs Elysées or the Tuileries or even the Louvre, but the Val d'Aosta.

Then Tom sat back and clapped his hands against his thighs, as if perceiving something obvious, missed through stupidity. 'You should have come with us. By God, Will, why on earth didn't you? It would've been marvellous. We would've claimed those boulevards as our own.'

'Perhaps,' Will answered, rising to leave. 'Perhaps.'

This is what's there, mostly: mundane encounters that merge in the mind, into a jumble of art gossip, trivial discourse and foolish, interminable debate. Nothing as sharp as that long-past summer. Will thinks of the night in the ice house and the lurching piggyback that followed; the feel of him there, of his back and his trembling arms, the sweat-slicked curl at the nape of his neck. These are moments, now, that only he can attest to. That live on in him alone. Heaviness collects in Will's stomach; the buckling of his left knee makes him list slowly to the side. Beau Lascelles winds up his eulogy, makes some excuse or other and departs. A minute elapses, maybe longer; and an attendant is attempting to prise Will from the wall, where he's perilously close to dislodging a view of St-Germain-en-Laye with his shoulder.

Morland is there, swatting the attendant away. 'What did he say, Turner? Will he do it?'

Will rights himself and the skewed print. He lifts a forefinger to release the hot tear that swims in his left eye. 'He will not.'

This sends the reprobate painter marching past the coin box and through the main doors, loudly declaring an intention to break every window in the blackguard's carriage. The others receive the news more philosophically, trying to console themselves with talk of a fund for a permanent structure, designed especially for Tom's panorama, which could be built up in Islington or one of the adjacent villages. Such a thing, they agree, must surely be possible.

The hall is closing. The viewing platform has already been cleared and the attendants are preparing to herd them, the last remaining visitors, out into the street. Will steps around the artists, peering back up the stairs, and manages to locate that fine passage of sky above the Monument. He wedges his hands into his pockets. Sniffs hard. Gives it ten seconds of his best attention.

A dazed crowd hangs in rags along the pavement, listening to the set-breakers begin their work inside. Morland returns, panting, claiming to have split the lip of a Lascelles footman – and proposing more drink, another tavern, a last tribute to Tom Girtin that will carry them to dawn and beyond. But Will is already off, back towards Charing Cross – towards Harley Street and the easels Father will have arranged in his painting room, standing in a circle with twelve feet of pacing space left in their centre. He waves a general farewell, deciding on colours and brushes, keeping that passage locked in his mind: the blackness of the rain storm, the shock of open blue, and then the paper lantern cloud, golden white, lit so perfectly by the sun.

Author's Note

Will & Tom combines the historical facts of J.M.W. Turner's visit to Harewood House in the summer of 1797 with a number of elements either invented or unverifiable. Most prominent among the latter is Thomas Girtin's presence in Yorkshire that year. Girtin had by then embarked upon the seasonal routine that governed the life of the professional landscape painter – touring in the spring and summer to gather in his materials, then working up paintings in the autumn and winter. He'd been to Harewood in 1796 and would go again in 1799, 1800 and perhaps 1801 as well, but it has never been established that he was there at the same time as Turner. It remains a clear possibility, though, and may explain the two figures in the foreground of Turner's eastern view of Harewood Castle; who they are, at any rate, if not why they're there. Across his six watercolours of the Lascelles estate, Turner was careful to present a picturesque rural idyll, filled with farmhands, haywains and wandering deer – which makes the sketcher and his companion, the sole intrusion of the outside world, all the more curious.

Girtin's brief biography contains many blank passages. Only two of his letters survive, and a handful of sketched likenesses; and a single, quintessentially Romantic portrait by John Opie, dating from around 1800. He was certainly adept at charming potential patrons, assembling a list of well-placed, often aristocratic admirers. But there were also signs of dissatisfaction with the system he was obliged to serve; rumours of radical and even revolutionary sympathies that ensured his exclusion from the Royal Academy, regardless of his obvious talent. Although prepared to accept the ongoing patronage of Beau Lascelles, other noblemen were turned down – notably Lord Elgin, who in 1799 was looking to recruit a draughtsman to accompany him on his embassy to Constantinople. Turner refused this commission also, on financial grounds; for Girtin, however, there appears to have been another element involved. He told a friend that when calling on Elgin he was kept waiting 'many useless hours ... between the hall and the presence-chamber' – like a tradesman, basically, or a servant. This he could not accept.

After Girtin's death on 9 November 1802, most probably from asthma, accounts of his character quickly diverged. A truly committed artist, claimed his supporters, as radical in technique as original in sensibility, poised to equal Turner if not surpass him; a reckless libertine, countered others – including his erstwhile master, Edward Dayes – slapdash in his work, whose excesses shortened his life. It is impossible to discuss him now without mentioning the quote attributed to Turner in old age: 'If Girtin had lived, I should have starved.' This is generally understood to be excessively kind – easy charity to a long-dead rival by the most successful painter of his generation, who was prone, in his later years, to occasional outpourings of sentimentality. What is certain, however, is that our view of Thomas Girtin as an artist, based as it is on two hundred or so watercolours, will always be incomplete. *Bolton Bridge*, his one documented oil painting, thought to demonstrate his superiority to Turner when shown at the RA in 1801, is lost; as is the *Eidometropolis*, the extraordinary work that dominated his final years.

A vast circular canvas measuring 18 by 108 feet, the *Eidometropolis* was characterised as the 'connoisseur's panorama' on account of its sophisticated light effects – which appears to have deterred the popular audience Girtin had hoped for. Those who did see it, though, were amazed. *The Morning Herald* remarked that 'the Briton stands enraptured ... in seeing his native place, the glory of the world, so finely and truly portrayed.' Obituarists asserted that this project, rather than his late watercolours, represented the true pinnacle of Girtin's artistic achievement. Despite this approbation, at the end of its nine-month run at Spring Garden the immense painting was left unclaimed. Girtin himself had given no indication of his wishes. Panorama were regarded as ephemeral, as entertainments to be consumed rather than artworks to be treasured and preserved; and it was on these terms that the *Eidometropolis* seems to have been sold, to the entrepreneur James Thayer. It was taken to the continent and exhibited in Paris, Amsterdam and Lyon. In 1807 there was a fire at Thayer's warehouse, destroying much of his stock – including Tom Girtin's panorama, it is assumed, as at this point it disappears from history. Had it survived, the *Eidometropolis* would now undoubtedly be counted among the foremost works of English art.

The Lascelles thrived in the years after Turner's visit. Having weathered the minor scandal of Mary Ann's elopement and accepted her merchant husband with apparent good grace, they applied themselves to the defence of the king's interest in Yorkshire parliamentary elections. In 1807, Henry Lascelles stood against William Wilberforce, with whom he had previously maintained an unlikely alliance, and the Whig Viscount Milton, son of the immensely wealthy Earl Fitzwilliam: three candidates running for two seats in the Commons. A contest of spectacular rancour ensued, drawing the attention of the nation. Lascelles was the loser, but the family's loyalty – they spent around a hundred thousand pounds, almost the cost of Harewood House itself – was noted; and when the political moment was right, just before the next election in 1812, Baron Harewood was made an Earl.

Beau Lascelles remained on the sidelines throughout all of this, devoting his time to porcelain rather than politics. He died in 1814, still unmarried, predeceasing his father by six years. Henry was left to inherit, and it is his descendents who bear the earldom today. The family would eventually succeed in mingling their line with that of royalty – the present Earl in fact has the distinction of being related to Prince William on both sides of the Prince's family tree. His grandmother is William's paternal great aunt, the sixth Earl having married Princess Mary in 1922 (proposing to her, allegedly, as a result of a bet at his club); and his fourth great aunt, none other than Frances Douglas, is William's maternal sixth great-grandmother.

The narrative of J.M.W. Turner's career is well established. Having achieved prodigious success in early life, he grew steadily more experimental with age, producing the paintings for which he's now arguably most famous in the 1830s and 40s – and alienating the same circles, often the same people, who had once lauded him so highly. It was in this mature period that the *Zong* finally made its appearance in Turner's work. *The Slave Ship*, originally entitled *Slavers throwing overboard the dead and dying. typhon coming on*, included in the RA Summer Exhibition of 1840, shows not the act itself, as the Abolitionist pamphlets had done, but the aftermath – the ship retreating into the distance, the hands of the jettisoned slaves raised imploringly from the waves as ocean creatures swim up to devour them. The picture was lavishly praised by John Ruskin, the great contemporary defender of Turner's late style, who wrote that it contained 'the noblest sea that Turner ever painted, and if so, the noblest certainly ever painted by man'; it was dismissed or derided by nearly everyone else. A sunset fills the sky and the colours are positively ferocious, a blaze of raw, expressionistic fury – but the storm itself is almost over. Slavery had been ended in the British Empire in 1833, following the abolition of the trade in 1807. The 'guilty ship', as Ruskin termed it, is from a different era, its masts and rigging silhouetted against the fiery horizon. *Slavers* can be understood as a counterpoint to the elegiac spirit of *The Fighting 'Temeraire' tugged to her last berth to be broken up*, which Turner had exhibited the previous year. The advent of steam had robbed mankind of a source of grandeur and grace; yet it had also overseen the ultimate cessation of the slave trade's barbarities. The *Zong* was an atrocity that belonged to the past.

Many books were consulted in the writing of this one, too many to list here; but particular mention must be made of Greg Smith's *Thomas Girtin: The Art of Watercolour* and David Hill's *Turner in the North*, both of which proved invaluable. Any errors or distortions are my own.

Sincere thanks are due to my editor, Katie Espiner, for her great expertise and perceptiveness, and unwavering belief in *Will & Tom*; Euan Thorneycroft, indefatigable agent and staunch ally; Louisa Joyner, Cassie Browne, Charlotte Cray and Ann Bissell; the teams at HarperCollins and A. M. Heath; the staff of the British Library and Harewood House; Jackman and Middleton, steadfast fellows both; my mother, who keeps the difficult questions to a minimum; my ever-supportive family; and Sarah, of course, my sounding board, beloved co-parent and dearest friend.

My lowest bow to you all.